THE MIRACLE MAN

DEVLIN THRILLER NUMBER 4

JAMES CARVER

PROLOGUE

Hugh Varley said a short, silent prayer to himself and asked God for the snow to stop. He checked his rearview mirror. The kids were exhausted; some lay across the double seats, and a couple of them were asleep, leaning against each other. Walking around the museum all afternoon had drained them, but the lecture in the planetarium at the end had really finished them off.

It was 6:30, and the night had begun to settle in. Snowfall drove at angles across the road, and the wind rang off the roof and windows of the school bus. Visibility was low, and truth be told, Varley, who had just got his school bus endorsement, wasn't so comfortable driving the bus in any weather. The size and the heavy steering were a big step up from his ten-year-old Toyota Camry.

The radio was tuned to a local rock station, and the familiar sound of plucked sitar strings caught Varley's ears. He turned the radio up a notch so he could hear "Paint It Black" over the wind and the wipers. Then he eased off on the gas and took a breath.

Concentrate.

Charlie Watts' drumbeat struck up, matching the swish of the wipers.

"Mr. Varley?" a boy's voice came from the back of the bus. "Can you turn the music down?"

Varley sighed and dialed the volume down.

Though the snow was getting stronger, it hadn't settled so much yet. The roads were still wet. Now and then, the wheels of the bus hit a pool of water and threw out hissing wings of rain.

Concentrate.

They had started out from St. Johnsbury in a light dust of snow. Varley had checked the weather before they left. There was a storm predicted to pass over south of the route back to Hinkley, so he didn't take any notice of it. Even if he had, what else could he do? They couldn't stay over in St. Johnsbury for the night—him with nine kids.

He squinted ahead. Way off in the distance, a pair of taillights winked through the blizzard, and a pair of headlights appeared, coming from the opposite direction.

It's fine, he said to himself. *Go slow, go steady, and concentrate. It's not like there's much traffic.*

Up ahead, he caught his first glimpse of Lake Vesper, and a wave of relief washed over him. They were only five miles out from Hinkley. He'd soon be parking up at Hinkley High School, and the kids would get their rides home from the waiting parents. Then he'd drive his Camry back to his house and finish that bottle of Seagram's. By himself.

Concentrate.

The signpost for Vesper Run Crossing and Hinkley came up on the right. Thunder rumbled overhead. He sensed movement and murmurs behind him. The kids' drowsiness had been disturbed by the storm. The sky flashed white, and the kids let out sounds of astonishment. For a moment, the lake and the flat landscape for miles around lit up. For a split second, the night was defeated, and the world was revealed.

Dear God, thought Varley. *Thundersnow.*

Then the night returned, and it was dark again except for a small twinkle of red and blue visible through the snow across the flat fields to the south. Varley craned forward to get a better view. Was that a police car? If it was, it was coming in from the south and going at a hell of a speed.

The road ahead was empty, and he couldn't yet see the Vesper Run crossing. If the police car was coming in from the south, then that would take it across his path. He had sped up a little since they hit the lake; now, he strengthened his grip on the steering wheel and slowed down, just in case...

DUE SOUTH of the Vesper Run crossing, another kind of storm was coming. A police car was in hot pursuit of a vehicle that had refused to pull over and was in one hell of a hurry to get away.

"Son of a bitch. That lightning was nearly a direct strike. You okay, Lori?"

"Yeah," Officer Lori Cassidy replied through clenched jaws. Her shoulders were hunched, and her eyes were fixed on the road ahead. "Can't see a damned thing through the snow. Whoever they are, they'd rather get themselves killed than caught."

Officer Kyle Ross picked up the receiver. "Dispatch, this is car P4. We are still in pursuit of a white Mercedes-Benz Metris with false plates heading north on South Hinkley Road. Vehicle speed is approximately ninety miles an hour... I repeat, ninety miles an hour in a snow squall..."

There was a crackle and whine, and then dispatch

responded, "Copy. Please be advised we have two state trooper cars on their way approaching from the east on Frost Hollow."

"Frost Hollow?" said Cassidy.

"Yeah. Another five minutes away, at least," said Ross. "And they aren't going to be going at ninety in this."

"Okay. Hold on tight."

Cassidy changed her grip on the wheel and accelerated. Ross slyly clamped a hand around the side of his seat. At this speed in these conditions, it would take hardly anything for the car to slide out of control.

Ross put the receiver to his mouth. "Dispatch, P4. Still in pursuit and coming up on Vesper Run Crossing."

The Mercedes was still barreling toward the crossing with no sign of slowing. They passed a gap in the trees that lined the highway. Through the gap and the snow, Lake Vesper could be seen in the distance, a thin strip of black spread out against the night sky. Ross saw something else too. Something that made his guts somersault.

"Oh my God..." Ross said in a low moan.

"What? What is it?"

"There's a bus... There's a bus coming up from the east along Route 5."

"What?" Cassidy took her eye off the road for a split second and glanced to her left. She caught sight of the distant silhouette of the bus just before it was hidden again by another stretch of trees.

"You think the Mercedes is gonna stop?" asked Ross.

"No. No, I don't. They've been driving like maniacs in the worst storm I've seen in ten years. I don't think they're going to stop for the devil himself."

"What is it that they got in the back of that thing?"

HUGH VARLEY DIDN'T HEAR or see the Mercedes until it was too late. The roadside by the crossing was overgrown and dense. Between the tall hedges, the out-of-control shrubbery, and the snow, it was impossible to see what was coming until you were right up on the junction. That and the bucketing snow meant the first time Varley caught sight of the white van was as it flew out of in front of him. Before he knew he was doing it, Varley had slammed the brakes and swung hard to the right, aiming the bus for the gap opening up behind the speeding Mercedes.

And it might have worked but for the sudden terrifying lurch the back end of the bus made as the rear wheels aquaplaned and lost their grip. A chorus of cries and animallike screams erupted. The bus was pulled into a violent sideways motion and swung around. A window shattered. Varley watched helplessly as the nose of the bus yawed wildly, sending the front wheel off the highway and down the steep bank into the black, blank unknown of Lake Vesper. The bus plunged into the water, engulfed and absorbed by the lake, which sucked it down in a matter of moments.

CASSIDY ROARED AND skidded to a stop yards away from black track marks that led off into the lake. She and Ross scrambled in blind, silent terror out of the car. The bitter-cold snow knifed down, and in the distance, they could hear the Mercedes' engine fading away. Standing on the bank, they looked back and forth for any sign of the bus in the black expanse of the lake.

But there was no bus. It was like there never was a bus.

The lake sizzled with snow and roiled in the wind but showed no sign of the vehicle or its passengers. If it weren't for the chaotic, looping track marks in the road, there would have been no evidence that the bus had ever been there.

Ross dove into the car and radioed dispatch. As he yelled into the receiver, he glanced out of the windshield. Cassidy was still by the lake, but she was taking off her jacket and shoes.

"What the hell?" Ross dropped the receiver and pulled himself out of the cruiser, but Cassidy was already racing down to the lake and dove in.

Ross skidded and stumbled down the muddy bank after his colleague and stood at the edge of the black water, already soaked to the skin. He couldn't see Cassidy anywhere.

"*Cassidy*!"

A thousand bullets of snow fell on the surface of the water, and there was another heavy rumble of thunder, but no Cassidy.

The sky flashed white, and the lake lit up like it was under floodlights, then receded into darkness. But no Cassidy.

Ross could hear urgent voices calling to each other on the police radio.

"Cassidy!" As useless as he knew it would be, he steeled himself, ready to plunge into the freezing waters. A splash and the sound of coughing and choking stopped him. Ross looked to his left, and ten yards away, a bedraggled Cassidy emerged, staggering and swaying toward the shore.

He rushed to her and helped her out of the water. She was shivering and convulsing.

"I couldn't see a thing," Cassidy whispered and then threw up a jet of water. She coughed and wretched some more till she could speak again. "It's blacker than hell down there."

"You're in shock. Here, let's get you to the car."

Though Cassidy was a force to be reckoned with, she wasn't big. Someone, Ross recalled, had once described her as a little punch of a woman. He lifted her in his arms and took her back to the cruiser and out of the merciless weather. The radio was buzzing with voices. Ross reached for the handset but stopped short. He had heard a sound from the other side of the highway. A groan. He looked across the road and saw a body lying in blood and shattered glass. He scrambled over the slick, dusted blacktop and crouched by the body. It was a girl, thirteen or fourteen.

And she was alive.

ONE

Three Weeks Later

DEVLIN'S second mistake had been to close his eyes just after they had passed the Canadian border. He didn't dislike Father Ramirez; it was just that he wouldn't stop talking. He was eager, still in training, and wanted to talk about the Montreal Catholic Convention they'd just been to in more detail than they'd lived it.

It was around seven in the evening, and they weren't due to get into Avery until the early hours of the morning. Ramirez had kept talking, so Devlin had closed his eyes and let the words wash over him. Ramirez soon got the message, and the monologue stopped. Shortly after, Devlin slipped into a deep sleep and didn't notice Ramirez make the wrong exit. He also didn't notice Ramirez take Route 89 and zigzag across Vermont, adding a couple of hours to their journey.

Devlin's first mistake had been to accept a lift from Ramirez, a trainee priest who had driven up from the Boston School of

Theology in a Nissan beater. But the Public Service Alliance of Canada was in a pay dispute and had brought Montreal Airport to a standstill with no sign of a deal. So Devlin took the offer.

The first Devlin knew of their detour was when he was woken by a knocking noise coming from the engine. He pulled himself up in his seat and listened intently to the banging.

"That doesn't sound good. Not good at all."

"Oh," Ramirez said breezily. "She makes all sorts of sounds, but this old beauty just goes and goes."

"How long has it been making that sound?"

"Since Newport."

"Newport? When did we go through Newport?" Devlin sat bolt upright. "Wait...are we on the 91?"

"Yeah. I thought it would save time switching from the 89."

Devlin checked his watch. "I highly doubt it."

"Well. We're making good time, I think."

The knocking sound was getting louder.

"You do have roadside assistance?" asked Devlin.

"Of course. I'm with the AAA. But we aren't going to need any roadside assistance. Trust me..." Ramirez had barely gotten to the end of his sentence when the knocking sound became a grinding sound, and every light on his dashboard started to blink.

"Oh no... No..." stammered Ramirez. "No...dear God..." The car began to lose power, forcing Ramirez to switch on his turn signal and pull over on the grass shoulder. He slammed his steering wheel in disbelief. "That is the first time it's ever done that."

"I would hope so."

"Or anything like it. She's usually so reliable. I swear to you." He shook his head. "This is so embarrassing."

Both priests checked their cells.

"No signal," they said in near unison.

"I saw a rest stop back in Newport," said Ramirez. "But that's gotta be..."

"Pop the hood," said Devlin, who was already getting out of the car. Ramirez pressed the catch and got out of the car. Devlin inspected the engine with his cell light.

"Looks like the engine's blown," said Devlin.

"That sounds bad."

"That's 'cause it is."

"Shoot. That's gonna cost me a bundle. I guess I can walk until I get a signal and call assistance."

Devlin closed the hood and looked around. He checked his watch again. It was just past nine, not late, but the highway was empty. "Or we can try and flag a car down. Get a ride to the next rest stop or town." He looked at Ramirez's collar and shirt. "The fact we're priests often helps in these kinds of situations."

They had stopped along a bend in the highway. Devlin walked over to the other side to get a better view of the road going north.

"You know the car is okay," Ramirez called after Devlin. "I know it's old, but it's an okay car. Reliable. I got it serviced before I left Boston. Got it checked over, and there was no problem."

"It's been serviced?"

"Yeah. Just before I left Boston."

"You should go to a different guy."

Ramirez threw up his hands. "Well, who knows? Maybe you brought bad luck with you?"

Devlin didn't answer, and Ramirez pushed his hands into his jacket pockets, stared down at the ground, and looked awkward. Devlin took another look back down the bend and began to walk north along the shoulder.

"Where are you going?"

"I can see lights," Devlin shouted back.

"What?"

"A little further on. Looks like a bar or a motel."

The two priests trudged along the roadside, checking their cells now and then for a flicker of a signal but getting nothing. After half a mile, they passed a green sign with the words "O'Leary's Roadhouse." An authentic Irish "Welcome" was painted in a gothic font. A little further on the grassy roadside opened onto a graveled road. The road led down to a parking lot overlooked by a weathered, single-story building with faded green exterior walls. A tilted shamrock-shaped sign that creaked in the breeze hung from the edge of the roof.

"Looks like a dump," said Ramirez.

"A dump with a pay phone," said Devlin.

Inside, the heavy scent of aged wood and stale beer hung in the air, and Irish folk music played out from cheap, tinny-sounding speakers. The interior was dimly lit, with flickering neon signs casting a glow over the worn-out wooden tables and scuffed bar counter. The ceiling was covered with dusty Guinness memorabilia, faded Irish flags, and photographs of loyal patrons.

The bar was divided into two main areas. There was a square of worn-out hardwood floor with a small stage in the center for bands, and the other section was filled with mismatched chairs and tables. The walls of the bar were decorated with peeling shamrock wallpaper, displaying photographs and newspaper clippings from past St. Patrick's Day celebrations and local events. A lonely jukebox had been shoved in the corner.

There was only one bartender, a grizzled-looking guy wearing sandals, jeans, and a Jerry Garcia T-shirt. About half a dozen regulars leaned against the bar, nursing beers or sipping on whiskey.

The bartender nodded at Ramirez and Devlin as they approached the bar.

"Fathers, welcome. What can I get you?"

"Just a Coke, please," said Ramirez.

"Coke for me too," said Devlin.

"I see it's gonna be a big night," replied the bartender.

"We've broken down," said Devlin. "And there doesn't seem to be much of a signal round here."

"Oh, this place is a dead zone, Father," said a stout old guy in a shabby leather jacket and a peak cap, propping up the bar and staring into half-drunk Guinness.

"It's famous for it," added the bartender.

"But works in our favor too, if you know what I mean..." said the old guy, tapping his red nose.

"Do you have a pay phone?" asked Ramirez.

"Out back." The bartender pointed to a narrow hallway leading to the restrooms.

"I'll go make a call," said Ramirez.

The bartender served up the drinks, and Devlin took a stool by the bar.

"You on the wagon, Father?" said the stout guy with a knowing look.

"I gave it up a while back," replied Devlin. "It wasn't doing me any good."

"I should do the same, but I ain't got the willpower. Where you headed?"

"Boston way."

"Is that an accent I can hear?" The bartender had a glass of beer in his hand and had leaned in.

"Yeah," said Devlin. "A faint one now. I lived in Belfast until I was nine."

"My folks were from Meath," said the bartender. "Billy here is from Dublin."

"Like yourself, I came over a long time ago," said Billy. "When I was a young man." He raised his glass. "Here's to the old country." The other two raised their glasses.

Somewhere out in the night, a distant rumble could be heard over the piped music, and the bartender and Billy shared an uneasy look.

"Well, that didn't go so well," said Ramirez, returning from the pay phone. "Roadside assistance won't be for a couple of hours at least. They don't have anybody within fifty miles of here."

"You're welcome to pass the time here. We got rooms, too, if you need them," said the bartender.

"Thanks," said Devlin.

The distant rumbling had got much louder and was now identifiable as a swarm of engines. Devlin watched the bartender twitch and feel under the bar for something, probably a baseball bat or a gun.

"You got trouble coming?" asked Devlin.

"Maybe," said the bartender. "This last week, we've had biker gangs roaming up and down."

"Damn nuisance," said Billy. "Don't know what the hell business brought 'em here."

"We never had bikers up here before," said the bartender. "They seem to have come out of nowhere."

The roar of engines was deafening now, and half a dozen headlights lit up the frosted windowpanes. The regulars exchanged murmurs and curses, and the bartender looked tense.

The door swung open, and six bikers in colors strode in. Most had bandanas around their heads, and patches covered their grease-stained denim vests.

Five of the men sat around a table, and one of them, built

like a tank with a thick gray beard and a ponytail, came up to the bar, stood between Devlin and Billy, and slammed the counter.

"Well," he rasped. "Just what we were looking for. A mick pub."

"Watch your language," said Billy into his pint.

"No offense, old man. I got nothing against the micks."

Devlin noticed a six-inch-long scar across the biker's throat, which explained the rasping quality of his voice. His arms were bulked up and worked out to massive proportions with boulder-like biceps and triceps. His hands matched the rest of him; outsized and gnarled, they looked like they could each hold a medicine ball.

The biker turned to the bartender. "We'll have three bottles of whiskey, and what beer you got here?"

"I'm not serving you," replied the bartender, screwing up every ounce of his courage.

"Come again?"

The bartender pointed to a swastika badge on the biker's shoulder. "I ain't serving anyone in my bar who wears one of them."

"You heard of the First Amendment?"

"Yeah, I have, and you're free to go anywhere you like. But not here, not with that thing."

"This is America. I'm free everywhere I go."

"I ain't serving you."

"Then I'll come over the bar and serve myself and put you in a wheelchair on the way."

"Listen," said Devlin, swinging around on his stool to face the biker. "The man says he won't serve you. It's his bar. So, I suggest you and your friends find somewhere else."

The biker looked at Devlin, who was finishing his Coke and placing the glass down on the counter. "Who are you?"

"A man looking to keep the peace."

"Huh? Is that so?" The biker grabbed Devlin's collar and ripped it away from his throat. He held it up to Devlin's face and crushed in his huge fist. "Peaceful enough for you?"

"Like I said," said Devlin. "This place isn't for you or your friends. You should go."

The biker suddenly grasped Devlin's head with both dinner-plate-sized hands and pulled him up from his seat. Stools crashed to the ground, and glass shattered. Then, as quickly as he'd lunged at Devlin, the biker let go. Both men staggered back, and the biker lifted his right arm. A long, jagged shard of glass was lodged in his side below his armpit. Before he could reach around to pull it out, Devlin had double punched him in the throat and followed up with an oblique kick to the left knee. The punches didn't do much, but the biker groaned from the impact to his knee. The two men paused, and the biker straightened up. He dragged out the glass blade from his side, dripping with globs of blood, and smiled. The other five bikers hadn't even bothered to leave their chairs; they were just sitting back and enjoying the spectacle.

"You think this is going to help you?" said the biker. "This kind of shit is just foreplay to me."

"Then let's get down to the main event."

The biker advanced on Devlin again. There was a shout from the bartender, who threw a baseball bat across the bar, which Devlin caught. Then, from outside, a police siren started up. The sound of the siren changed everything instantly. The biker looked over at his gang mates, and without a word, all five rose from their chairs and filed to the door.

"Next time, Father," rasped the ringleader, turning back to Devlin, who was still brandishing the baseball bat. "I'll crush your skull like an egg and watch your brains pour out of your eyes."

Within seconds, the gang had left. A swarm of engines

roared and rode away, and for a moment, the bar was silent. Then, the sound of a police siren filled the bar, and blue lights filled the windows.

"Well," said Billy into his pint. "He sure had a way with words. For a Nazi."

TWO

"You want to put that down, sir?" A short, blonde police officer had entered the bar and stood with her fists on her hips. She was looking at Devlin, who was still holding the baseball bat.

"Oh, it's not him, Officer," called out the bartender. "In fact, this guy saved the whole situation."

"What happened to your shirt?" asked the officer.

"Someone tried to de-frock me," replied Devlin.

"Who called the police?"

"I did," said a regular who, along with a few others, had come out of hiding in the restroom.

"There was a biker gang here, Officer," said the bartender. "Same one that's been crawling round the neighborhood this past week. I wouldn't serve them, and they weren't happy about it. The Father here stepped in. God bless him. The man's a hero." The regulars broke into a round of applause, along with whoops.

The officer surveyed the bar, the shattered glass, the blood on the floor, the upturned stools, and the clapping customers. She spotted a camera bolted high up on the wall at the end of the bar.

"You got CCTV?"

The bartender shrugged. "Yeah. But it never works, and it's too expensive to fix."

"Well, somebody had better fill me in with the details."

"You're a lot quicker than the AAA," piped up Ramirez.

The officer took statements in turn from the barman and some of the regulars. The last two she spoke to were Devlin and Ramirez. When she was through with them, she put down her notebook and studied the two priests. There was music still playing from the speakers, and the regulars had returned to their glasses and conversation. With the aid of drink, the bar had settled back down remarkably quickly from the recent altercation.

"So," said the officer, looking at Devlin. "You single-handedly fought off a biker gang?"

"I didn't fight them off. I bought some time. Enough time, it so happens, because you turned up. And they left quicker than I would have expected too."

"Why d'you say that?"

Devlin shrugged. "I don't know. But it only took one siren to spook them."

"Well, they probably thought more sirens were on their way." The cop sighed and shook her head. "I don't know what's going on around here lately. Those bikers turned up out of the blue a few days ago and haven't left. That's on top of everything else." She turned to Ramirez. "And your car's broken down on the highway?"

"That's right. I've called roadside assistance, but they're still not anywhere near."

"How bad's the breakdown?"

"It's bad," said Devlin.

"Yeah, it's bad," agreed Ramirez.

"Engine's blown," said Devlin.

"Look, why don't I drive you to Hinkley?" said the officer. "It's my town. I was only called out here because the state troopers were busy. I know the guys who run the town garage. I can get a tow for you. If it's a blown engine, even the AAA aren't gonna fix that roadside."

"That'd be great," said Ramirez.

"Is there anyplace you'd recommend to stay over?" asked Devlin.

"There's a couple of motels. You could also try St. Paul's Church. Father Wilson is the priest there. I don't know how it works with you guys, but could he help out, maybe?"

"Maybe," said Devlin. "We could try Father Wilson first. Sound good to you, Father Ramirez?"

"Yeah. Sounds like a good course of action. I'm just a bit anxious about leaving my car though."

"I'll get it towed into Hinkley first thing," said the cop. "With all due respect, Father, from what you say, no one's going to steal it."

Ramirez nodded. "I guess not."

"Our luggage is back in the car though," said Devlin.

"I'll drive you back to get your luggage, and then we can head to Hinkley. Name's Officer Cassidy, by the way. Officer Lori Cassidy."

"Father Devlin," said Devlin. "Thanks for your help."

"I'm Father Ramirez."

"Okay, Fathers, let's go."

THEY DROVE BACK to the spot where they'd left Ramirez's Nissan. Ramirez sat in the back with Devlin and replayed the events in the bar in his mind. He'd never seen a real fight. Kids scrapping in playgrounds and the streets were the sum total of his experience, and he'd always been a witness and definitely not a participant. Watching two adults going at it with damaging force was a first for him. It had been a white-hot explosion of violence that Ramirez was still recovering from.

Since he had first met Devlin, Ramirez had been struck by the older priest's almost unnatural stillness and calm. A large man, maybe six three or four, Devlin had piercing blue eyes that could go right through you and a presence that put Ramirez in a state of awe. And then there were the rumors he had heard about Devlin. Vague rumors about Devlin's past, about unusual events. Ramirez had been as unsettled by the rumors' lack of specific details as much as the strangeness of them. Rattled by the drama of the evening, he took a slow breath and fastened his gaze on the window and the roadside flashing past.

They pulled up behind the Nissan, and Devlin and Ramirez pulled their luggage out of the trunk. Devlin put on a clean clerical shirt and collar by the roadside. Then, they drove back south, took an off-ramp a few miles down the highway, and got onto a parallel road going back north. The road north wound through low hills and pine trees, which soon gave way to farmland and a large lake. They passed a gas station and old wooden buildings scattered by the road that looked in need of attention. Further along, smarter white and pale gray houses began to appear, which signaled the start of the town proper.

As they neared the town, Ramirez felt a change in Devlin's attitude. He seemed to become agitated, even a little pained. They rode on for a while longer, and Ramirez began to notice lit candles and framed photographs facing outward in some of the windows.

"What happened here?" Devlin's question rang out of the dark and took Ramirez by surprise. Ramirez watched the police officer's eyes in the rearview mirror, trying to make out Devlin in the back.

"Sorry, Father?"

"The candles and the photographs in the windows. What happened here?"

"There..." The officer paused for a moment. "There was an accident. Three weeks ago. A...terrible accident. We lost eight high school children and a teacher in a traffic accident."

"That's awful," said Devlin. "I'm sorry for your loss."

"We all are, Father. Just as sorry as hell."

They drew up by a collection of white-brick buildings, in the center of which was St. Paul's Church. Its long, spindly gray spire rose above four black-and-gold clock faces. The white paint on the walls was weathered, and some of the bricks were cracked and chipped, but on the whole, the building looked in working order. They crawled up the roads between the buildings, past the church, and stopped by another white-brick building with a green pitched roof.

"Here we are," said Cassidy. "Father Wilson's residence."

"Thank you for your help, Officer Cassidy," said Devlin. "And I'm sorry again for the terrible tragedy you and your friends and family are going through."

Cassidy nodded. The two priests got out of the car, fetched their cases from the trunk, and approached the house.

"How...? How did you know...?" asked Ramirez.

"What do you mean?" replied Devlin.

"You seemed to know that something bad had happened here."

"You saw the candles and the framed photographs? Didn't you guess too?"

"Yes...but you seemed to sense something even before that... before we even got into the town."

Devlin shrugged. "Just experience, I guess."

"And what about the fight with the biker? That was insane.

How many fights have you been in? That can't have been your first."

"I was a boxer back in the day. But truth to tell, another thirty seconds with that guy and I would likely have been mincemeat. Baseball bat or no baseball bat."

Devlin rang the bell, and a thin, animated figure appeared at the door in a clerical collar, cardigan, and slippers. Ramirez was hit by a strong smell of liquor.

"Father Wilson?" asked Devlin.

"Yes?"

"I'm Father Devlin, and this is Father Ramirez. Our car broke down on the way back to Boston from a conference, and we're stuck for a place to stay until our car is fixed."

"Oh, I see."

"I understand there are motels in the town, but we wondered if you had any room to put us up for the night?"

"Oh, dear... The thing is, usually I would happily put you up for a night or more, even. But things aren't usual in Hinkley at the moment." Father Wilson chewed his bottom lip, then waved Devlin and Ramirez in. "Come in anyway, and I'll help sort you out with a motel room. And fix you a drink. You'll probably need one."

Wilson led them through to the living room. The place was cluttered with old and antique-looking furniture. Ornaments occupied nearly every surface space, and heavy drapes covered the windows.

"I'm drinking a late-night brandy." Wilson pointed to a crystal decanter and half-full glass on a side table. "Will you join me?"

Ramirez accepted, and Devlin declined. Wilson fetched a second glass, poured out two drinks, and sat in an armchair before leaning forward, his glass cradled in his thin fingers.

"You've both arrived at the strangest time this town has seen," said Wilson. "Maybe any town has seen."

"Officer Cassidy, who drove us here, told us about the eight children and the teacher who died," said Ramirez.

"Officer Cassidy drove you here? Well, she was the one that saw the whole thing happen. Lori Cassidy went into the lake to look for the children and their teacher."

"She went into the lake?" asked Ramirez.

"Yes. The bus carrying the children was driven off the road into Lake Vesper. Officer Cassidy was chasing a van with false plates, and the bus had to swerve to avoid the van. The driver of the bus, Hugh Varley, God rest his soul, lost control and... well..." Wilson stared into his drink. "Apparently, that part of the lake is one hundred and thirty feet, and the bus lodged right at the bottom. I've lived here all my life and never knew how deep that lake was. We all know now. It's as deep as hell itself. All of the children in the bus and Hugh perished. It was the worst night we've seen in a generation. Thundersnow. And the lake was pitch-black. The bus took them to the bottom, and they wouldn't have known which way was up or down." Wilson took another gulp of his brandy. "Not a soul in this town has been untouched by 'the tragedy,' as we call it now. I lost my nephew, Franklin."

Devlin and Ramirez offered sincere condolences, and Wilson nodded, then took a deep draft from his glass.

"You must have been under such a strain," said Ramirez. "And the funerals..."

"There haven't been any funerals," replied Wilson. "The bus is still down there. With those children in it. The divers went down and said it was jammed hard into a narrow trench. Immovable. The Vermont Underwater Recovery Team are still trying to work out how to bring the bus back up. Apparently, it's a near impossible logistical feat."

"So, are they going to be able to do it?" asked Ramirez.

"They say they think it can be done in theory, but we're still waiting. In the meantime, the families have petitioned the probate court for presumption of death certificates so we can move on at least in simple administrative terms." Wilson looked upward and genuflected. "It's like the town took in a breath one night three weeks ago, and we're still waiting to exhale... The worst of it is the rumors."

"What rumors?" asked Devlin.

Wilson shook his head wearily. "No one actually saw the bus go into the lake. I mean, the very moment it went in. Neither Lori nor Officer Ross saw the exact moment. So there have been all sorts of rumors that the children are still alive somewhere. It all goes back to some other hearsay that Hugh Varley was a member of some doomsday cult in his youth, back in the nineties. And that he has kidnapped them."

"What doomsday cult?" asked Devlin.

"I don't know. Waco or some such. But it's not true. It's some wicked rumor put about by a wicked person."

"But hold on," said Ramirez. "You said yourself the bus is lodged at the bottom of the lake."

Wilson nodded his head vigorously. "Yes, it is. It's a hurtful, vicious, and utterly absurd rumor. If it weren't so hurtful, it would be amusing, I dare say." Wilson stared into his drink hopelessly. "Fourteen," he said bitterly. "Franklin was fourteen. He had seen nothing of life. It's a damned hard time to be a priest, is all I'll say."

"Have they found who was driving the van?" asked Devlin.

"No. Police and volunteers have combed the county and come up with nothing. Not a thing. No one knows who was responsible. It might be someone in the town. Equally, it could be someone from the other side of the state or the country."

He coughed and looked up at Devlin and Ramirez. "Let me

make a call. There's a motel not too far from here that has rooms. I know the owner somewhat."

"We're really sorry to impose at this time, Father Wilson," said Ramirez.

Wilson waved a hand and stood. For a moment, he lost his balance and nearly toppled. Devlin was out of his chair, ready to assist, but Wilson managed to steady himself.

"Apologies. A rush of blood to the head. You weren't to know. It was your bad luck to break down. Where's my damned cell...?" As the question left his mouth, a tinny rendition of "Amazing Grace" came from the side of the armchair he had been sitting in. Wilson dove a hand down the side of the cushion and pulled out his cell. He glanced at the screen and suddenly looked ashen.

"If you don't mind, I should take this in another room."

Devlin and Ramirez waited in silence as Wilson spoke in hushed tones in the hall. When he returned, he looked even worse.

"I...I told you all the children on the bus died," said Wilson. "That wasn't quite accurate. One girl survived. She was thrown from the bus before it entered the lake. But she was extremely badly hurt, and the doctors didn't encourage us to hold out much hope. In fact—" He paused, pressed a hand to his mouth, and took a breath through his nose to steady himself. "—I just got a call from her father, asking me to go over and perform last rites."

Devlin rose. "We've already asked too much of you. We can find..."

Father Wilson put out a hand. "No. Actually, it's a real help to have you here. To talk to other priests. It's been so lonely and hard, I can't tell you. In fact, I'd like you to come with me. Please come with me. I need someone to drive me, anyway. I've had too much to get behind a wheel. My car's around back in the garage." Wilson's speech had become noticeably slurred, and Ramirez wondered if he even had it in him to get to the car. But he seemed to find the sobriety he needed to lead the way to the garage. He slumped into the back seat, Ramirez got into the passenger seat, and Devlin took the wheel.

THREE

"I've done everything I can to make Elizabeth comfortable. She won't be in pain."

Dr. Rick Hudson was kneeling by a single bed, examining an unconscious teenage girl. His knees clicked as he rose and glanced at the morphine drip. He looked around at the other people in the room, a woman and two men standing in a rough semicircle around the bed, and said quietly, "I'll wait for Father Wilson."

The older of the three, the teenage girl's father, Hank Wendig, a large man with a heavy reddish beard and short gray hair, nodded. "Thanks, Doc."

"No problem, Hank. I'm so sorry I couldn't do more."

Wendig nodded. "You've done more than anyone else in the world for us."

"If only there had been a moment," said the woman. "A few minutes to say goodbye." She was slight and gaunt; her eyes were permanently teary, and her shoulders were rigid with grief.

"I'm so sorry, Kathleen," said Hudson, his own eyes red with emotion and fatigue.

"I should be grateful," Kathleen continued. "At least she

didn't die at the bottom of a freezing black lake, imprisoned in a bus. Of all the mothers, I was blessed...in a way. I just wanted to say goodbye."

The younger man, as tall as his dad but slimmer with a blond buzz cut, put an arm around his mother. "I'm sure she can hear us, Mom. I know she's heard us say goodbye."

The doorbell rang, sending a small shock through each family member, who knew it must be Father Wilson. Wendig went to the door.

"Father Wilson," said Hank somberly. "Thank you for coming."

"Not at all, Hank," replied Wilson, and Hank caught a blast of brandy breath. Wilson's eyes were bloodshot, and he looked unsteady.

"Are you okay, Father?"

"Quite so. Quite so."

"How are Jack and Betty?"

"Distraught over losing Franklin. Like all of us, Hank. Like all of us."

Hank looked over Wilson's shoulder to the car waiting outside the house.

"Who's in the car, Father?"

"Oh, sorry, I should have said. They're two priests who are staying overnight here on the way back to Boston. They kindly gave me a lift over as I'd...I'd had a couple of brandies."

"Tell them to come in."

"They wouldn't want to intrude."

"They shouldn't wait out in the car. And besides, I'd fill the house full of priests right now if I could."

Wilson nodded. "Understood."

Father Wilson fetched Devlin and Ramirez from the car, and once in the hallway, they introduced themselves to Hank in respectful tones. Then, Father Wilson went through to the front room, stumbling on his way. Elizabeth was lying in the bed they had made up for her when she had been sent home from the hospital once it had been decided nothing more could be done. Devlin and Ramirez were seated by Hank in an adjoining room connected by an archway where they could see Father Wilson give last rites to the girl.

Father Wilson got down awkwardly into a wooden chair by the bed. Sweat beaded on his forehead, and the color drained from his face. He searched his jacket pockets and pulled out a small gold pot containing the Oil of the Sick. His hands, which had been trembling, began to move erratically. Then, he stopped and put a shaking hand over his mouth.

"Oh dear, I don't... I'm afraid I don't feel well at all. I feel quite faint."

The family and Dr. Hudson exchanged glances.

"Can I get you some water?" asked Hudson.

"Yes, but...I feel very faint... Could... Could Father Devlin administer the anointing, perhaps? I'm so sorry, Hank...Kathleen..."

"That's okay, Father," said Kathleen. "I know it's been hard on you too. Father Devlin? Would you?"

Devlin had already appeared at the archway entrance to the room. "Of course. Doctor, if you and Father Ramirez could help Father Wilson up."

Ramirez and Hudson lifted an increasingly ill and helpless Father Wilson out of his chair and steered him to the adjoining room where Devlin had been sitting.

Devlin sat in the chair by the bed and picked up the Oil of the Sick that Father Wilson had left on the floor. Ramirez brought Father Wilson's stole to Devlin, and Devlin placed it on his shoulders.

For a long while, Devlin did nothing. He only watched the girl in silence. Then, he laid hands on Elizabeth and began to anoint her forehead before moving on to her hands. Though he was a big man, his hands moved with extraordinary lightness and sensitivity.

Father Wilson could be heard moaning softly in the next room, and a clock on the wall ticked on as Devlin recited prayers. In a whisper, he concluded with a final blessing, his last words so faint they were no longer audible. The silence that followed was profound, and nobody stirred while Devlin attended to the girl. All those witnessing the last rites had become transfixed by the ritual.

Suddenly, Kathleen flinched. "Dear God..."

"What?" asked Hank. "What is it, Kathleen?"

"No... No, it can't be possible... There..." Kathleen's arm was outstretched, her finger pointing at Elizabeth. "There... It happened again..."

"What? What happened?"

"I think... Her... Her eyelids moved... Elizabeth's... They moved..."

Hank, Kathleen, and their son moved closer in.

Devlin had stopped his prayers. He was looking at Elizabeth's hand, which had begun to move and close around Devlin's fingers.

Moments later, Elizabeth's eyes flickered open.

HANK SAW Devlin to the door. Ramirez and a faint Wilson were already in the car waiting. Cries of joy could be heard from the living room as Kathleen Wendig wept and kissed her living daughter's face.

The two men stood silently in the doorway, facing one another.

Hank was for a long time lost for words. Eventually, he said,

"What happened, Father? What happened between you and Elizabeth?"

"Honestly, I'm not sure."

"Did I...?" said Hank. "Did I just witness a miracle? Did I, Father? Did I witness a miracle?"

Devlin looked Hank directly in the eyes and said calmly, "I don't believe it was a miracle. I believe there may be many things, interconnected things that just happened to your daughter, that are difficult to separate. God willed it, of course. After all, she was spared from the lake, and now she's been spared again. But it is important to acknowledge there may well be medical reasons, too, for what just happened that we don't yet know."

Hank folded his arms. "You're awful damn skeptical for a priest, aren't you? Shouldn't you just take it as the work of God? End of story?"

"Actually, in the end, the most important thing isn't what I believe. The most important thing is you going back to your daughter and being able to hold her and love her again. Miracle or not, it's the rarest kind of gift."

Hank's words caught in his throat, and for a while, he was simply unable to speak. "Thank you, Father," he muttered eventually. "I don't know what happened just now, and neither I'm damn sure does Doc Hudson. But thank you." Hank suddenly threw his arms around Devlin, held him tight, and sobbed into his shoulder. The sobs faded, and he drew away a little embarrassed. He pulled himself together as much as he was able.

"Good night, Father."

"Good night."

FOUR

"No points for guessing you're Father Wilson's guests."

"That's right," said Ramirez.

The lady at the Hideaway Motel reception was a thin, hard-looking woman in her sixties, with her gray-and-black-streaked hair pulled tight into a ponytail. She wore no makeup and had a web of fine lines around her mouth and eyes and stronger lines across her forehead and down her cheeks, engraved by a lifetime of heavy smoking.

"I don't usually take guests in at one o'clock in the morning, but it seems you got connections in this town."

"Thank you. We're grateful," said Ramirez.

Devlin and Ramirez had dropped a recovering Father Wilson off at the rectory, who had protested he was well enough to be left alone once he'd had some painkillers. He was also clearheaded enough to be able to call ahead and book two rooms at the motel he had suggested earlier in the evening.

"Your car broke down, didn't it?" said the receptionist, who took a toot on her vape stick.

"That's right," said Ramirez. "Officer Cassidy, who drove us into Hinkley, said she knew someone who could fix it."

"I know."

"You know?"

"There's only one repair shop in Hinkley, and my eldest owns it, and my other son works for him. That's where your car'll be, and it'll be in good hands, Father."

"Oh... Great."

"I got two adjoining rooms. Follow me."

She picked two keys off hooks on a board behind her, came around from behind the desk, and walked out of the office. The priests picked up their suitcases and followed her out into the night.

"I'm Kay Kane," said the woman as she led them past the other mostly dark motel rooms. "People know me as Ma Kane. I run the Hideaway, and like I say, my boys run the repair shop. Though the younger one, Ted, sometimes helps out here too. How's old Father Wilson? Bet he was soused."

"He's been hit hard by the death of his nephew," said Devlin.

"Yeah, that's true, no doubt. But what was his excuse for the last twenty years?" Ma Kane came to an abrupt stop. "Here's your rooms."

She handed the two pairs of keys over.

"No smoking, no pets. Office hours are 8:00 a.m. till 9:00 p.m. Put the 'Maid' sign on your door if you want your room serviced or the 'Do Not Disturb' sign if you don't. Rooms without any sign will be cleaned automatically. All house rules are available from the office."

Then, she headed back to the office, trailing a sweet cloud behind her.

Father Ramirez had been silent on the journey to the rectory and then in the taxi to the motel. It was only now, alone outside their motel rooms, eyeing Devlin warily, that he spoke.

"You know that there are rumors about you, Father Devlin?"

"Are there?"

"Yes."

"Well, I'm not one for gossip, so..."

"Neither am I, believe me. The rumors are that strange things happen around you. Unaccountable things. I dismissed it as nonsense...but I've only spent one evening with you, and already, I have seen enough to add another volume to those rumors. I mean, first, the fight with that maniac biker in the bar."

"Like I said, I was a boxer. I've used my fists."

"So you say. But most people have never gone toe-to-toe with a Nazi biker. You should know it's really not a normal occurrence. And then there was the way you sensed something was wrong in Hinkley. And then, to top it all, what happened with Elizabeth Wendig? I've never seen anything like it. That girl came back from the dead...and it happened when you anointed her, touched her..."

"Father Ramirez, before you believe all the rumors you've heard, you should consider one thing: if strange things happened tonight, it's because we've arrived in a town hit by a terrible, once-in-ten-generations tragedy. The place is full of trauma and a need to believe. And in those kinds of circumstances, strange things can happen. Will happen. And not because of me."

"That's not what Elizabeth's family think. Or Elizabeth. And it's not what they were saying when we left."

Devlin ran fingers through his black, wavy hair and sighed. "The need to believe in this town is...well, you can feel it radiating from every house. There's a dreadful thirst here. That's the last I'll say on it, Father. I'll see you for breakfast, and then we can go see about your car. Good night."

Devlin went into his motel room, and Ramirez stood outside his door for a few minutes, pondering the day's events and the conversation he'd just had with Devlin. There was, he concluded, something about the older priest that was unlike anything else he'd encountered. But maybe Devlin was right—he was only a young trainee priest, twenty-two, inexperienced in so much, and perhaps a little more levelheadedness was needed. Ramirez suddenly felt a little ashamed of how carried away he'd become in the presence of the older, more experienced Father Devlin. Ashamed that he'd revealed his immaturity and rashness. Maybe he should have kept his mouth shut about the rumors he'd heard. Kept his mouth shut, period. Feeling regretful and a little embarrassed, Ramirez, realizing how damned tired he was, decided to turn in.

INSIDE HIS MOTEL ROOM, Devlin spent a few minutes unpacking essentials. Then, he sat on the bed and channel-hopped for a while but couldn't find anything to settle on. He picked up his cigar case from the chipped dresser and went out for a smoke.

The motel was deadly quiet. The rooms, most of which looked unoccupied, were in a one-story long row that looked out onto the parking lot. Up to the north, at the head of the motel, was the office and lobby. Down to the south was what looked like utility rooms. The office and lobby formed a horizontal shape at one end, and the utility rooms did the same at the other so that the whole complex formed an "I" shape with a parking lot on either side.

Devlin looked out over the mostly empty weed-strewn lot and smoked his cigar down to halfway. A wind from the east came and went, and a light rain started up. Somewhere out in the night, Devlin was certain he could hear a drone-like sound. The sound of swarming engines far away that seemed to be moving east into the wind.

Ramirez had been right, of course. There was something about this town, and Devlin had felt it as soon as Officer Cassidy drove them into Hinkley—an immense loss and bottomless despair. It had almost overwhelmed him. And the instant he had laid a hand on Elizabeth Wendig, he could feel her returning. He had a certain feeling from somewhere deep within him that had he been at the Wendigs' house half an hour later, it would have been too late, too late for anything or anyone to bring her back.

Just like the places Devlin had been to before—Halton Springs, Sag Harbor, Avery—he had been called to this place at this time for a reason. Not just for Elizabeth Wendig but for another thing he had sensed, something unknown that at this very moment was spreading through the community. He could nearly smell it. That was why he was here, now. But none of this could be made known to Ramirez. Devlin had to be free to operate independently. To do what he always did. To face down the dark forces out there in the midst of Hinkley.

Devlin took a stroll down toward the motel entrance, passing the motel rooms and arriving at the utility rooms. As the wind came and went, he caught the scent of something sharp and acidic that seemed to come from the first and largest utility room. This room had a door with a push bar. Devlin took a look around. The whole complex was silent; not a soul was about. He pushed the bar, and the door swung open. Inside the windowless room, the acidic smell was a little stronger. He found a light switch by the door and turned on the strip lights. In the hard, bright light, he could see cleaning supplies, folded bed linen kept on shelves, and carts for room service. Stacked in the corner of the room were half a dozen boxes of cat litter. Devlin guessed the acid smell must be cat urine. He turned the light off, shut the door, and strolled back to his room, finishing his cigar along the way.

FIVE

The Hideaway Motel didn't serve breakfast, so early the next morning, Devlin and Ramirez went looking for a place to eat. The motel was a five-minute drive from Main Street, so they headed toward the center of town and found a diner on the main drag.

Burke's Diner was a well-kept one-story cream wooden building with a bay window at each end and white-and-red striped awnings. They sat in one of the booths. Devlin ordered the ham steak breakfast, and Ramirez ordered french toast.

"I'll be darned happy to get out of this town," said Ramirez. "I got a thesis to finish by the end of May."

"What's it on?" asked Devlin.

"Hispanic Ministry. Boston is one of the few colleges that do it."

"Where would you like to minister?"

"Puerto Rico. You ever been there?"

"No. No, I haven't."

"You traveled at all?"

"Oh, sure. Before I was a priest, I traveled plenty."

"How so?"

"I was with the Air Force, so I was stationed all over."

"The Air Force? You flew planes?"

"No. I was a detective. Office of Special Investigations."

"So, you looked into crimes?"

"Crimes in the Air Force."

"What kinds of crimes?"

"All kinds of crimes."

"Murder?"

"Yep."

"Drugs?"

"Yep."

"Shootings?"

"Like I said, all kinds of crimes."

The food arrived, and Devlin's cell buzzed. It was Officer Cassidy.

"Your friend's car's with Roy Kane's auto shop," said Cassidy.

"We know. We're staying at the Hideaway Motel, and we met Roy Kane's mom."

"You met Ma Kane? Okay, well, she is the authentic Hinkley experience. You've seen it all now."

"Yeah. I would have felt cheated if I hadn't."

"I just spoke to Roy. They're looking at the car right now. Roy said for you to call by in the morning."

"Okay. We're having a bite to eat at a place called Burke's Diner."

"You're at Burke's? Well, the repair shop is only about a hundred yards further down the strip."

"Ask how long?" said Ramirez, gesturing to get Devlin's attention.

"Did he say how long it'd take to fix?" asked Devlin.

"No, he didn't," replied Cassidy.

"Okay. Thanks." Devlin hung up. "She doesn't know. Eat up, and we'll go find out."

Roy's Autos was on a lot at the lower end of Main Street. It was a plain, white-bricked garage with a corrugated roof. They found Roy Kane inside, working on a 1969 Pontiac in mint condition. He stuck his head out from under the hood, saw the two priests, and swung out from under the Pontiac.

"Hi," he said, standing and wiping his hands with a rag. Barrel-chested and bearlike with curly brown hair and a bushy beard, he looked like the kind of guy you'd lay money on being last man standing in a bar fight. His exposed forearms were covered in a mosaic of mostly blue tattoos. "You two are the priests that broke down last night?"

"That's right," said Devlin.

"You have my car?" asked Ramirez.

Roy Kane nodded. "It's round back."

"That's quite a car," said Ramirez, looking admiringly at the Pontiac.

"Belongs to one of the families that own a waterfront property on the lake. They can afford it up there. Follow me."

They walked around to the back of the garage, where Ramirez's Nissan was parked. On the way, they passed a younger, fair-haired man working on a flatbed. He was a slightly smaller, fairer version of Roy but still a solid six foot. His forearms were covered with tattoos too, though of mostly red and yellow variety.

"This is the guy who owns that Nissan, Ted," Roy said to the fair-haired man. The two shared an amused look.

"So, this is the owner of Hinkley's very own supercar?" said Ted.

"Ha! Yeah, this is the guy. Don't be offended by me and my little brother, Ted. We don't mean any harm," said Roy, chuckling.

"I wasn't offended," replied Ramirez.

"In that case, I'll be sure to try harder next time," said Ted, and the two brothers laughed again.

Out back, the three men stood around the Nissan, and Roy Kane put his hands on his hips. "It's a big job."

"Tell me the worst," said Ramirez.

"The connecting rod has gone. As well as fixing the rod, you'll need new engine seals and gaskets, cylinder head bolts, connecting rod bearings, and the engine and cooler lines will need flushing."

"How... How much?"

"Well, usually it'd be upward of two thousand..."

"Usually...?"

"Yeah. But I can shave off a couple of hundred. I mean, if you think she's worth saving."

"I can't afford another car, that's for sure."

"Well, then, I'll get her back on the road. After all, there's one miracle that already happened in this town." Roy looked at Devlin. "I'm a cousin of the Wendigs. I heard what happened last night with Elizabeth. They're saying it's God's work she's alive. That it was a miracle you performed on her."

Devlin shook his head. "I think her family's belief and science brought her back."

"Well, that's a reasonable-sounding explanation, but that's not the way people are looking to write it up here." Roy Kane stroked his beard and squinted at Devlin. "Did you feel anything? Did you feel God working through you?"

"I couldn't say that I did."

Roy Kane laughed. "There'd be some priests who would be on TV giving interviews and doing a whole circuit. Why not you?"

"I don't want to be on TV."

"Well, I guess if you can't be sure it's a miracle, then no one can." Kane looked at the pathetic Nissan. "But I'll tell you now, I'll bring this old wreck back from the dead."

"How long will it take?" asked Ramirez.

"It'll take the week to do. I got other customers I can't leapfrog."

The two priests headed away from Kane's back lot and stopped for a moment in the morning sunshine.

Ramirez shook his head. "A week?"

"Listen, I can rent a car and drop you back in Boston," said Devlin.

Ramirez considered the suggestion. "Yeah, that would work. I could get a friend to drive me back here to pick up my car when it's ready. There must be a car rental place somewhere around." Ramirez checked his cell. "There's a place in Littleton that does pickup and return."

"Fine. I'll rent a car from there. First though, we should go see Father Wilson. Say we're leaving."

They walked further up Main Street, took a right, which led downhill past more stores, and turned off into the collection of small side roads and buildings that surrounded St. Paul's. So far, the streets had been relatively quiet, but as soon as they got within sight of the church, that changed. A crowd of people were waiting on the sidewalk and the steps in front of the church.

"What's going on?" asked a baffled Ramirez.

"If this is the turnout for Mass, then I need to find out Father Wilson's secret."

As they got closer, they could see that many in the crowd were holding crucifixes and were part of a line stretching into the church. Devlin and Ramirez snaked their way through the crowd, their clerical collars easing their way through. Inside, they found even more people forming a line up to the altar. By the side of the altar, Father Wilson was enthusiastically talking to a group around him. He spotted Devlin and Ramirez, made his excuses to the group, and came over to the two priests.

"Fathers, I'm so glad you're here. Something wonderful has happened." Wilson's eyes shone with happiness. "A chink in the dark, a ray of sunlight at midnight."

"What?" asked Ramirez.

Wilson pointed to the statue of the Virgin Mary in an arched recess in the wall. "The Blessed Virgin Mary..."

Devlin and Ramirez looked at the statue over the heads of the crowd.

"I can't see anything," said Ramirez.

"Go closer," Wilson urged. So Ramirez and Devlin got as close as they could without cutting in line and saw the cause of the commotion. On the Virgin Mary's cheek was a faint streak of clear liquid, which seemed to start from the corner of her eye. The thin trail glistened in the light from the arched windows.

"Is that a tear...?" asked Ramirez.

"Yes," replied Wilson breathlessly. "She has been weeping since I came in first thing this morning. It's another sign that God is willing to intervene in our lives and can take away our suffering."

"Another sign...?" said Ramirez.

"As well as Elizabeth Wendig. As well as her miraculous recovery." Father Wilson didn't wait for a reply. He saw someone in the crowd he knew and went to greet them.

"Condensation," said Devlin flatly, shaking his head and looking at the statue. "It's condensation."

Ramirez looked shocked. "That's very cynical, isn't it? Are you a priest or a skeptic?"

"The two are not mutually exclusive. I've seen plenty of things that have no earthly explanation, but this isn't one of them."

"Well, take a look around. No one else here seems to agree with you."

"Like I said, it's a town in grieving that wants to believe."

Father Wilson returned, still beaming. "I've already reported it to the archbishop's office. I rang an hour ago and had the most inspiring conversation with the archbishop."

Devlin's cell had started to buzz. He took it out and looked at the screen. "Excuse me, I need to take this."

Devlin went and sat in a pew in the front row and took the call while Wilson continued to enthuse and chatter away at Ramirez.

"Isn't it wonderful?" said Wilson. "It's restorative to the faith at a time when we couldn't need it more."

And Ramirez had to admit, despite Devlin's skepticism, that the feeling of devotion and belief the weeping statue had aroused was quite inspiring. And the statue did seem to have something of an aura around it, glowing in the light from the high church windows.

"I've just had a call from Cardinal Hermes," said Devlin, returning with his cell still in his hand.

"The cardinal? What does he want?" asked Father Wilson.

"Apparently, you rang the cardinal's office, as well as the archbishop, this morning to tell them about the statue and Elizabeth Wendig."

Wilson's cheeks reddened. "Ah. Yes, yes, I did. I felt a duty to report what had happened. It would have been negligence not to tell the cardinal too. But why did he call you?"

"I know Cardinal Hermes from back in seminary. He's an old friend. Because of your phone call, the cardinal has been on the phone to the archbishop, and they've asked us, myself and Father Ramirez, as visiting priests to begin a preliminary investigation into the weeping statue...and Elizabeth Wendig."

"Wait... Us...?" said Ramirez.

"Somehow, the archbishop knew we were both here," said Devlin.

"I told them," said Wilson. "I believe the weeping Virgin Mary is connected with the Wendig girl's recovery, and I told them that you were both present for that. But why would he ask you, Father Devlin? Why wouldn't they send someone from the archbishop's office?"

"Because we're here, and Cardinal Hermes knows I worked as a detective."

"Oh, I see... I didn't know..."

"But I have to be back in Boston for college. My thesis..." said Ramirez.

"Father Ramirez," said Devlin. "Trainee priests don't get to investigate miracles. I'd grab the opportunity with both hands. They'll push back the deadline on your thesis for this. We're here now on the business of the archbishop and a cardinal."

"I guess..." replied Ramirez, beginning to see the advantages of the situation. "But...won't the fact you were directly involved in Elizabeth Wendig's recovery make you...biased?"

"We're not exactly the FBI here, kid," said Devlin. "It's just a preliminary investigation, and we happen to be on the spot. If there's a follow-up investigation, it will be far more official and senior."

"What shape will your investigation take?" asked Wilson.

"The cardinal wants us to take factual statements from the most relevant parties, including ours, and collect photographic evidence. I'll feed that back to him and the archbishop, who'll then make a decision about referring to the Vatican."

"The Vatican?"

"If the archbishop decides to refer it."

"So, what will you do first?" asked Wilson.

"If you can clear a space, Father Wilson, maybe Father Ramirez can take some video of the statue on his phone."

"Sure," said Ramirez.

"Then we need to interview witnesses."

Father Wilson went to speak to the people at the head of the line and move them back.

"You know," said Ramirez, getting his cell out and warming to the task they'd been given. "I could really get into this. It's a pretty rare opportunity. And if it gets me in front of the cardinal..."

"It could sure help with getting a ministry in Puerto Rico."

"Yeah... This does mean you're going to have to approach all of this with an open mind."

"My mind is plenty open."

SIX

"Hinkley is on its own now, Cassidy,"

The words rang through Officer Lori Cassidy like she was hollow.

"That's it?" said Cassidy. "Three weeks of help and then nothing?"

Chief Sean Garland was at the lectern, taking the roll call. Tall, topping out at six four, and bald as a coot, Garland was sandy colored from head to foot—sandy eyelashes, sandy stubble, sandy forearm hair, sandy skin. But he wasn't standing to his full height. He was stooped, his eyes were dark, and he looked like hell. In front of him, sitting behind two rows of desks, were the three Hinkley PD patrol officers, including Officers Cassidy and Kyle Ross.

"I'm no happier about it than you," said Garland. "The bureau see it as a terrible tragedy, and they'll assist with any checks we need, but they're not able to put boots on the ground. We can't keep the extra state police and federal resources without any leads. If..." Garland checked himself and started his sentence again. "*When* we find something, then we'll request extra resources. In the meantime, Garratt Marshall has agreed to take his floatplane out on searches around Hinkley, and I will accompany him. Brandon PD has loaned us two drones we can use to survey the surrounding area for the white Mercedes van."

To Cassidy, it all sounded like nothing very much. "How far can the drones go?"

"I'm told up to three thousand feet."

"How much can a drone see from three thousand feet?" asked Ross.

"It can give us an incredible radius. Sergeant Fleisner will go out with the drone and set up at different points within a thirty-mile area."

"We have six officers, including you, Chief," said Cassidy. "We're not gonna get anywhere with that manpower. I'm really concerned the hunt for the van and the people who killed our kids may be effectively over."

Garland sighed. He leaned on the lectern and shifted his weight from one foot to the other. "Officer, I fought to keep the state police team here. I gave it everything. For three weeks, I've hardly seen my family or slept more than two hours straight. And now the state police are gone, I'll give this case everything till I die. And I expect you to do the same, Cassidy. The town expects you to. And if you can't promise that, then I'll take your badge now."

Cassidy didn't rise to the threat. In any case, she knew what Garland had said was true—he had put nearly every waking hour into finding the van. A couple of other patrol officers shared smirks, but it was water off a duck's back as far as Cassidy was concerned.

"The only other business," Garland continued, changing the subject like he was throwing a handbrake turn, "is with the Kane brothers' auto repair shop." Just the mention of the brothers' names caused a stir and murmurs. "Yeah, I know, it's a pain in the ass, and it's the same old problem. The manager of Dunkin' Donuts next door is complaining that the Kanes are parking vehicles in front of the side entrance they use for deliveries. Now, I can pick someone to go have a word with Roy and Ted, but it would make things much easier if one of you guys could volunteer." Garland looked around the room and saw no hands. He was about to call out an officer's name at random when Cassidy shot her hand up.

"I'll do it."

There was another murmur, and Garland looked a little surprised. "You sure, Lori? I mean, if it feels like there's a conflict there..."

"Leave it with me. Not a problem. Proud to serve."

CASSIDY AND ROSS drifted out into the parking lot. The Hinkley Police Department building was a plain, long, two-story wooden structure that could easily be mistaken for apartments were it not for the sign over the front door and the cruisers parked in front. It overlooked acres of green meadow and forest, repeating in uneven strips as far as the eye could see.

"For what it's worth, I believe Garland," said Ross. "He won't give up. And we won't give up, ever. We have to find that van."

"I believe Garland too. You think it was someone from Hinkley who sent those kids to their death, Ross? You think it was one of us?"

Ross looked out over the meadows and forest and thought for a moment. "I think it must be."

"Yeah, me too. Why would they have been going north? It

takes them straight through Hinkley. They had to be heading for Hinkley or hereabouts. Whoever killed those kids is someone we know. They must be a psychopath, or I don't know how they can get up each morning and go about their business with that on their conscience. But it's someone we all know."

SEVEN

"I don't know, Hank. Hand to God, I don't know."

"Can we run tests, Doc? Get Elizabeth to the hospital and do bloods? I mean, they must want to know what happened here. The professors and scientists and whatnot up at Rutland could get Nobel Prizes for this kind of thing." Hank Wendig took a sip from his beer bottle and wiped his mouth with the back of his hand.

"That's exactly what's going to happen," replied Dr. Hudson. "I've already spoken to the laboratory and Neurology. I've taken blood samples this morning, and I'll get them sent up to Rutland." Hudson got up from the workbench he'd been sitting on in Hank's garage. He held a bottle of beer in one hand and gesticulated with the other. "But I'm telling you, Hank, Elizabeth had multiple organ failure. There was no way she should have recovered, and not like that. Thank God she did, but if there's a medical explanation to find, I'll goddamned find it."

"You took a look at her just now, Rick. Did that tell you anything?"

Hudson took a sip of his beer. "Not a great deal, except she seems to have recovered out of all recognition. Her vitals are all heading back to normal. She's still in a wheelchair, of course, and I don't know how long that will be for. But I can see there are reflexes in her legs, so that's really hopeful. Has she said much?"

Hank shrugged his heavy-plaid-shirted shoulders and scratched at his beard. "A little. Not much. It's...Jesus...it's crazy... I still can't get my head around it..." He wiped a tear away from his eye, and Hudson put a hand on his shoulder.

"I can't imagine how it feels... To lose a daughter and get her back. But Hank, you did get her back."

"She doesn't move from the window, Rick. She just looks out onto the street all the time."

"Well, she's catching up on the last few weeks, and it's been weeks from hell."

Hank looked Hudson straight in the eye. "Do you think...? Do you think what happened last night had anything to do with that priest?"

"Devlin? No... Why? Don't tell me you're getting all mystical now, Hank."

"He's a strange-looking guy for a priest. I mean, he ain't exactly like your regular priest. Looks more like an ex-heavyweight. And...he kind of has a presence about him... Kathleen thinks it's a miracle, and I..."

Hudson put up a hand and said flatly, "I don't think it was the priest, Hank."

"I don't suppose you've heard what happened at the church this morning?"

"No... What happened?"

"Kathleen was down there for a Legion of Mary meeting. She said there was a crowd inside the church. Apparently, the statue of the Virgin Mary is weeping."

"Weeping?" Hudson didn't look convinced. "Oh, come off

of it, Hank. It's a helluva lot more likely there's a leak somewhere. That church is on the brink of collapsing. It's got more cracks than bricks."

"Kathleen seemed convinced, and Father Wilson has already contacted the archbishop to have it looked into. There's a line right down the street of people waiting to witness the miracle. They got candles, crosses, the whole shebang."

Hudson shook his head and sighed. "It's the strangest time I ever knew, Hank. Goddamn, but it's the strangest time." He finished up his beer and put it on the workbench. "I'm a doctor, and everything that has happened will have a medical or practical explanation. I gotta go. I gotta get back to the surgery. Thanks for the beer."

"No problem."

Hank opened the garage door and let Hudson out.

"I'll be in touch as soon as I hear about the test results."

"Thanks, Rick. Appreciate it."

Hudson left, and Hank was scooping up his empty bottle when he heard the doorbell go. He went through the doorway that connected to the kitchen, dropped the bottles in the trash, and opened the front door. Devlin and Ramirez were standing on the porch.

"Hi, Mr. Wendig," said Devlin.

"Hello, Fathers. What can I do for you?"

"We thought we might check in on Elizabeth," said Devlin. "Just to see how she was."

"Sure, come on in, both of you. You brought good fortune to our house last night, hell, I'd put you up in the attic room if I could. Come in."

"Thank you," said Devlin. "There is also another reason for our visit."

"Oh?"

"This is going to sound a little dramatic, but here goes.

We're here on business of the church. Father Wilson has reported two events in Hinkley as miracles. One of them being Elizabeth's recovery."

"I guess the other is the Virgin Mary statue?"

"You've heard about it?"

"Small town, Father. Small town."

"The archbishop's and cardinal's offices have asked that we do a preliminary investigation on their behalf."

"What does that involve?"

"If you were agreeable, it would involve us sitting down with you and taking a short statement. And speaking with Elizabeth too."

Hank thought for a moment, then said, "Sure. Far as I'm concerned, what happened was a miracle of some kind. Or as near to it as can be. Elizabeth is here too. I don't know if she'd be up to speaking, but I can ask."

The two priests waited in the hall while Hank went to talk to Elizabeth. As he had expected, he found his daughter in the living room, where Devlin had performed last rites to her the night before. The bed was still up against the side wall, but it was made up, and Elizabeth was sitting in a wheelchair by the window. She had been staring out onto the street when Hank came in.

"Elizabeth," Hank said softly. "There are two priests here to talk to you."

She turned her wheelchair toward her father. "Is it Father Devlin?"

"Yes, yes, it is. He wants to talk to you about what happened last night. Father Wilson believes it might be a miracle."

Elizabeth gave a tired smile. "Sure. I'd really like to talk to Father Devlin."

Hank brought the two priests in. They took the sofa, and Hank sat on the side of the bed.

"Hello, Elizabeth," said Devlin. "I don't know if you remember me from last night?"

"Yes, I do, Father Devlin."

"Good. This is Father Ramirez. He was here last night too."

"Hello, Father."

Elizabeth was still pale and terribly thin, but a little color had returned to her cheeks, and her eyes were bright and even lively.

"You look well, Elizabeth," said Devlin.

"You mean, I look well for a dead person."

"I just mean that you look well."

"Thank you. I feel better than I did, that's for sure. Like I'm back from the brink."

"I think your dad told you why we're here."

"Yes. Father Wilson thinks what happened to me was a miracle."

"Yes. And Father Wilson believes it was one of two miracles. The statue of the Virgin Mary at St. Paul's has clear liquid running from an eye, and he believes the liquid is tears and is the work of God."

"Wow. I guess it's a good job there are more priests in Hinkley now," said Elizabeth, grinning.

Ramirez had taken out his cell and placed it down on the coffee table in front of the sofa.

"Do you mind if we record this conversation, Elizabeth?" asked Ramirez.

"No. No, I don't. What is it you want to ask me?"

"About what you remember," said Devlin. "Do you have any memories of the crash or of what happened last night? When you became conscious?"

Elizabeth looked out of the window for a moment and considered her answer. Her fingers twitched on the arms of her wheelchair, and she frowned.

"I remember fragments of the crash. Images and feelings, but nothing I could put together that make much sense. The last thing I remember before I woke up was the bus back from St. Johnsbury. I remember falling asleep on the journey back. And then there was nothing. Blackness. I don't even mean a deep sleep. I felt like I was gone. I was nowhere. The next thing that happened was I felt a hand holding mine. The gentlest, strongest hand I'd ever held. I felt myself breathing, and then the blackness got lighter. And then I opened my eyes and saw you, Father."

"Do you think it was a miracle, Elizabeth?" asked Hank.

Without hesitating, Elizabeth said," Yes. Yes, I do."

"It sure sounds like one to me too," said Hank. "What do you think, Father?"

Hank, Elizabeth, and Ramirez looked expectantly at Devlin, waiting on his pronouncement.

"I think the next thing is to get the address and number of Elizabeth's doctor."

THERE WAS a promise of spring outside in the street. Kids had started playing out, and there was birdsong. The two priests got into a Chevy Malibu. It was one of two cars they'd rented from the rental place out in Littleton. Ramirez had a Toyota Corolla that he'd left back at the motel.

"It sounded pretty miraculous to me." Ramirez's eyes were lit up with enthusiasm. "The more I hear and see, the more I really get excited about what's happened in this town."

Devlin turned the key and put the selector into drive. His reply was flat and cool. "I really think we need to talk to Elizabeth's doctor."

EIGHT

Blind Archie Baker's house was a fifteen-minute drive from the center of Hinkley and not far from where the local road rejoined the interstate. A dilapidated farmhouse in seventeen acres of scrubland filled with scrap and garbage, it had few visitors.

Dr. Rick Hudson pulled in from the highway and trundled down an uneven dirt track canopied by overgrown trees. He stopped in front of the farmhouse that after decades of neglect looked more like a shack.

There was no sign of Archie on the porch, where he spent most of his time sipping iced tea with his dog, Troy. Hudson got out of his car and entered the house, pushing open the front door, which Archie only locked at night.

Despite his regular visits, Hudson never got used to the low-level smell of stale sweat, stagnant garbage, and dog mess. He held his hand up to his face so he could inhale the sweet odor from the cologne-soaked handkerchief tucked into his jacket sleeve. It was an old trick used by social workers he knew, and he always had it prepared for his house visits to Archie.

The first floor was one big living room with a couch, TV, a wooden table and chairs, and a temporary bed on the floor made from cushions and a sleeping bag. The table was covered in bits of cable, unwashed plates, and old *Sports Illustrated* and *People* magazines. At the back of the room was a small kitchenette. Flies hovered over the trash can, the sink, and the dog bowl.

"Archie...?" There was no answer and no sounds from upstairs. No barks from Troy either. Hudson checked his watch. It was five past two, so he was pretty much on time, and Archie couldn't have gone far, even with Troy leading him.

Hudson came back out onto the porch and heard a bark from further down the track. A few moments later, Troy appeared with Archie following. Archie wore his usual stained overalls, overcoat, and thick black glasses.

"Hey, Archie. I was beginning to wonder where you'd got to."

"Just me and the mutt taking a walk, Doc."

Hudson watched Archie and his dog approach the house with rising interest. For a man with 5 percent vision, he seemed to be going at quite a clip. So it wasn't entirely unexpected when Archie hit his foot against a brick half sticking out of the earth and took a stumble. Hudson leaped over the porch steps and helped Archie to stand.

"You okay, Archie?"

"Damn brick. Place needs a cleanup, but who's gonna do that?"

Troy led Archie up onto the porch and sat him on the swing chair, with Troy curling up at his feet. Hudson sat beside him.

"So, how's tricks?" asked Hudson.

"I'm doing okay, Doc."

"Glad to hear it. Mind if I check you over?"

"Do your worst."

Hudson went to his car and got his medical bag from the trunk. He set about giving Archie the once-over and took some blood. Once he was done, he sat back in the swing chair and crossed his legs.

"So, what's the story, Doc?"

Hudson nodded. "Good. Your blood pressure is better than it's been in some time. And you're looking pretty well too."

"Yeah?"

"Yeah."

"You been out walking around the yard, Archie?"

Archie laughed. "Been doing more than that, Doc."

"Really?"

"I've been down to Frost Hollow."

Hudson shifted forward in the swing seat, hardly able to believe his ears. "Frost Hollow? But that's...that's gotta be a three-mile walk."

"Two point six miles. Each way. That's what my cell phone says on speaker."

"Frost Hollow? Archie, that's too far, way too far. I'm all for you getting exercise, but that's a long walk for someone with..."

"For a blind man. For ol' blind Archie Baker."

"For someone with 5 percent sight."

There was a pause, and Hudson could see that Archie was pleased with himself about something. Like he was about to reveal a long-held secret.

"You wanna know something, Doc? Something pretty incredible?"

"What?"

Grinning, Archie beckoned the doctor closer and whispered, "I'm getting better, Doc."

Hudson nodded. "Like I say, you're looking well, and your blood pressure—"

"Never mind my goddamned blood pressure. It's my sight I'm talking about. My eyesight is getting better."

"Better how?"

Archie thought for a moment. "It's like the blurred colors I could see in the center of my vision, they're coming into focus more. Every day since last Sunday, it's got a little bit better. It's got so I expect it in the morning when I wake up. That I'll get a little more definition. A little more sight."

Hudson sat back in the swing chair. He discreetly removed his own steel-framed glasses, tucking them in his jacket pocket, and said, "Turn and look at me, Archie."

Archie turned toward Hudson and looked straight at him. Hudson lifted Archie's dark glasses up and examined his eyes. He took a good look and concluded to himself that the old man's eyes didn't look like they were getting any better. They were not in good condition. The sclera was yellow and bloodshot, and his irises were so dark they were indistinguishable from his pupils.

"Okay, Archie. Now tell me, what can you see?"

"I can see you, Doc. Your face."

"Good. Tell me more about my face."

"I can see the outline of your face, gray and black hair, mustache..."

"Okay... Anything else?"

"Glasses..."

"Right," said Hudson. He replaced Archie's glasses and sat back into the swing chair, satisfied he'd put a pin in Archie's bold claims.

"You're not wearing any," said Archie.

"What?"

"I had an idea you wore glasses, Doc. But you're not wearing any."

Hudson shifted forward again. "I do. I took them off."

"Aha!" exclaimed Archie. "Trying to trick me?"

"Not trick you. Just do a simple test."

"And I passed, didn't I, Doc?"

"Have you been into town for an eye test?"

"I'm going this afternoon. I made an appointment because of the changes. I tell you, Doc, I can see colors and outlines like I've never seen before. Not since before I started to lose my sight. I can see the sun and the moon. I guess it's a long way from what other people have, but Doc...I can see trees and birds in the sky."

"Here, let me take another look." Hudson removed Archie's glasses again and studied the old man's face. Now, as he examined Archie a second time, it seemed plausible to Hudson that Archie's eyes were perhaps a little more alert, more alive. Suddenly, Hudson had a notion the dewy lifelessness had gone, and it felt like Archie was looking at him.

"Tell you something else," said Archie. "When I go up to Frost Hollow, I saw something I never expected. I saw Jack and Betty's son, Franklin."

"You saw Franklin Kelly?"

"Yep."

Hudson shook his head and let out the mother of all sighs. "C'mon, Archie. Franklin died in the crash. You know that."

"I've seen him. I've seen the ghost of Franklin Kelly."

Archie seemed to be looking out now toward the overgrown yard. Hudson watched his eyes for signs of sight and cognition. He remembered the way Archie had stumbled over the brick, how he'd felt for the swing chair, and the Franklin boy lying at the bottom of the lake in a rusting bus that might never see the light of day again. What was more likely? Hudson asked himself. That this eighty-year-old registered blind man had started to recover his sight and see ghosts or that he was fooling himself? And it seemed to Dr. Hudson that the question answered itself.

"Archie, I don't think you should be going up to Frost Hollow by yourself."

"One, I'm not by myself—I got Troy. And two, like I told you, my eyesight's getting better. I'm telling you, Doc, my eyesight is getting better. It's a solid, one hundred percent fact."

NINE

"You finished with that flatbed yet?" Roy Kane's head slid out from under the Mustang he'd been working on, and he waited for his brother to reply.

"Yeah. She's all done and out back. I called Fisher to come get it." Ted Kane had been filing paperwork in the office at the back of the repair shop, which was partitioned off by glass. He stepped out into the workshop and took a swig from a can of Monster Energy.

"Okay," Roy replied. "Well, I got another delivery you could do for me." Roy pulled himself all the way out on his creeper and got to his feet just as a car swung haphazardly off the street and shuddered to a stop at the workshop entrance. The driver's door flipped open, and Ma Kane got out. She walked toward the boys with her distinctive dogged gait, impeded by a slight limp, carrying a vape stick in her hand.

"Hi, Ma," said Roy. "Everything okay?"

"Oh, sure, everything's whoop-de-do 'cept the whole town's lost its head."

The two brothers looked at each other and rolled their eyes.

"Yeah, we heard about it too," said Ted. "The Wendig girl and the statue. Hard to know what to make of it all."

"I know what I make of it," replied Ma Kane sharply. "People here are soft in the head, that's what. Morons. Everyone needs to get a grip of themselves." She took a toot on her vape stick. "But they won't. You hear that gossip about ol' Hugh Varley being a cultist back in the day? That he might have taken those children off?"

"Yeah, I did," said Ted. "Where'd that come from? Wait... was that you, Ma?"

Ma Kane let out a rattling laugh.

"Ma," said Roy. "That's just mean...but funny too."

"I know. I told it to Nick at the hardware store and said I heard it from Nelson at the gas station, and I told Nelson that I heard it from Nick at the hardware store. It was hours—hours, I tell you—before I ran into the Campbell woman, who told the whole thing back to me like it was straight from the *New York Post*." She took another toot on her vape and spouted out a line of jubilant smoke. Then, she turned suddenly serious. "Roy, you told Ted we need him to do another delivery?"

"Just now," said Roy.

"When does it need to be done?" asked Ted.

"Not till tonight. Same order, same place," said Roy.

"How's it going with the priest's Nissan?" asked Ma Kane.

"It's a piece of crap, is what it is," said Roy.

"How long to fix?"

"Three to four days."

"How long you tell them priests?"

"At least a week. I'll milk it for more. There's a couple hundred more bucks in that job I can squeeze out for sure."

"Good boy. I bumped up the room rate for them too. So that's extra in the kitty." She took another toot on her vape stick and let the smoke escape out of the side of her mouth. "Nothing gives me more pleasure than taking money from a priest. It's almost wrong how much pleasure it gives me. Even more than screwing over a cop."

Roy coughed. "Speaking of which...we got company."

Ma Kane turned to see a police cruiser turning in from the road, with Officer Cassidy at the wheel. The cruiser drew up by Ma Kane's car, and Cassidy got out and put on her aviator shades. The three Kanes eyed the police officer warily and made no attempt to hide their displeasure at this visit by one of Hinkley's finest.

"How you doing?" said Cassidy.

"All the better to have a member of Hinkley PD here protecting us," replied Ma Kane.

"I've never known you to need protecting," replied Cassidy.

"Can you get me a tax deduction on that, then, honey?"

"If I could, I would."

"Sure, I believe you."

There was an awkward silence, which Ma Kane broke. "Well, there's nothing to report here, Officer Cassidy." Ma Kane snorted two lines of smoke out of her nostrils. "Though the way things are going around here, I wouldn't be surprised if the angel Gabriel descended at any moment."

"Still no news on who those bastards in the Mercedes were, Lori?" asked Ted.

"No. No news, Ted."

"And there won't be," said Ma Kane. "Not now the state police and the bureau have gone home."

"They're still working the case," said Lori. "Just don't have boots on the ground."

"Sure. No boots on the ground," said Ma Kane.

"Brandon PD have loaned us two drones. To help with the search."

"Whoopee doo. We got a couple of flying toys. Eight of the

town's children and Hugh Varley dead, and we got a couple of flying toys. That truck and whoever were in it are probably halfway to Rio by now."

"Yeah." Cassidy took her sunglasses off and looked thoughtful. "See, I don't think they're halfway round the world. I don't think whoever was in that truck is very far away at all."

"What makes you think that?" asked Roy.

"Because they were on the local road. It forks off from the interstate and then rejoins it. That road's only purpose is to connect Hinkley to the rest of the world. There's no reason they..."

"Could have been lost," said Ma. "Could have been avoiding a jam on the interstate. Could have been picking up whatever here. Coming from someplace else, going someplace else."

"The interstate wasn't jammed that night. If they were picking up, then someone hereabouts would know about that and said. That leaves lost. Yeah, that's possible, took a wrong turning. But the way markers and signs are pretty clear coming up to the Hinkley exit, so they'd had to be driving with blindfolds on to miss those."

"Or high or drunk or both," said Ma Kane. "Things some people put into their bodies these days have a worse effect than blindfolds."

"It's a possibility. Anyhow, I just pulled in 'cause the manager from Dunkin' Donuts has made a complaint—"

"For crying out loud," hissed Roy.

"That pencil-necked moron? Again?" said Ted.

"—a complaint that you're blocking their entrance with your cars."

"We ain't blocking his entrance. We gotta go past their side entrance to get round back."

"The manager says you're parking there."

"He can shove it up his ass," said Roy. "That's BS."

"He's sent us photographs," replied Cassidy.

"Who's to say it's not him setting us up?" Ma Kane protested. "Putting his own car there, taking fake photos."

"Well, I'm doing my job and letting you know. If you say you're not blocking the entrance, then I'll tell him that's what you're saying." Cassidy started to walk back to her cruiser. "I'll tell him the police have done what they can, so he can go ahead with the lawyers."

"What lawyers?" said a rattled Roy.

Cassidy stopped by her cruiser. "Oh, well, Dunkin' Donuts is a big corporate beast with more money than we'll ever see. So the manager's been talking to their legal department. I said, listen, hold off, I'll try and sort this amicably. But he's like a dog with a bone, so I'd brace yourself for a fight and suggest you lawyer up. Lawyer up big-time. I'll see you all around." Cassidy got into her cruiser and took off.

"Uppity little bitch," said Ma Kane. "Thinks she's better than us. But we know that can't be... Don't we, boys?"

"You think it's true about the lawyers?" asked Ted.

"No. She's lying through her teeth, conniving little so-and-so. Legal department won't get involved in a goddamned parking dispute." Ma Kane sucked on her vape stick, and her mouth puckered around the plastic mouthpiece. "But we need to pick our fights, and this one ain't worth the effort. You boys leave the side entrance clear, you hear me?"

The brothers moaned and cursed in protest, and Ma Kane put up a hand.

"We got bigger fish to fry than that poor excuse for a man next door. Leave it for now, and I promise, further down the line, we'll give that pipsqueak something to think about."

TEN

"That's it," said Ramirez. "That's the lake those poor children perished in."

Ramirez was at the wheel, with Devlin beside him. They were driving north along Route 5, approaching the Vesper Run Crossing, headed for a meeting with Dr. Rick Hudson. The lake was spread out up ahead to their left.

"I couldn't think of many more awful, unfriendly, and cruel places to die."

"Pull over, will you?" said Devlin suddenly.

"What?"

"Before we get to the crossing. Pull over."

Ramirez did as Devlin asked and pulled up ten yards short of the crossroads. Devlin got out and walked to the junction where the roads met. It was a light spring day. Cool air and warm sun came and went with the clouds. He looked over at the lake. For a couple of minutes, Devlin hardly moved. He seemed transfixed by the lake, as if he were trying to see what lay at the bottom of it. Then, abruptly, he turned and looked at the road coming in from the west that went on to Hinkley and the road heading north. He pulled his cell out and unlocked it. He'd been scrolling through for a minute or so when Ramirez appeared by his side.

"What are you doing?"

"Just trying to get my bearings." He pointed to the road coming in from the west. "That's Old Boulevard. It's a minor road that cuts across the state, going underneath the interstate. Maybe it was once the main route in and out of Hinkley. It's the road the bus took on the night of the accident." Devlin consulted his cell again. "It heads east into midtown. The road we're on, Route 5, that snakes off from the interstate and joins up with the north end of Main Street, then snakes back off to the interstate. The only other turnoff is to the road that services the waterfront complex, and that ends somewhere in the forest to the northwest of the lake."

"So?"

"You'd likely only take either of these roads if your destination was Hinkley. I'd lay good money whoever was driving that truck is from Hinkley or was coming to visit someone in Hinkley. Which to my mind means the answer to who killed those kids is in Hinkley."

"Ah, of course, I forgot you were a detective. Well, that's all well and good, but that's not what we're here for, is it?"

Devlin didn't answer. Instead, he continued to squint into the distance.

Ramirez indicated the way back to the car. "Shall we?"

Devlin trudged back to the car, and Ramirez followed.

Back in the car, Devlin said, "I think you should take the lead on gathering information for the cardinal and archbishop. You should submit the findings."

"Why?"

"You're a bright guy. That's obvious to me. You're sharp, you have the years on your side, and you'll go far. Of that, I have no doubt."

"You can see into the future now?" Ramirez said wryly.

"In this case, maybe I can. And because I think it would be a great thing for you to have done. A great opportunity. You won't get experience like this again. I'm not ambitious. I have no desires career-wise. But for you, this would be a real feather in your cap, and I would be very happy to let you have it. And, like I said, it would be a real boost to getting that position in Puerto Rico."

Ramirez thought for a moment and then said, "Okay... Thank you."

"It makes sense, is all."

Ramirez started the car, and they resumed the journey north along the eastern side of Lake Vesper. Eventually, they came to a hard left turn, which went uphill before it leveled out into a smaller, recently surfaced road. On the left side of the road was a marina with boats and, further down, a floatplane. On the right were large wooden cabins that looked like vacation homes and, beyond that, stores and restaurants. Some of the buildings were still under construction and surrounded by scaffolding.

They parked, deciding to do the last part of the journey on foot, and passed a stretch of cafes and restaurants. Some were shut, and those that were open weren't busy. One place, a bar called the Boathouse, which had tables set out on a veranda overlooking the marina, was the exception. A group of kids, mainly boys in their late teens to early twenties, were talking loudly, shouting, and laughing hard. As Devlin and Ramirez neared the veranda, a funny-serious argument between two of the boys turned into pushing and shoving. One was tall and athletic-looking; the other was shorter and squatter. Both wore ski jackets, torn jeans, and high-tops. Curiosity and a kind of fear and excitement gripped Ramirez, and he couldn't keep his eyes off the unfolding scene as he passed by. The pushing and shoving between the two kids began to get serious rather than funny—a chair went over, and the argument turned into a standoff. And it might have become a fight right there and then, but the taller kid caught Ramirez gawping.

"Hey, Father Dumbass."

Ramirez, suddenly self-conscious, looked down at the road.

"I said, hey, Father Dumbass. What are you looking at?" The other kids were laughing and egging the tall kid on. "You got the hots for me? Is that it? I know all about you priest guys, what you like..."

"Ignore them," said Devlin. "Just ignore them."

"What a bunch of—" Ramirez felt a sudden thud against his back. Glass shattered on the ground and was followed by laughter and cursing. He and Devlin turned to see a Coke bottle in pieces on the sidewalk.

"I'll have a word with these clowns," said Devlin. But Ramirez put a hand on his arm.

"No," he said firmly. "Let's turn the other cheek."

Devlin reluctantly let it go, and the two priests turned their backs on the catcalls and curses and walked away in silence.

"They're just kids, Father," said Ramirez.

"They're not much younger than you."

"It's not worth the trouble."

Devlin and Ramirez passed more empty bars, cafes, and restaurants, and only a couple of other people. Further on were more cabins, but all of these were partly built. Cranes and flatbed trucks were parked on what was still a building site.

The address they had for Dr. Hudson turned out to be a double-fronted, gray, two-story house with bay windows that looked out onto the marina and the lake.

"So, like we agreed," said Devlin, "you take the lead. This is your rodeo. Okay?"

Ramirez took a breath and collected himself. "Okay."

Devlin clapped Ramirez on the back. "You'll be fine. Just fine."

Devlin rang the bell, and Dr. Hudson answered.

"Father Devlin, Father Ramirez. Hi."

"Thanks for seeing us at such short notice, Doctor," said Ramirez.

"That's okay. Come in."

Devlin and Ramirez followed Dr. Hudson down the hallway to one of two large living rooms that faced the lake. The furniture was minimal, and there was virtually nothing in the way of personal items on display.

"You been in Hinkley long?" asked Devlin, scanning the room.

"Couple of years," said Hudson. "I know what you're thinking. There's not much in the way of homely touches. Curse of the bachelor who works long hours, I'm afraid. Please, sit down."

Ramirez and Devlin took two armchairs by the bay window. Hudson sat in a rocking chair in front of a bookcase that covered a whole wall but was mostly empty.

"So," said Hudson. "You're here about the so-called miracles? This is part of a church investigation?"

"Just preliminary," said Ramirez, placing his cell on the coffee table. Devlin sensed the younger priest was a little nervy and tentative. "Do you mind if I record our conversation?"

"No. No, I don't."

Ramirez sat back and crossed his legs. "Once we've completed our inquiries, senior members of the church will make a decision about a more rigorous investigation. Correct me if I'm wrong, but I would hazard a guess, Dr. Hudson, that you're a skeptic?"

Hudson smiled. "What would you expect? I'm a medical doctor, a trained scientist." Hudson folded his arms and sighed. "So, who's saying it's a miracle, and what's the process?"

Hudson's directness threw Ramirez, and he took a moment to collect his thoughts and reply. "The two events we're tasked with looking into are the recovery of Elizabeth Wendig and the claim of the weeping Virgin Mary statue at St. Paul's Church."

"And is there a process set down for these kinds of investigations?"

"What we're doing is more of a first report," said Ramirez, gaining more confidence and composure. "If there is sufficiently convincing circumstance, then the bishop will request that a Vatican-appointed committee assess the evidence. The committee will include medical professionals like yourself, Doctor, and include medical professionals that are nonbelievers, like yourself."

"I see. And what can I do?"

"We need two things from you. First, what Elizabeth's medical diagnosis and prognosis was. Secondly, we would want your explanation as to how Elizabeth recovered on the night that we were called to perform last rites on her."

There was a silence as Hudson looked out the window, his mind ticking over a response. "Well," he began, his fingers interlaced and his thumbs pressed together. "Her diagnosis was that she had severe head trauma, five broken ribs, and spinal cord swelling that was completely resistant to treatment. The injury to her spinal cord was causing respiratory and multiple organ failure, and I and two consultants at Rutland had made a very definite prognosis: death, and death sooner rather than later. The night Hank Wendig called Father Wilson, she hardly had a pulse. As to the explanation of her sudden recovery, I'll admit, I don't have much in the way of a medical explanation. But we're waiting for Elizabeth's test results. Those results should tell us more about what happened to her."

"But you were convinced she was dying? You and the consultants?" asked Ramirez.

"Yes. Yes, we were. I don't know if that makes it a miracle though."

"No. There is another category this could fall into. The category of events that cannot be medically explained but which are not miracles."

"Quite. Quite so."

"Do you know when the test results might come back?"

"Elizabeth's tests come back tomorrow at the latest. Obviously, I can't just share those with you. That'd be something Elizabeth and her parents would have to give consent to."

"Father Ramirez," asked Devlin. "Would you mind if I asked a question?"

"Go ahead."

"What kind of treatments was Elizabeth receiving?"

The question seemed to puzzle Hudson. "Only treatments to stabilize her condition. To try and contain the results of her injuries."

"Would you mind listing them, for our record?"

"Well, antibiotics, of course, for sepsis control, microcirculatory and respiratory support for reperfusion, organ-targeted drugs, and the correction of coagulation abnormalities, acid-base imbalance, metabolic issues, and electrolyte imbalance. But I'm not sure how much that would mean to the layperson."

"I was a para-rescue in the Air Force. I had some medical training, which I used in the field and as a medevac," said Devlin. "Obviously, my medical knowledge is nowhere near the level of yours, and over the years, I've forgotten more than I remember. But what I think you're saying is that Elizabeth was given the normal treatments for someone in her condition. There were no other treatments tried that might help explain her recovery. Say experimental therapies?"

Hudson shook his head firmly. "Certainly not. Elizabeth wasn't some kind of medical experiment. Everything done for

Elizabeth was based on conventional, tried-and-tested medicine."

"Fair enough. I'm just trying to eliminate every other more reasonable explanation than a miracle." Hudson nodded and seemed to accept Devlin's explanation. "Please, Father Ramirez, go on."

For another half hour, Ramirez doggedly got Hudson to recount every medical interaction he'd had with Elizabeth Wendig until they'd exhaustively noted all the doctor's interactions and prescriptions. Toward the end, Hudson's patience began to fray, and he was only too eager when Ramirez pressed the Stop button on his cell to show the priests out.

Hudson walked with them down the steps and onto the road outside. The sound of a plane engine came roaring in from the sky, and the three men looked up to see a small yellow floatplane descending on the surface of the lake water. It skimmed off the water a few times, then slowed and angled itself toward the dock, gliding in.

"That's Marshall with the chief of police," said Hudson. "They've been out searching for the truck that forced the school bus into the lake. I'm gonna go over and say hello."

"You mind if we come too?" asked Devlin.

"No, no, I don't," replied Hudson politely, though it was reasonably clear he did mind.

Hudson crossed the road onto the dock and waited for the floatplane to sail in. Devlin and Ramirez followed and waited a few steps behind. A middle-aged man of average height in a denim jacket got out of the pilot's seat and tied the plane to the dock. Another man in police uniform scrambled out after him.

Hudson called out to them, and the two men waved back. The pilot climbed back into the plane, and the man in uniform walked over to greet Hudson.

"You find anything? Any sign of the truck, Chief?" asked Hudson.

"Nope. There's so much to cover." He rubbed his bald crown and sighed. "Truth be told, Rick, I'm not certain we will find it. Not certain at all."

"Are you saying you don't think it's still in Hinkley?"

"There's a real chance it isn't here. That whoever was in that truck got out as fast as they could once they saw the bus go into the lake. But I'm chief of police in Hinkley, and I gotta do whatever I can here in Hinkley. I can't search the whole damn state."

The pilot had got out of the plane and waved as he approached the group of four men. "Hey, Rick."

"Hi, Garratt," replied Hudson. "Chief here says no luck."

"Nah. But there's a lot of forest out there where that truck could have been stashed. Lot of terrain still to search."

"Nice plane." Devlin was standing by Hudson, admiring Garratt's floatplane. "Piper PA-12 Super Cruiser."

"That's right," said Garratt.

"Father Devlin, Father Ramirez," said Hudson, making the introductions without enthusiasm. "This is Chief Garland, and this is Garratt Marshall, who runs a floatplane business on the lake. Father Devlin and Ramirez are looking into..." Hudson paused, a little unsure as to how to phrase his next sentence. "Into a couple of events people are claiming to be miracles. Those people being Father Wilson, mainly."

"That so?" said the chief. "What miracles?"

"Like Dr. Hudson says," said Devlin, "Father Wilson has claimed Elizabeth Wendig's recovery as a miracle. And there's a claim of a weeping Virgin Mary statue at St. Paul's Church."

The chief and Hudson exchanged glances. "Well," said the chief, "what happened with Elizabeth is a kind of a miracle, I guess. From what I know, the girl came back from the dead."

"We've been asked just to gather the facts by the archbishop and cardinal's office," said Ramirez. "Then they'll decide whether to take it further."

"Damn town could do with a miracle or two," said Marshall.

"I'll second that," said Garland.

"So, you know your planes, Father?" said Marshall.

"I was in the Air Force," replied Devlin. "Detective though. Didn't fly. Before that, I was para-rescue."

"I was in the Air Force too. Maintenance. Where were you stationed?"

"All over. Ghazni for a while. Wright-Patterson. Spent my longest stretches there."

"I spent most of my time in Andrews Air Force Base. You in Hinkley long? I can take you up if you like."

"Thanks for the offer, but I'm not sure how much time I'll have."

"Let me know if some time comes free. I got a dHc-2 Beaver too. Still small, but it can take a couple more customers. On tours, out fishing, things like that. Both planes are beauts."

"I'll bet. Thanks for the invite. If I can, I'll definitely take you up on it. If you'll excuse us though, we have to get back. Thanks again for your time, Doctor."

"You're welcome," Hudson replied.

THE PRIESTS WALKED BACK across the dock to the car, and Hudson, Garratt, and the chief continued talking and huddled a little closer together.

"Miracles?" said Chief Garland, giving his scalp another rub.

Hudson shrugged. "Far as I can see, it's Father Wilson stirring it all up. That's why those other priests are out here talking to me. I'm not sure they even believe it."

"Father Wilson isn't the most reliable source these days," said Garratt. "He's getting fonder and fonder of a belt or two of brandy."

"Ain't that the truth," said the chief. "What happened with the Wendig girl though, was that normal? Was there a medical reason behind it? Jill spoke to Kathleen Wendig first thing this morning and told me all about it over breakfast. The way Kathleen has it is that she's convinced Elizabeth came back from the dead."

"Not back from the dead," said Hudson. "But it was... unusual... She was as close to death as you can be without actually dying. The consultants were certain, I was certain..."

"So you think it could be something...miraculous?"

Hudson sighed and shook his head. "No, Chief. No, I don't. Medical science is good. Sometimes it's astonishing. But there are cases when something happens, and we don't have an explanation. But the reason for that isn't an act of God. It's just that we don't know the reason. But in fifty years, a hundred years' time, we probably will. Besides, Elizabeth's test results will be back soon. So, it's very possible we'll get an explanation that removes all talk of a miracle."

"You ever seen anything like that happen before, Rick?" asked Garland.

Garland gave the question some thought and said, "No. No, I haven't. But I bet other doctors have. Or a doctor somewhere has. What can I say? I just think there's a perfectly rational explanation, and it ain't no miracle. And neither is the weeping statue. I mean, come on, a weeping statue?"

The three men chuckled.

"She's probably weeping for the state of Father Wilson's liver," said Garland. "I gotta get back to the station."

"Me too," said Garratt. "I gotta get ready for a couple who want me to take them out over Lake Champlain."

Hudson's cell began to buzz in his pockets. "See you around."

Hudson left the two other men and took the call as he walked back from the marina to his house.

"Dr. Hudson speaking."

"Hello, Doctor? It's Jim Healy."

"Hi, Jim. What can I do for you?"

"I'm sorry to call you direct..."

"That's okay, Jim. I told Jean she could call me direct."

"That's what she said."

"Everything okay?"

"Um...I'm not sure. I'm over with Jean now, and...well... It's kind of weird. Her right hand..."

"What about it? Is she in pain?"

"No. She's not in pain... Doc, she's got some feeling back in it..."

"What kind of feeling?"

"She can feel hot and cold. And this morning... This morning, she moved a finger... A finger on the paralyzed side of her body."

Hudson stopped with his cell jammed to his ear. What he was hearing didn't add up. Jean Cassidy's condition was severe, an inoperable tumor that was only going to get worse.

"She what?"

"She can move her finger. At will. I thought all the doctors said the side of her body would be paralyzed for life."

"They did... We did..."

"Then what's happening?"

For a moment, Hudson felt dizzy, like the world was moving around him. "I'm coming over, Jim. I'll be there as quick as I can."

ELEVEN

As a favor to desk sergeant Esserman, Officer Kyle Ross was keeping his seat warm at Hinkley PD. Esserman was out back, trying to persuade his wife to come home from her mother's after an unholy drunken fight the night before. The way Ross looked at it, he was undertaking an act of compassion for Esserman. He was helping mend a broken home. Though how much longer the marriage would last was attracting unfavorable odds at the precinct.

Business was quiet, and Ross was robotically scrolling through TikTok videos, so he didn't see blind Archie Baker and his dog until they were right up at the desk.

"Officer Ross," said Archie, who was in an "official" mode, his shoulders thrown back and chest thrust forward like he was standing to attention. He wore dark glasses and overalls over a faded Eagles T-shirt. Troy lay panting on the floor by his owner's feet.

"Hey, Mr. Baker," said Ross and then peered over the desk and down at the dog. "Hey, Troy, buddy. What can I do for you?"

"I'd like to report something. It's not a crime, but it is a police matter, I think."

Ross reached for a pen. "Okay. Sure. What is it you want to report, Mr. Baker?"

"A sighting."

"A sighting?"

"Yes," said Archie defiantly. "A sighting."

"Of what?"

"A boy."

"What boy?"

"Franklin Kelly."

The pen slipped from Ross's hand and dropped to the floor.

"What was that?" asked Archie. "You dropped something?"

"Uh...my pen." An astonished Ross picked his pen up from the floor and reset his face. "You said Franklin Kelly, Archie?"

"That's correct."

"Franklin Kelly who died in the Lake Vesper crash?"

"That's the one."

"But he's dead, Archie. Franklin Kelly is dead."

"Then I saw his ghost. Up at Frost Hollow. Three times I been up there this week, and twice now I caught sight of the boy running around and through the trees and other places." Archie leaned in on the counter conspiratorially. "'Course he thinks he can run around right under my nose. That's why I saw him. If it were someone else, then he'd hide. But he isn't so careful when he sees me 'cause he thinks I'm blind."

"But...you are blind, Archie."

Archie tapped his nose. "Not so blind as you might think. My eyesight is getting better."

"Is it?"

"Yup. You're wearing a dark blue shirt, dark blue tie, and a gold tie clip. Tell me I'm right."

"You're right." Ross stopped short of pointing out that all the Hinkley PD Officers wore dark blue shirts, ties, and gold tie clips.

"And you got a beard."

"Yeah, I do."

"See? Before, it was nearly all darkness I saw. Now I see colors and shapes." Archie rapped the countertop with his fingertip. "So, you take my statement, young man, 'cause this is important."

"Okay, Mr. Baker. I'm all ears."

Archie proceeded to give a very detailed statement to Officer Ross that began with the quality of sleep he'd had the night before, the breakfast he'd eaten, and a blow-by-blow account of the weather. The alleged sighting of the Franklin kid was the briefest part. He'd seen a black-haired kid he'd swear on his ancestors' graves was the Franklin Kelly boy running through the woods. Once he'd finished, he asked Officer Ross what he was going to do with the statement.

"Oh, take it to the police chief and maybe the FBI," Ross lied, which satisfied Archie.

A contented Archie left the station with his dog leading the way. Ross was considering whether to trash the statement there and then when Cassidy came in carrying a gym bag.

"Hey, Ross," said Cassidy.

"Hey."

"You filling in for Esserman?"

"Yeah, he's fixing things up with his wife. They both got juiced up yesterday and fought like cats in a bag. Now he's trying to smooth it over."

"I don't give it long."

"Me neither."

"Looks like it's quiet here."

"Yeah, except I just had Archie Baker in here wanting to give a statement."

"What kind of statement?"

"Brace yourself. He says he's seen the ghost of Franklin Kelly up in Frost Hollow."

Cassidy shook her head, squeezed her eyes shut, and opened them again as if trying to awaken from a dream. "Wait, let me get this straight. A blind man saw a dead boy."

"That's about the size of it. Though Archie says his sight's come back."

"No," protested Cassidy. "That makes even less sense. A man in his seventies who hasn't been able to see a fly on the end of his nose since he was in shorts can suddenly see."

"Well, he doesn't claim that much. All he says is he can see shapes and colors where before he couldn't see anything."

"Ross, we've had patrol officers up in Frost Hollow every day since the crash, and a drone, and a seaplane flying over there, and they've seen nothing. So how likely is it that a blind man...?"

"Okay, I get it," said Ross, putting up a hand and cutting Cassidy off. "I know, I know. It's stupid."

Cassidy pointed at the notepaper in Ross's hand. "That the statement?"

"Yeah, I was just figuring what to do with it."

"Tell me something, Ross. You want a career in the police force?"

"Yeah, 'course I do."

"Then trash it. Trash that piece of paper and thank the Lord you bumped into me before you went and tried to file it."

"Right. You think it's a bad idea?"

"I'm going to get ready for my shift. I've said what I think you should do, but it's plumb up to you, Ross, what you do with those ramblings you call a statement."

Cassidy headed into the station, and Esserman came in through the fire door at the back of the office with his cell in his hand.

"Hey, Esserman, you managed to get things straight with your old lady?"

Esserman ignored the question. "Anything to report? Anyone come in? Any calls?"

Ross discreetly crumpled up the notepaper he was holding into a small ball. "No. Not a thing. Quiet as a snowy night."

"Thanks. You can get back to the office. I'm good here now."

TWELVE

Hank Wendig opened his garage door just as headlights lit up his drive. A car came to a stop a few feet from where he stood, and Roy Kane got out.

"Hey, Roy," said Hank.

"Hey, Hank. Well, here she is, all the bodywork cleaned up and the fender straightened out."

Hank walked around the car, inspecting it. "Great job. What do I owe you?"

"Nothing, Not a nickel."

"No. I insist."

"You just take this as the Kane family's way of trying to help out. I wouldn't dream of taking a dime off of you right now. And Ma says the same. I'm under orders not to take anything."

Hank put out his hand, and Roy shook it.

"That's a damn fine thing to do," said Hank. "I appreciate it. Say, come around back for a drink. I got Chief Garland and Kyle Ross here enjoying a few cold ones."

"Why not..."

"Least I could do."

Kane threw Hank his car keys, and the two walked through

the garage into the backyard. Chief Garland and Officer Kyle Ross were sitting around a garden table out of uniform. They were both smoking and swigging from bottles.

"Roy," said Chief Garland. "How's it going?"

Hank pulled a bottle from a cool box on the table, opened it, and handed it to Kane.

"Not so bad, Jerry, not so bad."

"Roy just delivered my car," said Hank. "Straightened out the bodywork from that fender bender in Burlington for free."

"Good man," said Garland, and he and Kyle raised their bottles.

"Least we could do. How's Elizabeth, Hank?" asked Kane.

"Getting better. Every day. Physically, getting better. Mentally, she's got a way to go, what with the shock 'n all. I mean, given what she's gone through."

"I can't even imagine," said Kane, and Garland and Ross murmured in agreement.

"She sits by the window most of the day, just looking out into the road. It's taking her a long time to come to terms with everything that's happened."

Garland took a swig of his beer. "I swear to you, Hank, we'll find that van. We won't rest until we find it and the evil bastards that drove it. If I have to fly out with every day for the rest of my life, I will. We'll keep looking, and we will not rest."

"Amen," said Ross.

"Any news about the bus?" asked Kane.

Garland shook his head and swapped looks with Ross. "The Vermont Underwater Recovery Team are still drawing up a plan. They've done a full sonar survey and found that the bus drifted a hell of a long way from the entry point and wedged itself in a narrow trench. Right now, they're drawing up a plan and pulling together resources."

"Pulling together resources?" said Hank, his face reddening.

"This should all just happen. There shouldn't be any goddamned 'pulling together.'"

"I hear you, Hank," said Garland. "But a twenty-thousand-pound bus in a place that deep and far from the shore is a logistical nightmare. I mean, how do you get a crane or a winch out there, and how do you secure cables around something like that in a place like it's in? Last I heard, they were talking about mounting a retrieval next week. But they're determined to do it."

"I guess," said a placated Hank. He studied the bottle in his hand, then looked over sympathetically at Ross. "How's your family, Kyle?"

"It's a mess. Losing my niece has blown us wide open. We'll never recover. Never. But we have to take the small bits of goodness where we can." Ross stood and raised his glass. "Here's to Elizabeth and the holy miracle that brought her back to us."

Garland stood, and the four men raised their bottles in a toast.

"You think it's a miracle, Kyle?" asked Kane.

"I think it is," said Hank. "They haven't finished all the tests on Elizabeth, but nobody's given me anything close to a rational explanation why in a moment my daughter awoke and came back to us. No one."

Hank raised his glass, and the other three men followed suit. They all swigged, and for a moment, they were all silent in thought.

"I tell you what is going around the town that's straight-up BS," said Garland. "The story about Hugh Varley being in some Davidian-type cult and taking the kids away." Garland shook his head. "I mean, what kind of person starts a sick rumor like that?"

The others shook their heads and muttered disapprovingly.

"Just the worst," Roy Kane chimed in. "Evil..."

"Hey, you want to hear something even crazier?" said Ross. "I had Archie Baker in the station today. Says his eyesight's coming back."

The other three men guffawed.

"More likely, his wits are leaving him," said Garland, and they all laughed harder.

"What was he at the station for?" asked Kane.

"He keeps telling people he's seen the Franklin kid up in Frost Hollow."

The group went quiet.

"The old fool," said Garland. "He's a blind old fool who ought to know better than bringing up things like that in a town full of pain."

"Too right," said Hank. He shivered a little and swigged his beer. "Say, it's getting cold out here. If you've finished smoking, why don't we go inside and drink our beers in the warmth."

"Right you are," said Garland. "Lead the way."

Hank picked up the cool box filled with beer bottles, and they filed back into the house. Hank led them through the patio doors and into the living room, where Elizabeth was sitting by the window in her wheelchair. Hank and the other three men stopped.

"Hey, darlin'," said Hank.

"Hey, Daddy."

"We're just going to finish our beers in the kitchen. Where's Mom?"

"She's upstairs in bed."

"You're looking really well, Elizabeth," said Garland. "Looking great."

"Thanks, Mr. Garland."

"Anything you need," added Kane. "Anything you need, just let me, my brother, or my ma know."

"That's very kind."

"Can I get you something from the kitchen?" asked Hank. "Something to eat or drink?"

"I'm okay."

"You warm enough?"

"Yes, Daddy. I'm fine. I'll just sit some more, and then..." Suddenly, Elizabeth stopped, and the smile that had been playing around her gentle features vanished. She looked horrified, staring into the middle distance as if some dreadful realization had come over her.

"What's wrong, Lizzy?" asked Hank.

For a moment, Elizabeth didn't answer, and then she seemed to free herself from the grip of whatever fear had taken hold and forced a smile.

"Nothing. Nothing at all, Daddy. You all go and have a drink. You deserve one right now. I'll stay here for a while longer."

"You boys make yourself comfortable in the kitchen." Hank handed the cool box to Ross. "Take these, Kyle, and help yourselves. There's chicken wings and salad in the fridge." The three men went through to the kitchen, and Hank kneeled by his daughter.

"What's wrong, sweetheart? Tell me. I can tell something isn't right."

Elizabeth paused for a moment, unsure of what to say next. Then, she smiled broadly and said, "I just had a little flashback, is all. It's fine. It's not the first time. The doctors said that might happen. But it came and went, and I'm okay, Daddy. Trust me."

Hank's eyes were watery, and he put his arms around his daughter and held her tight for a while. Then he let her go and looked her in the eyes.

"I won't let any harm come to you again. Ever. The good Lord brought you back to me for a reason. And I will spend every breath I have looking after you."

Then, he rose and went to join his friends.

ELIZABETH'S SMILE FADED. She looked out into the street and bit her lip.

"Oh, dear," she muttered to herself. "Oh, dear, oh, dear, oh, dear."

Cars passed by, headlights swept back and forth, voices and laughter came through from the kitchen, and all the time, Elizabeth wrung her hands. Eventually, she picked up her cell phone, which had been lying on her lap, and began to swipe at the screen. The sound of the kitchen door opening and closing startled her, and she dropped her cell. She turned to see a figure standing in front of the door.

Fear again took hold of Elizabeth again. Elizabeth's wide eyes fixed on the figure standing on the other side of the room. Voices and laughter continued to come from the kitchen beyond.

"I won't say anything to anyone, I swear," whispered Elizabeth. "I promise you. I won't say a word..."

THIRTEEN

New York

Stress and adrenaline. It was what he lived off. That and coke. A line of coke for breakfast, a line before his first meeting, a line at 11:00 a.m., a line at lunchtime. Then, a line to pep him up for the first afternoon meeting, a line at 3:30 p.m., and from 5:00 onward, it was a line whenever the mood took him. A daily diet of stress, adrenaline, and coke was ravaging his body and mind.

He did a line on his desk, poured himself a whiskey and Coke on the rocks, and checked his watch. A quarter to nine. Like every night, he would not sleep tonight due to stress and stimulants. He wandered out to the rooftop garden and pool and sat on the lounger, watching the garden lights shimmer across the surface of the water. He looked out over the carpet of NY city lights and tried to block out his worries. But it was no good; the troubles that had hunted him for months hijacked his mind. He badly needed distraction. He reached into his pocket, pulled out his cell, and speed-dialed the number for his favored escort agency. As he dialed, he wondered half-seriously if they had a loyalty card scheme. The receptionist, who recognized the number, answered with a warm "Hello, Mr. Richards."

"I want two girls, two of the regulars."

The voice on the other end suggested two names.

"Can they be here in fifteen minutes? Then send them over."

He padded back into the house, unlocked the front door, and left it open a crack. Then, he took off all his clothes, dumped a bottle of Cristal into a silver bucket of ice, and placed it by the pool alongside a candy bowl filled with coke. He jumped into the pool and breaststroked back and forth a few times till he was out of breath. Then, he leaned against the side and kicked his legs, waiting for the girls to arrive. Five minutes passed, and he checked his watch. He glided over to the side of the pool and heard the front door open, so he backed into the center of the pool again and called out.

"Hey, I'm back here," he yelled. "Take your clothes off and jump in." He did a forward roll and let the silence of the water envelop him. Giddy with anticipation, he floated to the surface, opening his eyes, ready to feast on two high-class escorts coming to join him. As the water cleared from his eyes and the world unblurred, his heart flashed hot in his chest. Instead of two modelesque agency girls, he saw a big guy in a black balaclava and suit holding a gun and standing with his toecaps over the edge of the poolside. Before he even had a chance to take a breath, his body began to shake violently as impact after impact spasmed his body. Bullets speared into him, sending him back into the silence of the water.

A MILE DOWNTOWN, the underground parking lot for 28 Liberty Street was nearly empty. Half a dozen Teslas, a couple of Cadillacs, and a Lincoln Navigator were all that were left in the cavernous space. The elevator door opened, and a slim figure in a suit carrying a briefcase dragged his feet across the lot. He was tired and light-headed from a day of work that had started at eight and likely wouldn't end after he got back to his apartment. He waved his key card at the pillar between the front and rear car windows, but nothing happened. The side mirrors didn't move, and the door locks didn't unlock.

"Goddammit..." He waved the card again and got the same result. He stared at the card in disbelief.

"What?" he muttered to himself. "What the hell? You're kidding me. How much does this piece of junk cost, and I can't even...?" The sound of footsteps behind him made him jump, and he turned to see two men, one huge and one short, wearing balaclavas.

"Mr. Haaland," said the much shorter man in an Eastern European accent. The edge of a black mustache and a pronounced gap in his front teeth were visible through the balaclava mouth hole. "We disabled your key card."

"Who... Who are you...?"

"We're the collectors, Mr. Haaland. The insurance men. We protect the investment fund that funded your venture. You were given a final demand to settle your account, and we still haven't seen a deposit."

"I've been working since daybreak putting the money together, I swear to you. I will get it to you. I just need to round up a couple more investors."

"You were meant to make the payment seven days ago. You knew when you took the loan that it came with the strictest penalties for default."

"Twenty-four hours. Please. I'll have it for you in twenty-four hours, I swear."

"No."

"Then give me till morning. I beg you." Haaland got down on his knees. "Please, please give me more time. A few hours..."

The bigger guy had had his hands behind his back. Now, as he brought his hands into view, Haaland understood why. He had a gun in one hand and a metal tube in the other. He fixed the metal tube to the barrel of the gun.

"Oh, Jesus, no... Please, God, no..."

"We are paid to protect investments, Mr. Haaland," said the shorter guy. "And when a client defaults on us and we realize we have to give up our money, it pains us. But we simply mustn't let it tarnish our reputation. We must be seen to enforce the terms of our agreement."

Survival instincts kicked in. Haaland scrambled to his feet and darted right. He had only taken a few frantic steps when a shot rang out around the concrete walls, and his head flicked sideways. He collapsed against the wheel of a car parked a few feet from his own.

The short guy and the big guy watched their victim's body twitch spasm.

"Finish him," said the short guy.

The big guy emptied three more rounds into Haaland's head.

The short guy sighed, then pulled out his cell and made a call. "The final settlement has been made. Both parties have been removed."

He put the cell back in his pocket. The big guy removed the silencer from his gun, and they turned and walked back across the lot.

FOURTEEN

It was dark when Devlin and Ramirez returned from the waterfront. Devlin dropped Ramirez off so he could go to his motel room and call his college in Boston. Devlin said good night, lit a cigar, and then got back in the car. He drove over to St. Paul's, parked, and entered the church. Even though it was just after ten, the front two rows were occupied by people come to venerate the Virgin Mary. Devlin walked along the north side of the church between the wall and the ends of the benches. He stood in front of the statue and studied it for a long while, feeling the curious eyes of the other visitors on him.

Without exchanging words with anyone, he turned, left the church, and headed for the rectory.

Father Wilson came to the door in slippers and a cardigan. He was still looking clear-eyed despite the time of night, which Devlin was thankful for.

"I thought I should let you know our progress today," said Devlin. "We spoke to Elizabeth Wendig and Dr. Hudson."

"Oh, yes, yes, come in. Can I offer you a drink, Father?"

"No. Thank you."

"Come through. I was sitting out on the back porch."

Wilson led Devlin into the backyard, where there were two wicker chairs and a table on the patio.

"Please, take a seat."

They both took a chair. A bowl of nuts and a rocks glass half-full of what looked like a gin and tonic stood on the table. Father Wilson leaned forward and lifted his glass, taking a deep sip. He grabbed a fistful of nuts and fed them to himself individually as they talked.

"Are you sure I can't get you anything?" he asked.

"Thank you, but I'm fine."

"So, you've had a very industrious day?"

"We've covered some bases. Spoken to the main people involved, including yourself. I've also asked Father Ramirez to lead the investigation and put the report together."

Wilson stopped feeding himself nuts. "Why?"

"Because he's an exceedingly able young priest, and he will approach the task with more...vigor than I would."

"Vigor?"

"Yes."

Wilson chewed thoughtfully on a nut. "Well, I suppose this is just a preliminary exploration. Research, if you will, before a much more official and forensic investigation. Father Ramirez is very, very inexperienced, however. He's really only a student. I would like your assurance that you are overseeing his work."

"I can give you that assurance. Do you mind if I smoke?"

"No. Go ahead."

Devlin pulled out a Cohiba, clipped the head, and lit it up. He inhaled deep and long, then let the smoke out into the fresh night air.

"So?" said Wilson. "Have you or Father Ramirez drawn any conclusions yet?"

"It's not for us to draw conclusions. That's not what we've

been asked to do. We're here to lay it all out in front of someone paid a lot more than me and Father Ramirez."

"But you must have a view on it? As a priest...as a man."

Devlin picked a morsel of leaf from his lower lip and flicked it away. "I think a town full of grieving people and who are still in deep shock is very fertile ground for belief or despair."

"What does that mean?"

Devlin took another smoke and turned to Father Wilson. "The statue of Our Blessed Lady. It's sat in an alcove. There's virtually no gap between the head of the statue and the roof of the alcove. There are cracks on the statue itself. And cracks around the eyes."

"What are you saying?"

"If I moved that statue—and right now, that isn't possible with a constant line of visitors coming to see it—what are the chances I'd find condensation in the alcove? What are the chances the condensation is being absorbed through the cracks in the statue and then being discharged through fine fissures around the eyes?"

Wilson shook his head hard. "It's never happened before. Never."

Devlin nodded and sighed. "After all the town has gone through, there's an appetite in Hinkley for something else. Something that isn't pain. Maybe God has decided that's what should happen. That a town that has experienced enough suffering to fill a dozen lifetimes needs a sign. Or maybe people are finding what they need to find right now."

"It might be impossible to tell the difference between those two things. Belief, and it is belief we're talking about, can create extraordinary things." Wilson emptied his glass. "May I speak candidly?"

"I wouldn't have it any other way."

"I have heard rumors about you, Father Devlin. Rumors

from down in Avery. That, like the Wendig girl, you came back from the dead. Is that all idle talk?"

Devlin scraped his cigar out on the patio flagstone. "Yeah. It is, I'm afraid. Sorry to disappoint. But you know what priests are like. Just devils for a bit of gossip." Devlin stood. "Once Father Ramirez has finished the report, he'll send a copy to you."

Wilson stood, clasping his empty glass. He fixed his beady, red eyes on Devlin and said with total conviction, "What's happening here is miraculous, Father. I am one hundred percent certain of it."

DEVLIN LEFT THE RECTORY, started up another cigar, and decided to walk back into town. He got to the brow of Main Street and stopped for a moment. The street swept down before him like a giant concrete slide. The stores, cafes, and restaurants were dark. Streetlamps lit up the sidewalk and road. Fine rain floated down in a mist, and the wind blew a little. Devlin took a drag of smoke. In the distance, he heard that low hum of motorcycle engines again—the swarm of bikes. By the sounds of it, they were traveling somewhere south of the town center, maybe along the interstate highway, Devlin guessed.

Then, Devlin heard other, different noises that were much closer by. Sounds of laughter and shouting. The raised voices came from a side street off the main drag. As the voices grew louder and got closer, Devlin thought he recognized them. From around the corner about fifty yards away came a group of young men, the same group he'd seen up at the waterfront and who had mocked Ramirez. At the head of the crowd was a tall, swaying figure and, beside him, a shorter, pudgier figure.

Devlin stepped back into a shop recess and smoked some more. He watched the kids walk by, moving and changing direction in unison like a flock of birds. One of the kids was rummaging around in his jacket pocket, and as he did, a small, glassy object came free and fell onto the ground. The kid didn't seem to realize or care he'd lost the object and carried on walking and laughing with his friends.

A cop car appeared out of a side street, and the kids suddenly got jumpy and began to pick up their pace, disappearing over the brow of the hill.

Devlin stepped out into the street, and the cop car pulled over. Officer Cassidy got out.

"Late to be out, isn't it, Father?" said Cassidy.

"That's exactly how I like it. A late-night walk." Devlin took a smoke. "Who were those kids, by the way? They local?"

"No. They're not local. The tall kid, his father owns a few of the big properties on the waterfront. Vacation homes. His son and friends come up to party. They're all rich out-of-towners down from New York or Boston. They're boisterous but not generally a problem." Cassidy looked Devlin over. "Well, as long as you're okay. Father."

"Right as rain."

Cassidy nodded and climbed back into her cruiser. "You should get yourself to bed."

Devlin nodded. As he watched the cruiser move away, something on the ground glinted in his side vision. It was the small glass object the kid had dropped, lying in the join between the curb and the blacktop. He picked it up, studied it, and slid it into his pocket.

FIFTEEN

Cassidy was two-thirds through her shift. The town was quiet, and there hadn't been much in the way of action aside from meeting the priest, attending a suspected break-in that turned out to be nothing at all, and issuing a ticket for speeding.

She headed back through town to the gas station for weak coffee from their crappy machine. On Main Street, she passed Roy and Ted Kane's body shop and noticed a slit of light coming from under the steel shutters. She checked the time: 2:00 a.m. She drove on, filled her flask with weak coffee from the gas station, and, her interest piqued by the light from the auto shop, came back along Main Street, eventually parking on a turnoff opposite the Kane shop. From here, facing away, she could see the steel shutters and the slit of light through her rearview and wing mirrors.

It didn't take long for something to happen, ten minutes and a quarter of a cup of bad coffee. First, the slit of light disappeared. Then, the shutter unrolled and lifted, revealing a Dodge Charger and Ted Kane at the wheel. The Dodge's headlights flashed on, and the car slipped out of the shop onto Main Street and headed north. Cassidy stuck her flask in the cup holder, reversed out of the side road, and followed, keeping a good distance behind the Dodge.

There were hardly any other cars on the road, so Cassidy had to keep a long way back. She kept her eyes glued to the Dodge's taillights, which were little red points of light in the distance. The Dodge drove for a quarter of an hour. Half a mile short of the interstate, it turned right, and its taillights disappeared. Cassidy came to a stop on the opposite side of the road from where the Dodge had turned off. She turned off the engine and killed the lights.

He's at blind Archie Baker's place, thought Cassidy. *What's Ted Kane doing at blind Archie Baker's place at two thirty in the morning?*

She turned the cruiser through a gap in the tree line and brought it to a stop on a band of scrubland that bounded the forest beyond. Then, she got out, walked back to the tree line, and scooted across the highway to the entrance to Archie Baker's drive. Keeping to the edge of the dirt track where the neglected bushes and trees crowded in, Cassidy edged her way along until she could see the front of Archie's farmhouse. Ted Kane's Dodge was parked in front of the door. Kane had opened the trunk and was heaving a round container out. He lugged it over to Archie's porch and lowered it onto the ground. Then, he got back into the Dodge, spun it around, and came back down the track. Cassidy stepped back and into the overgrowth while the Dodge rumbled past. She waited until it had turned back onto the highway and the sound of the engine had faded into nothing, and then she went to investigate.

Cassidy triggered a security light bolted to the front of Baker's porch, and it lit up the item Ted Kane had left: a three-gallon glass carboy full of clear liquid. Cassidy twisted out the stopper and inhaled the fumes.

"Moonshine. That it? A 2:00 a.m. drop off for a jar of moonshine?"

She put the stopper back in and looked up at Archie's door.

"Fill your boots, Archie. Here's mud in your eye."

Cassidy retraced her steps back to her car and finished a normal night shift in Hinkley by snaking through the western suburbs and back down Main Street. She passed the Kane brothers' shop. The shutters were down, and the lights were off.

"Moonshine." She shook her head and laughed. "The Kanes. Great criminal masterminds of Hinkley." Then, she headed back to the precinct.

FIVE MINUTES after Cassidy had driven by, a thin strip of light between the shutter and the sidewalk flickered on. The shutters rolled up, and Ted Kane stepped out into the street. Two headlights appeared over the brow of Main Street, and a black Yukon cruised toward him. Ted stepped back, and the Yukon turned into the garage. Ted followed the Yukon in and shuttered down behind it. Roy Kane got out and nodded. Ted nodded back.

"You do your deliveries?" asked Roy.

"Sure did. You?"

"Sure did. It's been a very productive night altogether. Let's go tally up."

SIXTEEN

Officer Kyle Ross was nursing a sore head. The drinks with Hank, Chief Garland, and Rob Kane hadn't finished till one thirty in the morning. There had been laughter and then plenty of tears as alcohol teased out the raw pain they kept locked up during the day.

Coffee flask in one hand and keys in the other, Ross unlocked his cruiser and did a once-over check. Then, he climbed in and drove out of the Hinkley PD parking lot to start his shift. He'd only just turned right onto the narrow road going west toward the town when his radio crackled into life and Esserman's voice came over the airwaves.

Ross picked up his receiver and checked in.

"This is Ross, go ahead."

"Can you take a trip out to Frost Hollow? We got Archie Baker calling in a sighting up there," said Esserman.

"What sighting?"

"Errr... He says he's up there and he's seen... He says he's seen the Franklin kid."

A little shaky still from booze and a late night, Ross felt anger and tears rising up in him. "Are you kidding me? He's blind, for crying out loud. Legally blind. How can he see anything, let alone a kid that died at the bottom of Lake Vesper? I mean, it's insane."

He heard crackles and silence while Esserman digested Ross's reaction.

"It wouldn't hurt to take a look-see, Kyle," said Esserman. "Then we can say we ticked that box and move on."

Ross sighed and shook his head. "Attending reported sighting."

"Thanks, Kyle."

Ross drove through Main Street and then onto the road leading to the interstate. He passed Archie Baker's house and found the turnoff into Frost Hollow. It was a narrow track walled with trees on both sides, with only space for one vehicle. Every so often, the track opened up to allow vehicles to pass. Eventually, he came out to a clearing where the forest gave way to plains. He parked by a turnstile that marked the beginning of what locally was called Frost Hollow, about forty acres of rolling plains bisected by a stream that frosted over every winter.

Ross picked up the receiver and called dispatch. Esserman answered.

"Frost Hollow's a big place," said Ross. "Any idea where Archie actually is?"

"He says he's up by Rook's bridge."

Ross got out of his cruiser, climbed over the stile, and walked out into the open fields. A ten-minute walk east took him to Rook's bridge. As he approached, he could see Archie standing in the middle of the narrow wooden bridge, with his dog sitting faithfully by his boots.

"Archie..." Ross called out as he stepped onto the bridge.

"Officer Ross," replied Archie, turning to greet him. "Thanks for coming out."

Archie faced Ross, staring directly at him. For a moment,

the breath caught in Ross's throat, and his body lost all motion. He stood still, transfixed by Archie Baker's eyes. They were round and bright and shining. The whites of his eyes were white, and the blues of his iris were crystal blue.

"You know," said Archie. "I never noticed before how handsome you were, young Michael Ross."

"You... You can see...?" stammered Ross.

"Of course. That's what I've been telling people all along. My eyes. They're back."

SEVENTEEN

Devlin and Ramirez went for breakfast in the same diner they'd been to the day before and sat in the same spot. The place was empty, and service was fast. Devlin had the steak and eggs, and Ramirez had the omelet. Ramirez picked at his food and took long, thoughtful gaps between mouthfuls. From time to time, he tapped his fork on the side of his plate.

"What's up?" asked Devlin.

"Nothing."

"Then eat your food, and don't play it like a drum."

"Okay, dad."

Ramirez took another mouthful, chewed it over, swallowed, and sat back in his chair. "Boy, I'm bushed. I was up until three in the morning, typing up the recorded conversations and uploading photographs. There are only two things I'm waiting on. I still haven't got any word on Elizabeth Wendig's blood tests from Dr. Hudson, and no word on my car either." He tapped his fork against his bottom lip. "I do wonder if I'm being ripped off. It is the only auto repair place in town, after all. But once I get the car back and get back to Boston, I can get the Hinkley report into a final shape, and you can look it over before it goes to the archbishop and the cardinal."

Devlin nodded and beckoned the waitress over and paid the bill. A tired Ramirez stared blankly into the mid-distance.

"Well, I'd say your work here is done," said Devlin.

"Yep," replied Ramirez, yawning. "I think I'm home and hosed." He took a sip of coffee and considered Devlin for a moment. "So, what's the deal with you, Father? I've spent not even a week with you. I've seen you go toe-to-toe with a Nazi biker, seen a girl come back from the dead in your presence, and I don't know the first thing about you."

"You can read it in my memoir."

"You're writing a...?"

"It was a joke."

"Oh. Okay. Nice swerve. So where are you from? Who are your family?"

"They're mostly dead."

"All of them?"

"I have a brother...somewhere. We haven't spoken for..." Devlin ticked off the years in his head. "Fifteen years or thereabouts."

"Why not?"

"Personality clash."

"Sounds like an understatement. What did your parents do?"

"My father was a cop. My mother worked part-time at lots of things to make ends meet. We moved all over. We were from another place, trying to find our feet in a big country."

"What other place?"

"Belfast in the north of Ireland."

"What were your parents like?"

"My father was...difficult. We fought hard and a lot. My mother was better. I moved out soon as I could."

Devlin's cell buzzed.

"Hello? Father Wilson...?"

Devlin listened intently for a stretch as Father Wilson spoke fast and without breath on the other end.

"Sure," said Devlin. "Text me the address, and we'll come over." He put his cell down by his empty plate.

"What is it? What did Father Wilson want?"

"He says there's been another miracle."

Ramirez's mouth fell open. "No? Another...?"

"Another one."

"What kind of miracle?"

"Father Wilson says it's a healing miracle. An old lady with paralysis claims she can move." Devlin took out a fresh cigar and pointed it at Ramirez. "You might be done with Hinkley, but it looks like Hinkley isn't done with you."

They'd left the rental back at the motel, so Devlin and Ramirez took a cab to an address a few miles east of the town center. The house they were looking for sat on a couple of acres of land on the V-shaped intersection where one lane split into two. A collection of white wooden buildings surrounded by trees and bushes could be seen as they approached the fork in the road. The cab driver took one of the forks and turned left into the front yard.

Devlin paid the fare, the cab drove off, and the two priests approached the house, which was the largest of the wooden buildings on the lot. Other smaller buildings were scattered around the house; sheds and garages that seemed positioned without purpose or planning. Four cars had been parked on the edge of the grounds by a chicken-wire fence. One of the cars was a police cruiser.

A tall, thin, elderly man in a cardigan who was expecting Devlin and Ramirez answered the door.

"Father Devlin, Father Ramirez, I presume. I'm Jim Healy. I'm the one who called Father Wilson. Come on in."

Healy led them through a doorway off the hall into the front room that smelled of fresh flowers and polish. Armchairs and a couch covered in floral prints were grouped together in the center of the room, facing a TV. Behind was a long dining table and french windows. Numerous vases holding flowers decorated the mantelpiece and other surfaces.

Sitting in the armchair with a blanket across her knees and a walking stick leaning against the armrest was a woman at least as old as Jim Healy but who looked much frailer. Her gaunt face and body were thin to the bone, and a fine gray fuzz covered her scalp.

Father Wilson was sitting on the end of the couch nearest to the woman. His hand lay on the woman's arm. Dr. Hudson was standing by the window, sipping at a mug.

"Father Devlin, Father Ramirez," said Father Wilson. "Thank you for coming."

Dr. Hudson nodded at the priests. He looked tired and harassed.

"Please, sit down," said Healy as he sat on the couch. Devlin and Ramirez took the empty armchairs.

"Jean," said Healy. "This is Father Devlin and Father Ramirez. They're here looking into all the...the events that have happened in Hinkley these past days."

Hudson sighed, sipped his coffee, and looked out of the window.

"Hello, Father Devlin, Father Ramirez," said Jean.

"Tell them what's happened to you, Jean," said Father Wilson. "The sudden change in you."

Jean looked at Devlin and Ramirez, her watery eyes magnified by her glasses' thick lenses. The large, round, plastic frames looked outsized on her thin, fragile face.

"I have a condition, Fathers," said Jean. "In fact, many conditions. But specifically, an inoperable tumor on my spine, which has irreversibly paralyzed one side of my body, my right arm, and leg. Nothing can be done for it except manage the discomfort so I can live as best as I can. And I don't complain about that. I've had the life the Lord meant me to have and lived longer than a good many folk. But I wasn't getting any better. Only worse. Ask Dr. Hudson."

Dr. Hudson didn't comment either way, and his face remained impassive.

"Anyhow... Yesterday, I started to get some feeling back in my right hand. At first, I thought it was my imagination. Hope over reality. But the feeling got stronger. Then, when Jim came back from town, he left the front door open, and I felt a faint draft against the back of my hand. So, I blew on it, and sure enough, I could feel my own breath. Then I got..." She stopped for a moment and seemed to stifle emotion. "I got Jim to touch the back of my hand...and for the first time in eighteen months, I felt his fingertips." She brought her left hand up to wipe the tears falling from her eyes. "And only a few hours ago, this happened." She glanced down at her right hand and moved the fingers very slowly in a wave motion. "I can move my hand. The Lord be praised. My hand that has been paralyzed and without feeling since two winters ago."

Father Wilson turned to Devlin and Ramirez. "I think this is more of what we've already seen. The Wendig girl's miraculous recovery. The weeping statue. This is not normal, far from it. I submit it's the work of the Lord, and at the very least, you must report this back to the archbishop and cardinal too."

"Sure," said Ramirez. "I can take statements..."

"Maybe not right now," said Healy. "Today's been enough for you already, don't you think, Jean?"

"Maybe so. Maybe you could come visit tomorrow, Father?" said Jean.

"Of course," said Ramirez.

Devlin looked over at Dr. Hudson, who had resumed staring out of the window. "What's your opinion, Doctor?"

Hudson turned from the window to address the room. "I don't have a ready explanation. But that doesn't mean there isn't one. If everything that couldn't be explained was chalked up to miracles, we'd still be living in the dark ages. I've taken blood from Jean, and I'll get tests run on them. It may be there's remission that has begun on its own accord, or there's been some movement in the tumor that's eased up pressure on the nervous system. That's two possibilities I can think of off the top of my head, and there will be more."

Father Wilson was about to speak, but the sound of feet descending the stairs stopped him. Lori Cassidy appeared in the doorway.

"I didn't realize we had a social gathering in the diary," said Cassidy.

"Hi, Lori, sweetheart," said Healy. "We were just talking over what's happened to your nanna."

"You okay, Nanna?" asked Lori.

"I am, darling. In fact, I feel better with each passing hour."

"That's good to hear, Nanna." Cassidy looked over at the priests. "Hello again, Father Devlin."

"Hello, Officer Cassidy. I saw the police car but didn't realize it was yours."

"Yep, I'm on shift and ducked back to see Nanna. Hey, Father Ramirez."

"Officer Cassidy," replied Ramirez.

"So, what do you think?" asked Cassidy. "You think it's a miracle?"

"The doctor was just saying there are other possibilities," said Ramirez.

"Dr. Hudson thinks everyone's going plumb crazy in Hinkley, don't you, Doc?" said Cassidy.

"I think there's going to be a perfectly rational explanation for everything," said Hudson. "But this is a town that deserves a hundred miracles, whether or not they've actually happened." Hudson put his mug down and picked up his coat. "Thanks for the coffee, Jim. I better get back to the surgery so I can get Jean's sample off. Father Wilson, Lori, Father Devlin, Father Ramirez..."

Hudson left, and Devlin and Ramirez stood.

"We can get more of the medical details from Dr. Hudson," said Ramirez. "And if you're agreeable, Jean, I'd like to get the results of your tests when they come back. Then we'll add that to the report I'm submitting to the archbishop."

"Of course," said Jean. "I understand it's all got to be done properly, by the book. But I've lived a long time, and I know what's science and what's faith. And what's happening to me isn't anything to do with any doctor. It's to do with the Lord."

"I believe you," said Ramirez.

Devlin pulled out his cell. "I'll call for a cab."

"No need," said Lori. "I'm driving to the precinct. I'll give you a lift."

"YOU SAID YOU BELIEVED MY GRANDMOTHER." Lori Cassidy was looking in her rearview mirror at Father Ramirez, who was sitting in the back seat. "So, you think it is a miracle? What's happened to her hand?"

"I believe your nanna believes it," said Ramirez.

"That's just a get-out-of-jail answer, ain't it?" She looked across at Devlin in the front passenger seat. "And you?"

"I don't know."

Cassidy gave a short, wry chuckle.

"What do you think?" asked Devlin.

"I think Nanna's like me, a fighter. She's had to be, and so have I."

"How so?"

Cassidy looked out of the side window, sighed, and turned her gaze back to the road. "My mother left when I was three, and my father died when I was four. So, Nanna and Grandpa brought me up. Although Grandpa Jim isn't my biological grandpa. That's why he's a Healy and me and Nanna are Cassidys. My real grandpa upped and left too. Bit of a family tradition, you might say. Anyhow, Nanna caught a good one in the end—Jim—and the three of us are tight-knit 'cause we had only each other to rely on. Nothing came easy. So, when I see Nanna's disease getting better, it's 'cause I think the disease never met anyone like Nanna before."

"Why did your mother leave?"

"I don't want to talk about it. Truth of the matter is the whole town would rather not talk about it."

They drove on for a little while longer without conversation. Then, Devlin took out a Cohiba and turned it in his fingers, studying it.

"Those kids last night..." said Devlin.

"What about them?"

"Hinkley seems a strange place for a group of teens to come to out of season, don't you think?"

"I suppose I assumed they were rich kids enjoying having the run of the waterfront and their rich daddy's big house." Cassidy looked at Devlin. "Are you getting at something? 'Cause if you are, you better cut to the chase."

Devlin slipped his Cohiba back into his pocket and pulled out something else.

"After you pulled up last night and the kids moved on, I found this." He held the object up for Cassidy to see.

"That's a meth pipe," said Cassidy.

"It is."

"How would you know what it's for?"

"Before I became a priest, I worked in the Air Force as a detective. Office of Special Investigations."

"Huh..." She looked him up and down. "Kind of figures. Big, ugly guy like you doesn't look like he was built for just Mass. So, you think these kids are on meth?"

"Don't you?"

"Looks that way."

"So where are they getting it from?"

Cassidy looked across at Devlin, and this time, she was almost laughing. "Wait, you think someone's cooking it up here? In Hinkley?"

"Why not?"

"Because this place is a two-horse town. We'd know about it. It's far more likely these rich kids are bringing it with them."

"What about the bikers?"

"What about them?"

"The only thing that saved my ass that night was you turning up. They scrammed as soon as they heard the siren. Now, as much as I'd like to believe a gang of Nazi-loving bikers only need to hear a police siren to run away, I think it's far more likely they just didn't want to risk it. They're more likely running drugs, maybe meth, out of Hinkley."

Cassidy thought for a moment. "That gang only appeared around a week ago."

"So?"

"Well, why would they start running meth now? Out of the blue?"

"The whole town is looking one way at the moment, caught up with what'd happened. Police have their hands full. That could mean opportunities for others."

"You wanna leave that with me?" said Cassidy, looking at the pipe Devlin was holding. "There are evidence bags in the glove compartment. Open one up and drop that in for me."

"Sure." Devlin found the bags and pulled one out. He dropped the pipe in and sealed it up.

"Lay it on the dash for me, where I won't forget it." She eyed him again and shook her head. "Ain't you a box of surprises?"

EIGHTEEN

Officer Ross and Troy had followed Archie across the plains of Frost Hollow, down into the bottom of its deep dip, and up the other side. Archie didn't move so fast, and at times, Ross feared he'd lose his footing and they'd have to get him back to a hospital somehow. But the old man was on a mission. On top of that, he seemed like he was high, high on the new sight he'd been given.

The three of them had scaled the other side of Frost Hollow and stood panting on its rim.

"Are you sure you're okay, Archie?"

"Better than I've been in fifteen years," replied Archie.

"You sure?" Ross was looking at Archie's face. His eyes, which at first sight had seemed so clear, so shining, on closer inspection looked a little less healthy. The irises, Ross noticed, were violet. And the rims of his eyes were red and inflamed.

"I know I am," said Archie defiantly and pointed. "There... The Franklin kid's there... He's in an old hunting blind on the edge of the woods."

Ross looked over to the edge of the woods and saw a rickety, elevated shack on top of a wooden frame.

"Come on, Troy," shouted Archie. "Let's show Officer Ross we're not crazy ol' bastards."

Archie and Troy set off again with Ross in tow. They came to a stop on a rocky strip of land in front of the hunting blind.

"Well?" said Archie. "You'd better go investigate."

Ross shook his head, not quite able to believe he'd followed a lunatic old man and his dog out into the middle of Frost Hollow. Even so, he felt duty bound to settle the whole thing once and for all. He got a foothold on one of the lower planks of wood that crisscrossed the legs and held the structure up. He was about to plant a second foot in the triangle of timbers when the bush behind the hunting blind rustled. Troy barked, and through the leaves and branches, Ross caught sight of a black mop of hair darting away. Ross swung off the frame and sprinted into the woods in the direction the mop of black hair had gone. Behind him, he heard barks and shouts. For what must have been a whole minute, he ran as fast as he was able, convinced he'd lost track of his quarry. He stumbled out into a small clearing, stopped, and listened intently, scanning the immediate woodland. Nothing. No sound. No movement. And then the bush to his right opened up, and the black mop appeared again, flashing across Ross's path. Ross flung himself forward and made a diving tackle, ending up on the forest floor face-to-face with his prey.

"Franklin?" said an astonished Ross.

Two large, tearful brown eyes peered out from a fringe of black hair.

"Am I in a lot of trouble...?" replied the boy.

NINETEEN

Franklin Kelly was sitting in an office chair that had been rolled up by Ross's desk. He hid his face under his fringe, and his fists were balled up on his squeezed-together knees. An empty pizza box and a half-drunk two-liter bottle of Pepsi lay by his feet. He was pale and thin with big dark circles around his eyes and wore a faded set of Nike sweatshirt and pants. His own clothes had been wet, ragged, and mildewed. And he had stank. Stank so bad it was hard to be near him. So, he'd been told to shower in the cops' bathroom and been given some of Cassidy's old gym kit she kept in her locker. Dr. Hudson had been in to check him over and then left to make a house call.

Ross was sitting at the desk, typing on his keyboard. Cassidy, Esserman, and Chief Garland stood around him, looking like they'd caught a ghost. Which they had.

"So, you never went on the school trip?" asked Ross, repeating the key points in Franklin's statement.

"No, sir."

"And when you heard about the crash, you didn't know what to do."

"No, sir."

"You were round at your cousin's place, and he didn't know you were there?"

"Yes, sir. Marcus, my cousin, he's out most nights working late at Hennessy's on the waterfront. He's got a PS5, and I have a spare set of keys, so I let myself in. Then, at about ten o'clock, I saw other kids talking about the crash on Snapchat. So, I checked the TV and saw the news. I just felt so awful about it all. Like it was my fault. This was my punishment..." He paused and bit at his nails. "And then I thought there might be a way...a way that things might be better for me. See, my stepdad, he's... he's strict. And most of the time, he doesn't want me around, anyway. He just wanted to be with my mom. Have her all to herself. Up until she passed. And after that, me just being around him made him angry. So, I thought this could be an answer, for him and for me..." Franklin's head dropped, and he stared at his balled-up fists. "I knew by the first night I'd made a mistake. That I'd done something really dumb. But by that time, I figured I made everyone think I was dead." Franklin's eyes started to well up, and he scrunched his face. "And if I ever did go back, I'd be hated for it... Or maybe go to jail... Or something..."

"You're not going to jail," said Ross. "And no one's going to hate you. It's just the opposite. We're all relieved you're alive."

"Amen," said Esserman.

"What did you eat?" asked Chief Garland.

"I stole a set of my cousin's keys for Hennessy's storeroom. They had boxes of potato chips and nuts and candy and soda. I slept there most nights when it was too cold in the blind."

"You survived off bar snacks for three weeks?"

"Yeah, I guess. Are you gonna arrest me for that?"

"No. No we're not, Franklin."

"Kid's a damn survivalist," said Esserman.

"We're just glad you're here," said Garland. The other adults nodded and made heartfelt noises in agreement.

"We need to get you back to your stepdad though," said Garland. "Have we got hold of him?"

"No," said Cassidy. "He's out of state with work and hasn't answered his phone."

"Any other next of kin?"

"My only other family are over in Detroit," said the boy. "And I haven't seen them in four or five years. Since before Mom passed. I mean, there's Uncle Peter...Father Wilson, I mean..."

The cops looked at each other.

"We should tell Father Wilson, but I'm not sure he'd be the best hands to put the kid in right now," said Chief Garland.

"Franklin's dad works for a haulage company," said Esserman. "So he'll surface sooner or later. We'll just have to keep trying. In the meantime, we can put him up at ours."

"Is that okay with you, Franklin?" asked Garland.

Franklin nodded. "Thanks, Mr. Esserman."

"Yeah, thanks, Tony," said Garland.

"No problem at all. Me and the wife will be happy to look after you for as long as you need. Why don't I make a call, and Linda can make up the spare room for you, Franklin?"

"Thanks, Officer Esserman."

"No sweat at all. You're alive, and we're all grateful for it. You stay here, and when Officer Ross is done, I'll drive you to ours."

Esserman waddled out of the office. Garland rubbed his chin and said, "Anyone else know about this yet?"

"Nope," replied Ross.

"Except for next of kin, let's keep it quiet for now. Give the kid here some breathing space. For a day or so."

"I'll have to talk to the school, social services, all the referrals will need to be done," said Ross.

"I know, but in a day or so. Okay?"

"Sure thing, Chief."

"I'll call Rick Hudson, too, and tell him to keep it to himself."

"What about Archie Baker?" said Ross. "We should let him know not to blab."

"I'll go see him," said Cassidy. "By the way, is he okay? He looks terrible."

"He keeps saying he can see again," said Ross. "And he can...up to a point. But his eyes... I'm no optician, but they don't look quite right."

"How blind exactly was he before?" asked Cassidy.

"He had a little vision. Five percent. But when I was up in Frost Hollow with him, he seemed to be able to walk and even run fine without Troy."

"He could run?" said Cassidy, astonished.

"He was no Usain Bolt, but yeah. He could run."

"You think something's going on here? Like what happened to the Wendig girl?"

Garland and Ross looked at each other and shrugged.

"I spoke to my nanna this morning. And she says she has feeling and movement in her arm," said Cassidy. "She swears it's some kind of miracle."

"Come on, Lori," said Ross. "You buy all of that?"

"I don't know. How can Archie Baker be running over Frost Hollow if he's blind?"

Ross thought for a second and then said, "He had some vision before."

"Five percent," said Cassidy. "You said 5 percent."

"Yeah. But he said himself he could always see some outlines, some shapes. And he's been up to the Hollow with

Troy and his other dogs for most days for most of his life. He knows it like the back of the hand. And, yeah, now he says his sight's better, but not like he can see for real, like it's restored, like we can see."

"What can he see?" asked Cassidy.

"He says he can see like we can, but it's all glowing, in primary colors." Ross shrugged. "Search me what that means. And he sure doesn't look like someone who's been hit by a miracle. He looks like something's not right with him. Not right at all."

"When I speak to Dr. Hudson, I'll suggest he pays Archie a visit," said Garland. "Whatever's going on with Archie, I think it needs a doctor to look at him and right away. But first, I'll go tell Esserman to make sure he and his wife keep this to themselves." Garland left the office to find his desk sergeant.

"You want anything else to eat or drink?" Cassidy asked Franklin.

"I'm fine, thanks, Officer."

"Well, I'm supposed to be out attending a vehicle burglary on Tall Pines, so I better scoot." Cassidy kneeled in front of Franklin and held his hand. "We're all so happy you're okay, Franklin. That's the truth. Welcome back. Tonight, you'll be sleeping in a warm bed."

Cassidy left, and Ross set about finishing up his report. Franklin took a small sip from the Pepsi bottle and looked around the room.

"What's that?" asked Franklin.

"What's what?"

"The pictures of the white van?"

Ross turned and looked over at the dry-erase board with photos of the white Mercedes-Benz Metris stuck to it. "It's a van we're trying to find. In fact, it's the van responsible for the school coach crashing into the lake."

"Huh..."

"Me and Officer Cassidy were—"

"I've seen a white van."

Ross dropped his pen and turned to Franklin. "You've seen it? Where?"

"Well, I couldn't say a hundred percent it's the same one, but it's a lot like it. The same shape, same badge. Saw it being driven out into Walton Woods. 'Bout two miles from the old hunting blind."

"When?"

"Not long after I ran away. I remember it 'cause it was dark, and the van was being driven over fields with the headlights off, making a hell of a racket."

"Who was driving it?"

"It was dark. I couldn't see."

Ross pulled out a notepad from a desk drawer and handed it to Franklin with a pen. "I want you to think about where you saw it and draw me a map. Understand?"

"Sure."

For the next ten minutes, with Ross's help, Franklin drew out the area he'd been hiding out in and the main landmarks he could remember. Ross didn't really know how much he could trust the map, but there seemed to be a clear diagonal east-west line from the hunting blind through Necker's Brook, stopping short of a fire trail. From what Franklin was saying, he would have seen the white van heading out to Necker's Brook.

Ross went to find Esserman in the front office, but he was on the phone. Ross banged on the reception window, and Esserman turned to acknowledge him.

"I'm just on the line to Linda," said Esserman. "I'll come take the kid. Give me five."

"Where's the chief? I got something that could be important."

"He's gone home," Esserman replied and went back to his call.

Ross considered what to do. He could call the chief, or he could get Cassidy's help, but he was suddenly struck by a third option, an idea of how he might be able to find out fast if the kid was right about the van. He made a call on his cell, and the person on the other end picked up.

"It's Officer Kyle Ross. I got a real big favor to ask. We might have a lead on the white Mercedes. Would you be able to fly me up to Frost Hollow?"

"Sure," replied Marshall. "For something as important as this, I'll damn well make time."

"Appreciate it. And I'll get the chief to sign off for a fuel reimbursement. I'll be over in about fifteen minutes."

Ross got off the phone and looked through the glass door into the main office. Franklin was swigging Pepsi and wiping his nose with the sleeve of Cassidy's sweater. He could take Franklin with him, he thought. That might make things faster. But the kid had been through enough. Ross had the map and an airplane; that ought to be enough, he reasoned to himself. He went back into the main office and took Franklin through to the front office, where Esserman was still on the phone.

"Franklin, Officer Esserman will look after you. I gotta split on urgent business. Is that okay?"

"Sure. That's fine."

"I'll come check on you. Promise."

"Okay."

TWENTY

Ross drove out to Route 5 and headed north up to the waterfront. He parked up next to the marina, where Garratt Marshall's seaplane was moored. Marshall was standing on the water's edge by the wing of his plane.

"Hey," said Marshall as Ross approached.

"Hey, Garratt. I can't tell you how much I appreciate you dropping everything and helping out."

"Are you kidding? No question, bud, no question. You got new intel on the van?"

"Yeah."

"Where from?"

"I'm afraid I can't tell you that. Not currently. I'm under orders."

"No sweat. Where do you want to go?"

"Up over Walton Woods just before you get to the fire trail."

"We looked over that way. Must have flown over that area a dozen times or more."

"I know. But I have to act on what I've been told."

"Sure. Sure. I get it. Anyhow, we can't be too thorough when it comes to finding the scum who killed those children. I can land in Blackwater. It's a few minutes' walk from the east bank."

"Perfect. Thanks, Marshall."

"Jump in, and I'll fire the old girl up."

Ross squeezed into the seat behind Marshall, strapped himself in, and put on the passenger headphones. The Piper PA-12 Super Cruiser was an ancient two-seater, and as the plane rolled forward, the engine whirred like a thousand rattling parts of old metal. They were putting a hell of a lot of faith into an antique, thought Ross.

Through his headphones, Ross heard Marshall talking over the clanking engine.

"I know she sounds a thousand-year-old, Kyle, but she's as safe as any commercial flight you've ever taken. Safer. These Pipers are a thing of beauty."

They lifted up and rose smoothly into the sky, and Ross began to believe his pilot. Leaving the gray, flat expanse of Vesper Lake behind them, they turned, banking eastward, and soared high over Route 5 and strips of isolated houses surrounded by plains and forest. In five minutes, they had crossed the dip of Frost Hollow and continued northeast. Ross could already see the hunting blind below where he'd found Franklin Kelly.

"If we keep on toward East Haven," said Marshall, "we'll hit the fire road. You just keep a lookout."

Ross scanned the woodland below for any glimpse of white in among the trees. Acre after acre passed beneath him, but nothing that wasn't more canopy or grassland. Neither he nor Marshall saw anything other than forest. They got to the fire trail, and Marshall banked around for a return sweep.

"This time, I'll go in a little lower."

Marshall dropped altitude, which brought the forest into

higher resolution. They did another sweep back toward Frost Hollow but came up with nothing.

"I'll swing around again," said Marshall.

Marshall took a wide circle and came back around. The sun's angle was low and sharp, causing Ross to squint. Sunshine lit up the cockpit, and as Ross fumbled in his jacket pocket for his sunglasses, a flash of light went off in his peripheral vision. Instinctively, he swung his head down and left toward the source of the flash. Another pinpoint burst of sunlight reflected off something below. Ross jerked around to Marshall, who was still scanning the landscape ahead.

"Turn around," said Ross.

"What?"

"Turn around now and go back exactly the route we came."

"You've seen it?"

"I don't know. I've seen something."

Marshall did the turn, and they headed back east. Ross looked out of his window, examining the forest below. The sunlight played around the cockpit, and then Ross saw what he'd hoped he'd see. A flash of light below. The flash had come from within a cluster of pines.

"Down there," said Ross. "The circle of pines. Something's reflecting back up from the middle of the circle. Is there anywhere you can land?"

"Necker's Brook leads into Bitter Creek. I can put us down there." Marshall pulled to the right and veered over the snaking brook. They flew over a wooden bridge, and shortly after, the brook broadened out into Bitter Creek. Marshall took the plane down, and Ross felt a crosswind jostle the craft sideways. Marshall was forced to fly into the wind and use the gusts as brakes as the floats touched down on the surface of the lake.

"Wow... That was smooth. Good flying," said Ross.

"When the water's flat like this, it's like landing on a cloud."

Marshall drifted the plane to the bank. The two men scrambled to the shore, soaking their boots and pants. Marshall tied the mooring rope to a tree that jutted out over the edge of the water.

"Okay," said Marshall. "You're the pilot now."

Ross nodded, and he headed off south, walking back to the head of Necker's Brook, where he followed its course until they got to the wooden bridge. At the bridge, they struck out east, and after a mile or so, Ross could see the cluster of pines.

"That's the place I saw the flash coming from," said Ross. "Could be a windshield, a hubcap, or a mirror, maybe?"

"Maybe..." said Marshall, but he didn't look convinced. Ross suspected Marshall was losing faith, and he couldn't blame him. This was turning out to be a search for a needle in a haystack.

"I'll get the chief to sign off on that repayment," said Ross. "And I'll make sure there's extra in it to make up for this. Especially if we don't come up with anything."

"I'm here out of civic duty, Kyle, not obligation. I'll do what's needed of me willingly."

"Thanks, Kyle. I would have got the chief to pay up front, but I was in a hurry to get out here. I didn't have time to let anyone know what I was doing. Figured I'd use my initiative and square things with everybody after."

"You didn't tell anyone?"

"Nope."

"I get you. I'd be exactly the same. No sense in jabbering about doing it. Just get on and do it." Marshall's pace suddenly faltered, and he clutched his right leg. "Hold up for a second. Leg's playing up. Bad knee, I'm afraid."

"Sure thing."

Marshall bent over, put his hands on his legs, and took a couple of breaths. Then, he straightened up and smiled. "Okay. All good."

They were yards away from the pines now. As they approached, they could see the outer edge of the cluster was more dispersed, the trees further apart. But toward the center, it got thicker and darker, and the bramble had grown a couple of feet off the ground. Ross stamped out a route through the bramble into the inner ring of trees. Amongst the sweet scent of wood, leaves, and brambles, Ross smelled something else. Something thicker, coarser. Something man-made.

"You smell that?" said Ross.

Marshall shook his head. "Smell what?"

"Gasoline," said Ross. "I can smell gasoline." He redoubled his efforts and battled through the thick brush. Ahead, he could see a mound of shrubbery, leaves, and branches between the pines that rose out of the bushes. The mound was square-shaped, and Ross began to sweep some of the brushwood away. As he cleared the debris, it became clear to Ross that hidden under the piled-up shrubbery was a van. But the van wasn't white; it was black. Scorched black. It had been torched, then covered in brambles, earth, and branches. On top of the mound was a broken-off wing mirror lying face up that had only been partially covered.

"That's it," said Ross. "That's gotta be it. We've found it. They drove it out here and torched it."

"Goddamn. Son of a bitch, Kyle, you've done it. You spotted a flash of light from a wing mirror from up in the sky. Got the eyes of a damned hawk." Marshall laughed and clapped like he was applauding Ross. Ross laughed too.

"What mastermind did this?" said Ross. "They went to the trouble of driving all the way out here, setting the thing alight, covering it in earth and branches, and then left a wing mirror on top."

"Yeah... What mastermind?" Marshall agreed, his laughter

fading away. "I just wish you hadn't told me you'd come out here without telling anyone else, Kyle."

The change of tone in Marshall's voice made Ross turn around. Marshall had a gun in his hand and was pointing it at Ross. Before Ross could ask Marshall what the hell he was doing, he heard a pop. His ears went numb and started to buzz. The strength left his body, and he dropped to the ground, where he lay on his side, unable to move. Ross didn't feel any pain, but he was certain he was bleeding from his stomach.

He heard Marshall speaking. Marshall sounded reasonable. Kind even. "I want you to know, Kyle, that I didn't come out here planning to kill you. It just turned out that way."

There was one more pop, some more pain, then nothing else.

MARSHALL SLIPPED HIS COMPACT SMITH & Wesson M&P Shield back into his jacket pocket. Then, he made a call on his cell.

The person on the other end picked up but didn't speak.

"I've started the cleanup," said Marshall, then ended the call.

TWENTY-ONE

"I've started the cleanup." That's all the voice on the other end had said.

For a while, the recipient of Marshall's call stared at his cell phone in dumb wonder. Then he called back, and it went straight to voicemail. So he called again, and again, and again, but each time, it went to voicemail, and he wasn't going to leave a voicemail. He wasn't a complete idiot. The line of work he found himself in required a kind of buttoned-up restraint that would drive most people crazy. One day, it might well drive him crazy. *Don't ever acknowledge the tightrope you are walking along*, he thought. Once you placed your first foot on that thin piece of cord, you simply had to keep on walking and never look down. And besides, he reassured himself, he wasn't knowingly doing anything terrible. He was just one small part of a larger process he had no idea about and didn't wish to know anything about. He talked to his CEO, who of course knew more than he did, but how much his CEO knew was up to his CEO. He was the second part of the chain. He knew very little about the first part of the chain and nothing about the third part of the chain.

Just a cog or a link. Whatever the analogy, he was a bit-part player.

He stood up and smoothed down his jacket. One of his office walls was half brick and half glass, which meant he could see into the operation next door and keep an eye on his employees who knew even less than he did.

It was time, he realized, to call the next part of the chain. The third part.

He walked to the door and pushed it shut. He went back behind his desk and picked up the phone.

It rang twice.

"Yes." The voice on the other end, the third part of the chain, was curt.

"One of our people just rang in. The guy out in Vermont."

He heard the third part of the chain sigh. "What now?"

"He says he's started a cleanup."

"He said what?"

"He said he's 'started a cleanup.' Those were his exact words. That's all he said. Nothing else. He put the phone down."

"You tried calling back?"

"Yeah. He won't answer."

"Jesus."

"What should I do? I mean, I just need to let you know, don't I?"

There was a pause. "Ditch the cell."

The phone went dead. Dial tone. Just what he'd expected and hoped. He'd passed a piece of information up the chain. Job done.

"STARTED A CLEANUP?"

The third part of the chain sat back in his ergonomically designed office chair and cursed. He looked out over the Seattle business campus and cursed again.

"Started a cleanup?" he said again, hoping just repeating it might lessen the starkness of the phrase. It didn't. He shook his mouse and woke up his screen. For half an hour, he looked through his fund folders and thought about his bottom line. It only confirmed what he already knew. One fund was his bottom line. The fund that was presently giving him heartburn. He threw himself back in his chair. He thought about the fourth part of the chain: the enforcers. The enforcers of this fund were what one might term "shady," existing in a legal twilight where some of their endeavors were legitimate, and others were not so much. And those enforcers could become very nasty very quickly. Especially if they knew one of their most profitable investments was in danger of running into terminal difficulties.

Should he ring the fourth part of the chain? The people who, if you wanted to sleep at night and hope for a better future for your children, you never wanted to meet. Or even believe existed.

Maybe not yet. Maybe the cleanup would work out okay. Maybe he should just hold off raising the alarm with the fourth part of the chain, for the time being.

TWENTY-TWO

Lori Cassidy made it over to Archie Baker's bright and early. She was there to check in with him and ask him to keep the discovery of the Franklin kid on the down-low for the time being. When she got to Archie's place, she found two things she wasn't expecting: Father Ramirez and the strange spectacle that was Archie Baker's eyes.

Archie's eyes looked like plates. In the gloom of his tar-paper shack, it seemed to Cassidy at times like his eyes were shining. Like some energy source behind his eyeballs was fluxing yellow light through his bloodshot corneas.

"We've called Dr. Hudson out, Archie," said Cassidy.

"The doc ain't gonna be able to do anything. What's happening to me isn't science. It's something else. Like what happened to the Wendig girl, like what happened to the statue, like what I heard happened to your nanna."

"How did you hear about Nanna?"

"This town is too small to keep secrets long."

"I know for a fact that ain't true, Archie. A white van blew through here and killed a bus filled with children and Hugh Varley, and we still haven't found it. I've been a cop thirteen years, and I'll bet you there are things have happened in this town I still don't know about."

"Maybe so. But Father Ramirez here must think there's something in what I'm saying, or he wouldn't be here." Archie nodded across at Father Ramirez, who was sitting in an old office swivel chair rescued from a tip with a leather satchel on his lap. Cassidy was sitting next to him on a wicker chair, much of which had unwoven and didn't make her feel particularly secure.

"You're right, Mr. Baker," said Ramirez. "I've been asked by the church to look into the claimed miracles in Hinkley. May I ask you a few questions?"

"Go ahead."

Ramirez slid out a notebook, pen, and his cell phone from his satchel. He placed the cell on his satchel and held the notebook open in one hand, ready to write.

Archie laughed. "Who'd have thunk it? Ol' blind Archie Baker, miracle maker, being investigated by the church. Will the pope get to hear about this?"

"If it's decided a miracle has taken place, then yes. But the process would be long and thorough."

Archie clapped his hands and rubbed them. "Then we'd better get started."

Ramirez nodded, thought for a moment, then asked, "When did you start to get your sight back?"

"A few days ago. Sunday morning was when I really noticed things starting to get a little clearer."

"What medical condition do you suffer from?"

"It's called retinitis pigmentosa." Archie said the words slowly so he could get through them without tripping up. "Had it since a kid. Been going blind all my life. Slowly."

"What medications are you on?"

"A heap of them. You'd need to get a list from my doctor."

"I'd need your permission in writing for that."

"Then I'll write it down and give it to the doc. Anything to get this business to the pope."

"Are there any treatments to improve your sight?"

"No. None. It's a done deal."

"On Sunday morning, when you first noticed your sight improving, was there any event around that time you'd associate with the change?"

Archie thought for a while about this one. But after giving it a long consideration, he shook his head. "Nope. Nothing."

"And is your sight still improving?"

"Maybe. Thing is, it's not like it's getting back to normal. It's like I see the world, but it's all glowing, shimmering. Like everything and everyone is radiating. And different things radiate different colors, different energies. Like you, Father Ramirez, you radiate a steady glow. But you, Lori"—Archie turned his eyes onto Cassidy, and the orb of energy behind them seemed to intensify—"you radiate a fierce orange glow. Like you're burning. The only person I seen didn't have a glow was Officer Kyle Ross. When I saw him out on Frost Hollow, it was like his glow was fading away. Hardly any of it left."

Ramirez looked at Cassidy, who rolled her eyes.

"You got more questions for me, young man?" asked Archie.

"A few more, I think. Just a few more."

TWENTY-THREE

The Boathouse was one of the few bars that had already opened along the Marina. Others were in the process of being built, some were being fitted out, and others were already marketing for the launch night. But only a few had opened preseason, and of those, the Boathouse was attracting a regular group, a dozen out-of-state rich kids who were all vacationing in the same three luxury lakefront timber-framed houses. The alpha of the crowd, the skinny, tall kid in a Tommy Hilfiger padded vest, held court here. At the head of the table on the veranda, looking out at the lake, they would breakfast and plan the day. Some were in their twenties, others a little younger, all carrying fake IDs, and all were on a vacation financed by rich parents.

"Hey, Ryan," shouted one of the girls in the group. She was blonde, fresh-faced, in a tight Ralph Lauren quilted winter coat with fur trim. "We driving into town again tonight?"

"Nah, let's drive over to Newport tonight. I've had enough of the town here. Everyone's so sad 'cause they lost their children in the lake." Ryan made a comic "boo-hoo" crying face, and the crowd laughed.

The stocky kid sitting next to him looked out at the lake and squinted. "You think they got all the bodies out?"

"Nah, they're all still down there," said the kid on the other side of him.

"Creepy."

"I gotta hit the head. Get another pitcher, will ya?" Ryan said and left the table. The restroom was at the back of the Boathouse and up a flight of stairs. He skipped up the stairs, pushed the door open, and felt a large-knuckled hand at his throat and his feet lift off the floor. Next thing he knew, his back was smashing against hard, cold tiles. Staring down at him was a dark, serious face inches away from his own.

"You?" he gasped. "Is this about what we did to the other priest? Your little friend? 'Cause that was only a joke, old man."

"You're gonna wish it was about that. And the name's Father Devlin." Devlin tightened his grip on him and leaned his weight into his fist.

"Get your hands off me, you asshole."

"No," said Devlin.

"I'll call the cops and get your ass put in jail. I'll tell them you assaulted me and other stuff. I swear, I'll say things about you that'll make your life unlivable—"

"Not if I call the cops first. Tell them what's in your pockets and back at your house."

"What the hell are you—"

Devlin pushed harder at Ryan's neck and dug a hand into his padded vest pocket. He pulled out a small glass pipe.

"You're carrying it around with you. You're smoking it openly at night in town. You know how long you'll get for this? Up to a year. If you're supplying your friends, then five."

"I got lawyers on retainer. This kind of thing would be chicken feed to them."

"Where are you getting it from?"

"Getting what from?"

"Is it the bikers?"

"Screw you."

Devlin slapped the Ryan's face.

"You... You hit me?" he whined.

"And I'll hit you up and down the place unless I get an answer. Is it the bikers?"

"No... No, it isn't the bikers. They run the meth out of the county, but I don't get it from them. It's the guy who runs the auto repair place in town. Kane. I get it from Roy Kane."

Devlin let him slump down onto the floor and stood over him, not moving.

"What...?" Ryan moaned. "What else do you want?"

"Of course," muttered Devlin. "The Kanes."

DEVLIN LEFT the kid on the floor and exited the Boathouse. He jumped into the Chevy rental and set off south, driving through town and back out to Ma Kane's motel, where he pulled up outside his room. He got out and surveyed the cracked, weed-strewn lot and the faded, weather exterior of the motel building. The day was dry and bright, and again, he felt the wind coming at him from the east. A wind that came up and out of the valley below. And then he heard the sound of swarming motorbike engines again. Like flies buzzing around.

TWENTY-FOUR

Father Ramirez had finished interviewing Archie Baker. He was standing by the front door, waiting for Cassidy, who was crouched by Archie's chair, having a few last words with him.

"Archie," said Cassidy in a low whisper so Ramirez couldn't hear. "We haven't told anyone else that you found Franklin Kelly. We're keeping it quiet for a day or so. Only a few people know: the cops, Dr. Hudson, and you. I'd appreciate it if you could keep it to yourself too."

Archie patted her hand. "Sure, darling. Won't say a word. You can trust me, Lori."

There was a knock at the door, and Archie gestured to Ramirez. "Open the door, Father. See who it is."

Ramirez opened the door. Dr. Hudson was standing on the rickety porch.

"Hello, Lori, Father..." said Hudson. "They calling out the priest before the doctor now? Very medieval, I must say." Hudson marched past Ramirez. "I've come to examine Archie."

"Come on in, Doc," said Archie. "Father Ramirez here was interrogating me as to whether I might be a living miracle. What with my sight getting better."

Hudson sat in the old office chair opposite Archie and took a good look at his patient's eyes.

"Dear God, Archie," said Hudson, alarmed. "What's happened to you?"

"That's what we're all trying to work out, Doc. I said to the Father, you could give him a list of the medication I'm on. For his investigation."

Hudson looked over at Ramirez and shook his head. "Really?"

"If this is taken up by the archbishop, independent medical experts will be consulted too," said Ramirez. "So best to have the most accurate picture of the current medical condition and treatment."

Hudson looked back at Archie. "Really, Archie? You're happy with all of this? A church investigation?"

"Delighted. I might get to meet the pope, Doc. And then, who knows? Maybe the Dalai Lama. Maybe even Bono..."

Hudson sighed wearily and nodded toward Ramirez. "Give me your email, and I'll send the list over."

Ramirez took a page from his notebook, scribbled down his email address, and handed it to Hudson.

Then, he and Cassidy left the doctor to examine his unusual patient and got into Cassidy's cruiser.

Cassidy started up the car, backed out, and circled around, then drove down the dirt track back to the highway.

"Thanks for the lift back to St. Paul's, Officer," said Ramirez.

"No problem. Where's Father Devlin?"

"I don't know. He got your call and asked me to come out. He's really handed the investigation over to me."

"You okay with that?

"I'm more than okay. It's an amazing opportunity. And fascinating." Ramirez looked side to side at the countryside spread out on both sides of the highway. "The longer I'm in this town, the more fascinated I become."

"Is that so? Say, what's the deal with Father Devlin, anyway?"

"Excuse me?"

"What's the deal with him? He doesn't exactly look like a priest, for starters. More like a boxer who retired a couple of fights too late. He's kind of remote a lot of the time, and...well, he's like no other priest I've ever met."

"He's...different. That's for sure."

"You known him for long?"

"No. But I've known of him."

"What does that mean?"

"I...I heard things about him before I met him. Gossip."

"What kind of gossip?"

Ramirez sighed and crossed his arms. "Ridiculous-sounding gossip...and also less ridiculous-sounding gossip."

"Okay. So, start with the less ridiculous-sounding gossip."

"He had a wife. Before he was a priest, obviously."

"Obviously."

"He doesn't know I know this, and I sure as hell wouldn't mention it to him, but I heard she was murdered."

"No way. How?"

"Shot by a guy, an addict who wanted money to get more drugs."

"That's awful."

"Yeah. And that's not all. She was pregnant, and he lost his unborn child too."

"Dear God. Poor guy." Cassidy shook her head. They drove on for a stretch, and Cassidy shook her head a few more times, thinking over what Ramirez had just told her. "And what about the more ridiculous-sounding gossip?"

"There's...stuff..."

"Stuff like what?"

"Stuff like..."

"Like...?"

"Like he's healed people."

Cassidy turned to Ramirez, astonished. "That's what people are saying happened with the Wendig girl?"

"Yeah."

"Are you gonna put that in the report? That he has a track record?"

"How can I? It's all just rumors I heard from other people. And the priest community is probably worse than any other group of people for rumors."

"Have you asked him?"

"No."

"You have to ask him. It's relevant."

"How can I ask him? It's just ridiculous gossip."

"That's not what you said. You said ridiculous-sounding gossip. You should ask him."

"I don't know about that."

"It's your duty."

"Okay. I hear you. Now, please, give it a rest."

"Okay, Father. But if I were you..."

"I know. I know."

Cassidy dropped Ramirez off at St. Paul's, where he was due to meet Father Wilson. Then, she drove back to the precinct. On her way through the lobby, sitting waiting for her in one of the banks of gray molded plastic chairs, was Devlin.

He got to his feet and said solemnly, "There's something you and I need to find."

"And hello to you too, Father."

TWENTY-FIVE

Cassidy felt a chill run down her spine as she pulled up in the parking lot by Ma Kane's motel. The same feeling of dread she always felt here. It was still mostly empty, apart from three cars and all the weeds breaking through the concrete. The Kanes would really be praying for a spring rush this year, thought Cassidy.

Devlin, who had gone ahead in his own car, was waiting for her on the other side of the lot. He was sitting on the curb outside his motel room, smoking a fat cigar. Cassidy thought back to her conversation with Ramirez. The rumors he'd heard about Devlin. It struck Cassidy that, looking at the man sitting smoking ten yards away, the rumors weren't so unbelievable. There was a crack and sparkle about the man. Something that lit you up and made you a little afraid too.

"How you doing, man of mystery?" said Cassidy, standing in front of the priest.

"I'm doing okay." Devlin stood up to his full height, stretched out his broad frame, then took a hit on his cigar.

"Well...?" said Cassidy. "There is such a thing as wasting police time."

"I think there's a lot of that been wasted already."

"Oh, yeah, wiseass? Do tell."

Devlin looked around as if waiting for something to happen. Then he smiled.

"You smell that?"

Cassidy sniffed at the light breeze and screwed her nose up. There was a faint but harsh and unpleasant odor coming from somewhere.

"What's that?" asked Cassidy. "Smells like...cat pee?"

"Come with me."

Cassidy followed Devlin, passing the motel rooms until they got to the part of the building that housed the utility room. Just like he had done on his first night in Hinkley, he pressed the push bar and opened the door. Then, he reached inside and switched on the strip lighting.

"Step inside."

Cassidy took up Devlin's invite and looked around. All she could see was exactly what she would expect to see: carts for the room changes, bleach, brooms, mops, spare towels, and bed linen.

"Am I supposed to be looking for something in particular?" said Cassidy. "Is this supposed to be testing my powers of detection?"

Devlin pointed at a stack of boxes in the corner.

"Kitty litter," said Cassidy. "Well, that makes sense, what with the smell of cat pee."

"Absolutely. So, here's the sixty-four-thousand-dollar question: where's the cat? I've been here two days, and I haven't seen a cat or a cat hair even. How long you lived in this town? You ever known Ma Kane to keep cats?"

"No. Never. I imagine she'd hate cats. Or anything cute and furry. And they'd detest her. She doesn't even like people."

"There isn't a cat, and there's never been a cat."

"So, what's going on? Clearly, you've got some theory about this."

"Yeah, I do. My theory is that smell isn't to do with cats. It's the smell of a chemical process producing ammonia or something like it. The cat litter is being used to mop up spills from that same chemical process. And that would tie into the pipe I found, the one you have. The pipe one of the rich kids staying up at the lakefront dropped. The rich kids who follow some flagpole of a kid around. The same flagpole kid I tracked down out at the Boathouse this morning and made him tell me where he got his meth from."

"I'm beginning to get the feeling you were a very good detective."

"Old habits die hard, or never die at all, I guess."

"Who is it? Who supplied the meth?"

"Roy Kane."

"Roy Kane?"

"That's what I said. I think there's a trail we can follow."

"What trail?"

"That ammonia smell. I smelled it the night I got here and whenever the wind comes over from the east."

"You think we should follow the smell?"

"Correct."

Cassidy took a deep breath and said, "Okay." Then, she walked back to the door, stopped, and looked back at Devlin. "Well? You invited me out here to find a meth lab, didn't you? So, let's go find it."

Back in the cruiser, Cassidy reversed, wheeled the car around, then headed out of the lot. She stopped with the nose of the cruiser pointing east toward the outer ring of Hinkley. They were on the brow of a lane that dipped into a steep gradient and gave them a view over squares, bands, and islands of greenery. Forest and plains stretched out as far as the eye could see and were crossed by a few narrow roads and dotted by farms and half a dozen isolated houses.

In the distance, a faint hum could be heard that rose to growl. Cassidy and Devlin looked at each other.

"The bikers," said Cassidy.

"I've been hearing them on and off since I got here. The kid at the Boathouse said they run the meth out of Hinkley. Across the state."

"Jesus. We were all just hoping they were a temporary irritant. A cloud that was gonna pass over sooner or later."

"That may be wishful thinking."

Cassidy cranked down her window, popped her head out, and smelled the breeze. Then, she ducked back in. "This road carries on southeast till you hit the old cemetery and then the state forest. There's a tangle of roads off to the south but only one road heading north."

"Let's go east," said Devlin, "and follow our noses."

They drove for a mile, doing a steady twenty, heading down into the bowl of woodland. Occasionally, they'd pass a house, an island of habitation hemmed in by trees along the roadside. For the most part, there was nothing but nature and the road ahead. Every five minutes, they'd stop and see if they could locate the smell of ammonia on the wind. A few times, they lost it, but then, when the wind from the east grew in strength, they picked it up again, and eventually, they came to a crossroads. There was the one road headed north on the left, and the first of more roads headed south on the right. The wind from the east had tapered off, and the ammonia smell had gone. The trail had gone cold.

"Which way now?" asked Cassidy.

"My guess is north," said Devlin.

Cassidy nodded. "It's less populated. South, there's a few more houses and a farm. So, you'd think north. Though the whole area's been combed in the search for the white van, so how would we miss a meth lab?"

"Maybe it just got started?"

"Maybe. But right now, we're running on wishes and guesses. We could be riding around for a week and not find..."

Cassidy stopped talking. A familiar sound had begun to swell in the distance. A chorus of engines that all came from the same direction.

"North..." said Cassidy. "It's gotta be north."

Cassidy took the left turn and kept her speed low. The forest on either side was a thick wall of green broken up by small tracks for hikers and bikes. About a couple of miles from the crossroad, they came across a track leading off from the road that was different from the others. It was wide enough to take a vehicle, and the ground was stony, like a driveway.

Cassidy pulled over.

"The smell. It's back," she said.

"Let's go explore on foot."

Cassidy tucked the cruiser up onto the earth bank that bordered the road, and they followed the track. After about a quarter of a mile, the track changed from stone to soil, and tire tracks were visible, embedded in the compacted surface. The path snaked around to the right and left as if it had no real purpose, no intended destination, but the tire tracks continued, and the smell of ammonia got stronger. Eventually, they came to a clearing that showed evidence of recent activity. Dotted around the clearing were blackened patches where the vegetation had been scorched away. About twenty yards beyond the other side of the clearing was an old, tumbledown barn. Behind the barn was a black Yukon.

"That's the Kane brothers' Yukon, I'm sure of it," said Cassidy.

"Dead spots," said Devlin, looking at the dark patches. "Where chemicals have been dumped."

"I've never seen that barn before. Looks like it's been here a long time though." Cassidy unholstered her Glock. "Let's go have a look-see."

The barn was scorched in parts, and the timber that hadn't perished and fallen away was rotten. Inside, Cassidy and Devlin found black trash bags stuffed full of empty Sudafed and Advil boxes, empty cans of starting fluid, and plastic soda bottles. All of it had been bagged up, ready to be shipped off and dumped properly. The smell of ammonia was even stronger now, like rotten eggs.

The sound of something cracking came from outside the barn, like a twig snapping or a foot on dry gravel. Devlin froze and put his finger to his lips. Cassidy moved to the doorway, Glock in hand, and motioned for Devlin to stay behind. She stepped outside.

A gnarly voice to her right barked at her. "Drop the gun, or I'll shoot you in the head."

The voice belonged to a biker with a red bandana and long goatee who was standing a few feet away with a gun aimed at her. She sensed movement to her left and saw another biker with a gun. She dropped her Glock, and the biker with the goatee motioned her to walk away from the cabin.

A third biker strode into view. He had a gray beard and a ponytail, but the most extraordinary thing about him was his physical build. His upper half was hugely overdeveloped, like a bodybuilder on steroids. Yet his legs were strikingly thin by comparison. And the other curious thing about him was his voice—it was rasping and strained. Cassidy immediately recognized him as the bikers' leader from the descriptions the customers at the Irish bar had given her a few nights before.

"It's not you I want," the leader rasped. "It's the priest I want. Come out, priest."

There was a moment's pause before Devlin walked out into the sunshine. The biker with the goatee pushed Cassidy to the ground and picked up her Glock. Then, he and the other biker stepped back to form a semicircle with a dozen other gang members who had emerged from the forest. They lined up behind their leader, who stood waiting for Devlin. All the time, the biker with the goatee kept his gun trained on Cassidy, who remained on the ground.

"I been waiting, Father," said the ringleader. "Imagine how happy I was to see you in this neck of the woods."

"You and me both," said Devlin.

"You dug that glass in deep, Father. Twelve stitches I needed. Put each stitch in myself."

"Twelve? That's one for each apostle."

"A joke. That's good. You made a joke." The biker had started to step toward Devlin, narrowing the space between them. "You won't be making jokes when I snap your spine in two and paralyze you from the neck down for the rest of your life. Run and we'll shoot you down, so you better stay and take what chances you have."

"I intend to."

The ringleader advanced a little further, and Devlin stood his ground, anticipating the first strike. His opponent was built like a brick outhouse. Like an Abrams tank. And like an Abrams tank, he wasn't fast, but he was immensely powerful. His first swing had the destructive power of a wrecking ball. Devlin leaned back and felt the wind against his chin. In the split-second opening that followed, Devlin landed a jab to the face. But the jab didn't even give the biker pause, and he retaliated immediately, thumping Devlin in the guts. The wind sailed out of Devlin, and hard on that came another in-swinger, which

Devlin ducked. On the way back up, Devlin took a direct jab to the face and then a rear-hand punch that nearly blinded him. Mere seconds had gone by, and Devlin could feel the strength draining from his legs.

His vision blurred, and Devlin could see the outline of his opponent, who appeared to be grinning. Two large hands clapped around his head and began to squeeze hard. Two thumbs were planted in Devlin's eyes and began to push. The crushing force was extraordinary. Devlin frantically grabbed at the biker's forearms, trying to prize his hands from his head. The forearms of his attacker were enormous and hard as granite. No matter how much force Devlin applied to them, they didn't give an inch. The crushing grew stronger. He could hear liquid swirling in his ears, feel his eyeballs slipping back into their sockets, and his whole head throbbed with terrible pain. There were only seconds left before his skull and his eye socket would be breached.

From somewhere in the periphery of Devlin's waning consciousness came the words "left knee." A memory from their previous encounter. Withstanding extreme pressure, his eyes and head close to implosion, Devlin stamped his right foot out blindly, about where he guessed the biker's left knee might be. He felt a hard connection and knew he'd guessed right when the pressure around his skull and eyes eased off fractionally. Now he'd located the biker's knee, he stamped out again, as hard and fast as he could. He kept on relentlessly stamping, knowing that this part of his opponent's body was somehow vulnerable, whether from an old injury, encroaching arthritis, or some other reason. The pressure on his skull began to lift as the biker reeled from Devlin's successive blows. Eventually, he had no option but to let go, such was the terrible agony Devlin had inflicted on his joint. The biker stumbled back, gripping his knee and cursing violently.

Devlin was free but could hardly see. His head was pounding with blood and pain. He could barely make out the bulky figure hobbling toward him. Maimed and robbed of full mobility, the biker was still dangerous, but now the field had been leveled. Devlin twisted to his left as the biker came at him and crouched low, springing up and upending his opponent onto the ground. Devlin found himself on the ground too. Scrambling down in the dirt, he put a knee on the biker's thigh, clamped his hands around his left ankle, and wrenched it forward. Joints and ligaments cracked, snapped, and split. The howl the biker gave out could have come from a dying bear. As they scrabbled around, Devlin became aware of a white mist rolling around him and the biker, moving across the forest floor. The smell of rotting eggs had become almost overwhelming.

A gunshot went off, and the two men froze. The biker disengaged and dragged his ruined limb away. Devlin, his sight returning, saw that one of the biker gang, a skinny guy with bushy sideburns, was aiming a pistol at him. He was aware of Cassidy on the ground to his left.

"You okay, Dwayne?" said the biker with the gun to his leader.

"Yeah... Yeah... I'm fine..."

However, the biker with the sideburns was only partly concerned with his leader's physical condition. His focus was on the thick white clouds covering the forest floor. "What's up with the white mist everywhere? What the hell is that?"

The other bikers were all also looking around at the mist gathering on the ground and murmuring curses and "what the hells?"

"No idea," said the ringleader, who was trying to get to standing but finding that his right leg wasn't up to the job. "Just shoot the bastard," he yelled from a kneeling position. "And the bitch."

The biker with the sideburns swung his barrel around at Devlin, but the sound of a distant scream distracted him. Then another scream came from the same direction, muffled but definitely human. And then a third scream came, and after came more screams, wild and unhinged and haunting, muffled with an eerie echo.

Cassidy looked about frantically. So did the bikers, who were just as disturbed by the screams. The biker with the sideburns returned his focus to Devlin and took aim again, intending to shoot. But before he could fire, the ground beneath him rumbled and seemed to lift up. Out of nowhere came a wall of intense heat, and then another wall of earth, branches, bits of brush, and rocks hit hard. Chunks of metal and glass followed. The bikers were thrown high and forward by the force of the explosion, and debris rained down like a bomb had gone off.

TWENTY-SIX

The Hinkley fire department sent out two Spartan fire trucks, their ambulance response vehicle, and a Chevy Idaho. The smaller of the two fire trucks was a Freightliner pumper, which had enough water to contain the fire at ground level and then deal with the blaze raging below ground. It took two hard hours to extinguish the last of the fires. Once that had been achieved, the firefighters had a chance to investigate what had caused the explosion and the fire and take stock of the aftermath.

A chunk had been carved out of the woodland, a crater about ten yards in diameter. Trees had been flattened, the blasted earth was charred black, an acrid chemical smell hung in the air, and there was no birdsong. Around half an acre of land had been devastated.

The bikers had taken the brunt of the blast and had sustained such serious injuries that they were all immediately transported away in ambulances for urgent ER care. Devlin and Cassidy had been only three or four yards further back but had, in effect, been shielded by the gang, who, standing in a semicircular wall, had absorbed most of the shock wave and debris. Apart from a few scratches and dirt stains, they were pretty much unscathed. They only needed a once-over from the attending paramedics before they were given the all clear.

"It's a damned freight container. An underground meth lab. Unbelievable." Captain Diaz was shaking her head and wiping the sweat from her brow. Her face was blackened with smoke and her eyes marked out with pale rings where she'd been wearing her goggles. She placed her helmet on the hood of the Chevy and shook her head again, then looked at Cassidy and Devlin with disbelief. They were standing back from the barn about forty yards away from the scorched rubble and devastation left behind by the explosion. Wisps of smoke were still rising from the ruins of the forest.

"They dug a trench into the ground," Diaz continued, "and lowered a freight container in there. They cut out an entry hatch at the top and covered the whole thing with earth. We found the remains of the roof. It was a meth lab—that's what the contents of the barn say loud and clear. But there's not much evidence left in the freight container of the actual lab. The heat in there was extreme. It baked up like a furnace and baked up fast before it went off like an almighty pressure-cooker bomb. I'll need to call the state fire marshal in to take over the investigation."

"Any human remains?" asked Cassidy.

"There are some charred bones, and from what little's left, it looks like bones from two bodies. But we're just firefighters, so that's a guess."

"State Police Crime Scene Search Team are on their way," said Cassidy. "I called the chief, and the Yukon is registered to Roy Kane."

"You know him?" asked Diaz.

"Yeah, I know him. Chief's with Kane's mother now, lady known locally as Ma Kane. She says the brothers left the motel in the Yukon this morning. Apparently, she's in full denial mode." Cassidy sighed. "There's not much more here than meets the eye. The Kane brothers were operating a meth lab, and it blew up and them with it. The bikers must have been helping them run the meth out of state, across the border, and maybe providing protection."

Captain Diaz was called away by one of the firefighters. Devlin, who had been looking thoughtfully into the distance, broke off from surveying the destruction.

"You thinking what I'm thinking?" said Devlin. "That the van you were chasing that night was being driven by the Kane brothers. That they were transporting equipment and materials to set up the meth operation here. That's why they didn't stop."

"The possibility had crossed my mind. But what about the bikers? It could have been them?"

"Maybe. But you said yourself that the bikers didn't show up until about a week ago. And that's what the bartender at O'Leary's said too."

"Yeah, they came a couple of weeks after the crash at Lake Vesper. I've got officers down in ER to question the biker gang and find out what they know. But whether it was them, the Kane brothers, or someone else, the sixty-four-thousand-dollar question is still where's the van?"

"We might not know the answer to that question, but we do know the next best thing, where to look for clues—the Kanes' body shop. And if we do it now, then we'll beat the Crime Scene Team to it."

Cassidy scowled at Devlin. "Firstly, the Crime Scene Team should process Ma Kane's motel and the Kanes' body shop. Secondly, 'we'?"

"The people best qualified to look at that place are local cops like you who know what they're looking for. And yes, I said 'we.' I got us to the meth lab, nearly had my head caved in by a Nazi biker, so I think I've proved my value a few times over. But of course, you could enlist the help of one of your colleagues back at the precinct. It's your choice, Officer."

Cassidy looked over at the two other officers sealing off the smoldering crime scene and the firefighters running hoses to the scorched open scar in the clearing beyond. Then she eyed Devlin, studied him.

"First of all, you can stop calling me Officer—it's Lori. Secondly, who the hell are you, anyway? You come into Hinkley, and all manner of weird things happen. Sick people come back from the dead, statues weep, and you literally sniff out a meth lab."

"Like I said, I have a past in the military."

"That's it? That's the explanation? Not according to your pal Father Ramirez, it isn't."

"What did Father Ramirez say?"

"That he's heard all sorts of rumors. Rumors that you can heal people."

"Well, the important word here is 'rumors.'"

Cassidy almost let the matter go there and then, but niggling curiosity drove her on. "He... He also told me that you lost your wife."

Devlin nodded, but his face didn't show a crack of emotion. "Yeah. That's not a rumor. That part's true."

"He said she was shot...while she was pregnant..."

"That's true as well."

"That's awful. I can't imagine how you came through that."

Devlin still didn't emit even a flicker of feeling. Whatever was happening was happening deep inside, away from Cassidy and the world. He just looked down at Cassidy, turning his hard blue eyes on her, and said, "You want the truth?"

Cassidy nodded.

"You may well not believe me."

"Tell me. I decide what I believe."

"I came through it because I was given a purpose. I'm someone who turns up at places in need of someone like me. Places where bad things have happened, and I was brought here for a reason. This town is locked up with grief and sin. I can unlock it. That's why I'm here."

Cassidy watched Devlin closely, trying to absorb the essence of him. Trying to decide whether to believe the crazy-sounding things he was saying. But nothing he said was crazier than the things that had actually happened.

"Did you really bring the Wendig girl back to life?"

"I genuinely don't know. But stranger things have happened in my presence."

"What about the other things that have happened here? My nanna? Archie Baker? Are they anything to do with you?"

Devlin shrugged. "I've yet to be convinced. What I do think is that the epicenter for everything that's happened in the last few days in this town is the night the children died in the lake. Everything since then has been ripples from that terrible catastrophe, and right now, my best use for this town is as a detective more than a priest. And right now, right here, I can help you. In a way no one else can."

"Can I trust you? You're like a fortress, some kind of castle. I met you a few days ago, but I have this feeling I could know you for a thousand years and not ever figure you out."

"You can most certainly trust me."

TWENTY-SEVEN

It was the fifth house call Ramirez had made that day. He'd been driving around town, chasing one tip-off after another. People all over Hinkley were calling Father Wilson either to report some astonishing medical turnaround in themselves or in someone they knew. Father Wilson would eagerly pass the information straight on to Ramirez with the expectation that Ramirez do the chasing up. This was only his fourth day in Hinkley, but the cases of claimed miracles seemed to be rising exponentially. If this kept on, they'd need a whole team of priests.

And then there was the question of Father Devlin. Ramirez had called him half a dozen times before he got hold of him. When he had finally gotten Devlin on the phone, he told Ramirez that he was caught up in something important but didn't feel obliged to tell him what the hell it was. As keen as Ramirez had been to take on the job of recording the events in Hinkley, he could really do with the extra help right now.

Ramirez pulled up outside the next address he had written down in his notebook. It was a colonial-style house on a quiet road lined with other colonial-style houses. He looked at the notes scribbled down during his phone conversation with Father Wilson: "Gary & Maria Burnett. Maria says MND symptoms suddenly reversing."

Ramirez was young and had never had to deal with ill health or being face-to-face with others who were in continual discomfort and pain. He had certainly never seen so many people close to death. Mortality had yet to become a reality to him. He took a breath and looked at his reflection in the rearview mirror. "Just get the facts, Ramirez. That's all you have to do. Simple." Then he slipped his notebook into his backpack and got out of the car.

He rang the bell, and a man in his seventies opened the door. His clothes seemed a little baggy on him, and his face was drawn, stubbled, and tired.

"Mr. Burnett?"

"Gary, please. It's Father Ramirez, isn't it?"

"Yes, Father Wilson passed on your details. I'm conducting an initial assessment for the church on events in Hinkley. The claimed—"

"Yes, yes," said Burnett, not waiting to hear the formal spiel. "Come in. Come through." Ramirez followed Burnett as he shuffled along the hall into a back room that looked onto the yard. The room had been cleared of most furniture except for two armchairs, a television, and a round table with a pile of exercise books on top. Maria Burnett was in a motorized wheelchair in the center of the room. She was much frailer than her husband, her physical movements seemingly almost entirely restricted by her disease. Her eyes darted across to Ramirez as he entered the room, but her head, which rested in a semicircular headrest attached to the wheelchair, did not move.

"Maria," said Burnett. "This is Father Ramirez. He's come to see your improvement."

Maria managed a smile.

"Please sit, Father. Would you like anything to drink? Tea, coffee...?"

"Thank you, no."

The two men sat in armchairs that faced each other diagonally across the room. Maria's wheelchair made a triangle. Ramirez took out a notebook and pen from his backpack, which he placed on the floor. He also took out his cell and placed that on his lap.

"Would you mind if I record our conversation?" asked Ramirez.

Burnett looked at his wife and shrugged. "I guess not. So, you're looking into all of the...things happening in Hinkley, Father? All of these miracles."

"I am."

"I do believe something special is happening here. That the faith of good people in a town broken with grief is being repaid. After a great darkness has come a great light."

Ramirez nodded. "I pray it is so. I really do. Thank you for calling Father Wilson." Ramirez turned to Maria. "Maria, I understand you have seen changes in your health?"

"That's right," Burnett interjected, speaking for his wife. "Isn't that so, Maria?"

"Yes," said Maria. "That's what you think, isn't it, Gary?" Her speech was slurred, slow, and hardly audible. Her words were more breath than voice, and Ramirez suddenly felt that reality in this room wasn't as solid as it should be.

"Yes. Yes, I do," said Burnett. "See, I've been keeping precise measurements of Maria's grip strength using the dynamometer. I take it every hour on the hour and have done since Maria was diagnosed with MND two years ago. Here, take a look at this." Burnett reached for the exercise book on the top of the pile on the round table. He opened it and passed it to Ramirez. "Go on, Father, take a look."

Ramirez flicked through the pages of graph paper on which columns had been marked out with a ruler and a pen. There were two columns on each page. In one column were numbers. In the column next to it were dates. Ramirez closed the exercise book and rested it on his lap.

"That's hard data right there," said Burnett. "Each book records three months. So, I take that data, and then I turn it into a graph. Time on one side and the dynamometer measurements on the other. Here. Look." He picked up another exercise book with graph paper, opened it up, and held it up for Ramirez to see. Across the first two pages, he'd marked out an x- and y-axis and plotted a graph just like he described.

"That graph is the measurements taken over this last month," said Burnett. "Can you see the pattern? It's going down like it has been for two years right until a week ago when it starts to even out and go up."

Ramirez studied the graph. A blue line traveled from point to point, and it was true, there was a slight change in the line's trajectory. But it was so slight and could so easily be a temporary blip. He looked from the graph up to Burnett's hope-filled face. Burnett looked over to his wife, his eyes shining with determined love.

"I just know there is some kind of mysterious agency moving among us," he said. "And it has alighted on this house, and it is working wonders on my own beloved wife. Maria's grip is getting stronger, and her health is returning. I just know it, Father. Praise be to God. And it's not just Hinkley."

"What do you mean?"

Burnett leaned toward Ramirez as if sharing a great secret. "I heard of an old people's home over in Lyndonville where the same thing's happening. People who have no right to be well unaccountably getting better. Defying doctors' expectations."

"What's the name of the home?"

Burnett rubbed his chin and shook his head. "I can't remember. I heard it from the guy who owns the hardware store—Nick. His dad's up there in the home in Lyndonville."

"Why is this the first I'm hearing of it? Do other people know about it?"

Burnett dabbed his nose with his index finger. "Maybe they want to keep it quiet."

Ramirez, not entirely trusting the authenticity of this new rumor from Burnett, changed the subject. "Have you discussed your wife's health with a doctor too? Dr. Hudson, say?"

"No. Hudson isn't our doctor. We go to Northeastern in St. Johnsbury for Maria. We haven't talked to a doctor yet about Maria's condition improving."

"Well, when you do, it would be really useful to know what they say. In the meantime, I'll take this back to Father Wilson and the archbishop with the other information I've gathered."

"You hear that, Maria? This will go to the archbishop." Burnett leaned over and placed his hand on Maria's. Maria managed a weak smile in return.

RAMIREZ GOT BACK into his car and reflected on his day. He had been to six homes, and if he was being honest with himself, all the cases were much more likely to be the product of desperate hope rather than miracles. Only Archie Baker and Jean Cassidy could be argued to be in any way exceptional. It seemed to Ramirez that there was an epidemic of delusion rather than miracles in Hinkley. Devlin's words came back to him, about a town in the wake of grief needing belief in something.

He rang Devlin again, and again, his cell went through to voicemail. Ramirez cursed Devlin. For a while, he sat in the car, wondering what on earth he was meant to do with all the testimony he'd collected. He looked at his notebook lying on the passenger seat and thought about going back to the motel and writing it all up.

"Screw that," he muttered and started up the car.

TWENTY-EIGHT

The auto repair shop was shuttered. Cassidy led the way around the back to a small parking lot crammed full of cars and pickups. The rear of the shop was a brick wall with one rear door. She gave the handle a try, but the door was locked.

"If we're here on police business, I could oblige," said Devlin.

"How?"

Without giving any warning, Devlin stepped back and rammed his considerable weight into the solid wood door. The woodwork shuddered and splintered, and a second attempt following fast on the heel of the first sent the door swinging open and set off an alarm.

"You're proving useful to have around," Cassidy yelled over the shrill blare of the security alarm.

"I like to think so."

They entered the back office. Everything looked normal. Like a working office waiting for its owners to return. Receipts lay in a stack on a desk. The coffee machine was half-full of cold coffee. Patriot Pennants and covers of *Sports Illustrated Swimsuit* hung on the walls.

Cassidy tried the door between the office and the workshop, and it opened.

Inside the workshop, there were four vehicles: a Chevy Impala, a Silverado, a Ford Pontiac, and Ramirez's Nissan beater.

Cassidy began to look around and search the vehicles. She started with the Pontiac, opening the driver's door and searching the glove box, footwells, and under the seats.

"Lori..."

Cassidy pulled her head out of the Impala. Devlin was standing back, looking over the four vehicles.

"What?" Cassidy shouted back.

Devlin walked over to the trunk of the Impala. "You should take a look at this."

Cassidy stood by Devlin.

"There," said Devlin, pointing to the area between the trunk and the rear fender. A thin line of red ran from the trunk and ended in a tiny bead.

"Wait there. Don't touch anything," said Cassidy. She left through the office and came back wearing latex gloves. She felt for the release, and the Impala's trunk lifted open. Cassidy stepped back and froze. Crammed into the trunk compartment was the body of Kyle Ross. His eyes were glassy and his face deathly pale. Blood had pooled and congealed on the carpet beneath him.

"Dear God. No... Kyle... Oh, God, no..."

Wedged in behind Kyle Ross's body was a battered, scorched license plate.

TWENTY-NINE

Seattle

A buzz came from the lowest drawer in the left-hand cabinet under his desk. He waited for the buzzing to stop, then went over to the door and locked it. He sat back behind his desk, took a key out of the pocket of his waistcoat, and unlocked the bottom drawer. The drawer was empty except for an old plastic flip phone. He took it out and dialed the missed number. After one ring, the person on the other end picked up.

"What's the situation?"

"The situation in the Vermont account has gone south," said the voice on the other end. "It's a complete and total mess. We need to call in the fourth part of the chain. We can't hold off any longer. You should have called them in when I called last time."

He sighed and rubbed his face. "Shit. Okay, I'll talk to them."

He snapped the cell shut and placed it in front of him. Then, he put his elbows on the table and clasped his hands together tightly. For a few minutes, he pressed his forehead against his hands, bumping them together repeatedly in quiet frustration. Then, he swung around in his chair and looked out of the window over the business campus and the other low-rise buildings. His office was in the largest building on the campus, which was situated a short drive north of Bellevue, Seattle. It was a low, sleek gray concrete building in the shape of a shallow V with smoky-brown windows. A building working hard to avoid any outward identity.

He took a quick, deep breath in through his nose, exhaled slowly through his mouth, picked up the cell phone, and dialed a number. There were two rings before the person on the other end picked up.

"Yes?"

"It's Taylor. I need to meet. Urgently."

"You can come now," said the voice on the other end. "I'll send a car to the ferry terminal."

The person on the other end cut off. Taylor put the cell back in the drawer, went to the door, unlocked it, and looked around his office, the bright, shiny, plush fixtures and fittings. Everything in the building, from the glass doors at the entrance through the lobby and into the elevator to the offices above felt like money. Lots of money. The building was designed that way. To give the people who came here confidence. Confidence that this ship was filled to the brim with money. And it was. Because this place sold something that lots of people wanted.

Taylor took the elevator to the underground parking lot and got into his Lexus. It was a three-leg journey he was going on. First leg was the car trip west to the Seattle waterfront. There, he picked up the Bainbridge Island Ferry. The third leg started at the ferry terminal parking lot, where he swapped his car for a chauffeured Bentley that was waiting to pick him up.

The chauffeur drove him a mile east and a mile south to

Wing Point. He turned off the increasingly narrow Wing Point Road and stopped on a narrow strip of graveled forecourt in front of a four-gabled three-story timber house. The house was tall and wide, backed by pines, and right on the shore of Eagle Harbor. The city skyline was visible over to the east through the March fog. Beyond the forecourt, stone steps descended into the green water of the harbor, and two jetties on either side of the house made crooked walkways out to the bay.

Taylor got out, and the chauffeur backed up and K-turned away. The big oak doors at the front of the house were open, so he entered and walked along the wide day-lit hallway into an octagon-shaped inner courtyard. An octagon-shaped swimming pool in the middle of the courtyard was surrounded by loungers, lawn chairs, and planters.

One of the loungers was occupied. A hairy, bald man with a thick black mustache in a short-sleeve shirt, shorts, and sandals was sitting in the middle lounger. Beside him, two men in suits were sitting in lawn chairs. All three were drinking from espresso cups. One of the suited men got up, approached Taylor, and patted him down. Then, he was beckoned forward. He pulled up a chair in front of the three men. The bald man took a sip from his espresso cup. His thick, matted chest hair sprung out over the top of his shirt, and he had a gap in his front teeth, which made his smile, on the odd occasion that he did smile, seem less like a smile and more like a threat. Like a wolf baring its canines.

"What is concerning you, Mr. Taylor?" asked the man with the gapped teeth in a thick accent, which Taylor knew to be Belarussian. He and his colleagues in the syndicate had created the necessary paperwork to get him into the US without any fuss.

"Your investment with us, Mr. Loban."

"Yes?"

"We're having a problem with the operational end in one of our districts."

"Go on."

"It's possible that problem might put our whole investment portfolio at risk. And, as we know, it is a very lucrative source of finance for many of our syndicate."

"And why come to me?"

"For the reason, or one of the reasons, I should say, that you were invited to invest in the first place. That you had certain resources that would be helpful, should push come to shove. And your recent termination of a troubled investment in Los Angeles was particularly impressive and tidy work."

"Yes, it was. Which district?"

"Vermont."

"I see." Loban sipped at his small cup and considered his position. "Of course, as part of the usual fee for this sort of work, we would need to agree to an increased dividend from my portfolio."

"I had given that some consideration."

Loban leaned forward and tapped his ear. "Tell me your consideration."

Taylor leaned forward and whispered a figure.

Loban leaned back. "I want twice that. No negotiation."

Taylor had anticipated his initial figure would be at least doubled, so he nodded.

Loban smiled and said, "Tell me everything."

So Taylor told Loban everything.

Loban took some time to think over what Taylor had told him. Enough time for Taylor to try to second-guess every possible answer.

Eventually, Loban spoke. He spoke slowly and as clearly as his thick accent allowed. "So, you are telling me the main contact in Hinkley is reporting that the situation is under control?"

"Yes."

"Do you think the situation is under control?"

"Yes...I think so. But I thought you should know because—"

"You thought I should know because if it isn't under control, if it gets out of control again, you have covered your ass. Better I know now before something bad happens."

"But I do believe the situation has been brought under control."

Loban tutted and shook his head. Then, he bared his gapped teeth and smiled a crocodile smile that didn't reach his eyes. "We have had for a long time a very good and profitable understanding, Mr. Taylor. It has been clear which side of things we handle. You handle the figures, and I handle the enforcement. In this case, you should have come to me right away. The first time that events diverted from their usual course, you should have alerted me."

"I'm sorry. You're right. I made a mistake."

"You made many mistakes. You let amateurs do our job. Clowns. Morons. I could have told you what was going to happen. I let you do your side of things. You should have let me do the job I take my money for, enforcing our terms. The longer you left it, the more work I have. The more money I take. You understand?"

Taylor's head dropped, and he shook it wearily. "Yes."

"I'm your firewall. I sell what you have to terrifying people. Powerful people in the worst parts of the world who pay a premium for commodities that come without scrutiny, ethics, or international oversight and sanctions. But the firewall works both ways. I have to protect myself too. And I will do whatever is needed to keep the firewall intact."

"What... What should I do...?"

"You go back to your office. There is nothing you can do now. You go back, and you wait for word from me. Wait out front. A car will take you to the ferry port. And the usual fee will be tripled for my troubles."

THIRTY

Garratt Marshall kept the yoke forward and brought the nose cone down. Through his headset, he could hear his passengers in the seats behind him laugh and talk excitedly as they made the descent. There was a slight bump as they hit the water, and then the plane settled, and Marshall steered the Piper across a placid, flat, and shimmering Lake Vesper toward his mooring spot. The whole landing couldn't have gone more smoothly.

"That was a great trip. What a place to fish," said one of the guys cramped in the back.

"It's a well-kept secret, so keep it to yourselves," said Marshall. "Very few locals know about that bend in the creek. I only spotted it 'cause I've flown over every inch of these parts a hundred times at least."

"A guy we know back in Boston recommended you," said the other guy. "We'll do the same too."

"Much obliged," replied Marshall. "I know other places even further out that are more difficult fishing, but the size of some of the brown trout is like nowhere else I've seen."

"We'll be back in late summer, so we'll definitely call you up. You do this every day?"

"Nope. I'm semi-retired, and this business means I can keep two planes running and keep some for profit."

"What did you work in?"

"I was an engineer in the Air Force. It's where I caught the bug for plane restoration. This plane would have been beyond my paycheck, but it came to me a wreck, and I spent years putting it back together. But it's as good now as it was new."

They had reached the jetty. Marshall powered down so he could cruise the last few yards and gently stop alongside the dock. He took off his headset, shifted his seat back, and then opened the door so he could judge the docking more precisely. Once he was close enough, he stepped from the pontoon onto the dock and tied up. He helped the passengers out with their fishing gear, which had been stored behind their seats.

Marshall escorted his guests back to their rental. He helped them pack the trunk and, after receiving a healthy tip, said goodbye. Then, he towed his plane up onto the ramp. Using a piece of engineering he'd put together himself, the front half of a specially modified Ford 4WD pickup with a hydraulic dolly on the front, he lifted and carried his plane from the ramp to his hangar that stood between two new lakefront condominiums. Once the floatplane and the modified Ford were stowed away, he shuttered the hangar.

Back out on the front, he stopped for a beer and a club sandwich at his favorite bar, then got in his pickup. He drove west past the bars and restaurants, past the zone of construction where new condos were being built. The road was clear, which was just as well as he had his eyes on his rearview mirror the whole way. He followed the road as it curved with the shape of the lake. There were few houses out this far, and eventually, he came to his own isolated lakefront property. Stick-built, one-story, and vinyl-sided, it was small and low-maintenance and a good fit for a middle-aged bachelor who was stuck in his ways.

Around the side was a double garage, where he spent most of his time when he wasn't down on the docks working on his floatplanes.

Marshall drove the pickup onto the grass shoulder in front of his house. He scanned his immediate surroundings, reached into his glove compartment, and pulled out his Smith and Wesson. Then he sat awhile in his car, studying his house for any signs of entry or disturbance. Once he was satisfied everything was just as he had left it that morning, he got out of the truck and slipped his gun into the band of his pants. He walked up the wooden stairs to the decking that fronted the house, put his key in the door, and opened up. Then, room by room, he swept the place until he was satisfied he was alone. He locked the front door, filled a tumbler with Maker's Mark, and set a chair in front of the window overlooking the street. He sat in the chair with the glass in one hand and the Smith and Wesson in another.

For a while, Marshall fought off sleep. He was exhausted. He'd spent most of the night tying up the loose ends. He shook his head in wonder and pride at what he had accomplished. He'd done it all alone, without any help, and it looked like he'd got clean away with it. Dear God! He let out a chuckle. What balls!

He stared at his hands, the same hands that had dropped Molotov cocktails into the Kanes' meth lab. He shook his head once more in disbelief. By Christ, those Kane boys were dumb as mules. Building a meth lab underground was about the most crazy-stupid, dumb-assed thing they could have done. They'd built themselves a sealed box full of explosive, toxic substances. They'd dug their own grave and built their own coffin. The Kane brothers had put a hatch in the roof of the shipping container they'd buried. All Marshall had to do was light the rag wicks of three bottles filled with gasoline and drop them through the hatch onto the hard floor below. He'd heard the glass smash and the flames spread. He'd heard the brothers' cries. Marshall shuddered. The cries were, without a doubt, the worst bit. Awful inhuman howling and weeping and screaming. Two men being cooked alive. He wondered if there would be a time to come when those cries wouldn't come back to haunt him. The cries hadn't been enough to stop Marshall though. He had put a sturdy length of wood through the metal hoops on the hatch and stepped back. The square metal plate shuddered from the brothers' frantic blows below as they fought to escape the already runaway fire.

Marshall had run. He'd run deeper into the forest. He ran as fast as a man of his age could run. Heavy-footed and ungainly, he couldn't even remember the last time he'd had to sprint. Behind him, he'd heard the violence of an explosion that told him he'd done the job as well as it could be done. The ground beneath him shook. Then, he walked through the forest back to his pickup, where Kyle Ross's body and the Mercedes license plate lay in the load bed under a tonneau cover. Now, the second part of his plan could unfold. Marshall drove to the Kanes' garage and parked around the back. He had bought a Wi-Fi interceptor generator online, and using his engineering know-how, he'd modified it so it would jam the security alarm. He picked the office door lock and put Ross's body and the evidence implicating him in the Impala. Once that was done, he went back to the marina and flew out to pick up the tourists he'd dropped first thing at a prime fishing spot. What a slick son of a bitch he was.

Now, he was waiting to be contacted. To be told what happened next. He'd called the number he had and told the next part of the chain that he'd "started the cleanup" and hung up. Whoever was on the other end had called back, but Marshall had gotten scared and hadn't answered. Then, finally, when he'd plucked up the courage, he'd called the number again but discovered it was disconnected. He was beginning to suspect that was a bad sign. He had taken things into his own hands in the most extreme way. The people he dealt with may not be pleased with his radical and highly risky solution to a problem he, after all, had created.

He shook his head and cursed. Why on earth had he got the Kane brothers involved in the first place? Sure, he was in a tight spot, but it wasn't his only option. He'd made the biggest mistake of all—he'd trusted his business with people that, in his heart of hearts, he didn't trust. He'd thought he'd get away with it. One time. That was all. He'd been counting on the Kane brothers not to screw up one time. And those half-witted morons couldn't even do that. And if those boys were dumb, then didn't that mean he, Marshall, was the dumbest of them all?

In the distance, he heard a car engine coming. His hand tightened around his gun, and he took a sip of bourbon. The engine got louder. Then, it passed by the house. The sound belonged to a minivan with a hard-shell rooftop cargo carrier attached. Two adults were in the front, two kids and a dog in the back. The car passed, and Marshall's grip loosened, and he took another slug. There was no point in being relieved. A car would come for him, eventually. It would stop, and the people inside would want to have the most serious kind of conversation with very possibly the most serious kinds of consequences. He could, of course, run, but it would look damn suspicious. And run where and for how long? His only chance lay in setting his case out. Sure, he made the mistake, but he also faced up to his mistake and did something about it.

Another car approached from the east, and Marshall waited.

Every car that came from now on could be the one.

THIRTY-ONE

Officer Lori Cassidy was sitting on a low wall outside the Kanes' auto shop. She was clutching her knees, and her shoulders were hunched. Her whole body was stiff, and her jaw was clenched hard. Chief Garland stood tall in front of her, throwing a shadow over her much smaller form. Behind them, the auto shop had been taped off, and forensics had arrived to process the scene. The second team called out to Hinkley that day. Red and blue roof lights whirled and cops, and crime scene officers went back and forth, in and out of the Kanes' shop.

"Goddamn, I'm sorry, Lori," said Garland. "It's like a punch to the gut. Those sons of bitches. If they hadn't blown themselves up, I would have turned them inside out with my bare hands for what they did to Kyle."

"But why kill Kyle? I mean... It makes no sense...?" Cassidy forced the questions out through gritted teeth.

"He must have found the van," said the chief. "The plates match the false plates you called in the night of the accident. I guess that's why the Kanes killed him. They were using the van to move their lab supplies, so they had to keep that secret and that they were responsible for all those deaths that night."

"I just can't get my head around it..." Cassidy's face was screwed up, trying to make sense of it all. "The Kane brothers were in the van we were chasing...and they caused the death of the children... It's too much to take in." Suddenly, her face unscrewed and became deadly serious. "Where's Ma Kane?"

"Down at the station."

Cassidy pulled herself to her feet. "Then I'll go interview her."

"You don't have to. I can talk to Ma Kane."

"We both know it's better I do it. There's more...more between us two..."

"Yeah, more to get in the way."

"Maybe. But maybe more to pull and twist on. You got any more from the biker gang?"

"A couple of them are fit to talk. The main guy, the one built like the Hulk, he's in a bad way, but we got some time with him. Unsurprisingly, he's not talking except to say one thing."

"What's that?"

"The bus crash had nothing to do with his motorcycle club. He's adamant. Says it's a matter of principle to tell the truth 'cause it's about kids. His members were nowhere near Hinkley at the time. First time they came up here was two weeks after the crash."

"You think he's telling the truth?"

"How can I trust the word of a meth-dealing biker?"

"I never saw them before about a week ago. Maybe the Kanes had only just got enough product and cash to make it worth doing a deal with them."

"Maybe. Maybe not. But the van's license plate was found in the Kanes' shop, so in terms of evidence, we couldn't ask for much more."

"I guess..."

Cassidy looked over the road to where Devlin was standing and smoking on a cigar. Garland turned to look at the priest too.

"What's he doing hanging around, Lori?"

"Him? He's the one who found the meth lab. He's the one who went hand to hand with the Incredible Hulk and lived to tell the tale. Twice. That's who he is. We oughta thank him."

"For what? All he found us was a hole in the ground and two dead men." The chief scratched his chin and said sourly, "There's something about him. Something off. We got cartloads of visitors still coming to the church every day to see the statue. Rumors of miracles like the world's gone mad. He seems to have brought all that with him."

"Did you know he was a detective? With the Air Force? I think he was probably a good one."

"Yeah, I heard that. But he's just a priest now."

"A priest some people say brought the Wendig girl back to life." Cassidy began to cross the road toward Devlin, and Garland caught her arm.

"Be careful, Lori. I've lived and worked in this town all my life, and I've never known anything like this. Something strange is working its way through the guts of this place...and its people too."

DEVLIN'S dark features were wreathed in smoke, but his hard blue eyes seemed to laser through the clouds and straight into Cassidy's soul.

"You okay?" he said.

"No. No, I'm not. I knew Kyle since he came here five years ago. I showed him the ropes. Mentored him. The whole thing has turned out so damn...ugly. I mean, in one way, it's all real damn neat. It all ties up now—we seem to know who's responsible for all the death and misery that's happened. But damn, this town feels like the ugliest place on Earth right now. I gotta go interview Ma Kane about all this. I'll see you later."

Cassidy walked off toward her cruiser, and Devlin felt his cell buzz. With a cigar in his mouth, he tried to read the dozen missed calls on his screen. Most were from Ramirez, but the last one was a voicemail from an unknown number. He listened to the message and heard the voice of Elizabeth Wendig.

THIRTY-TWO

Lori Cassidy entered the interview room, and Ma Kane's sour, thin, sun-damaged face wrinkled up like she'd smelled something nasty. Cassidy knew she had to tread with care. After all, this was a woman who'd lost two sons in one day. Though, observed Cassidy, even after such an enormous tragedy, Ma Kane still seemed able to keep grief from collapsing her. She was still that fierce force of nature she'd always been.

"Why're you here?" snapped Ma Kane. "I told the other cop all I had to tell."

Cassidy sat in a plastic seat behind a worn wooden desk that faced the white-painted cinder block wall. The way the desk was placed left a small space between the side of the desk and the wall where Ma Kane was sitting. It was a deliberate setup to make the interviewee feel cornered and exposed at the same time. It was not, Cassidy had to admit, the way to treat a woman in Ma Kane's position.

Cassidy shuffled her notes and sifted through them.

"I'm sorry for your loss. Truly, I am," said Cassidy.

"I've said everything I have to say. I want to go home and mourn my boys."

Cassidy paused and considered her next move. "You say you didn't know Roy and Ted were running a meth lab?"

"Ask the other guy. I ain't answering questions twice."

"Fair enough. What the other guy won't have told you is there was a search of your motel this morning."

"What? That's against my constitutional rights."

"We had a search warrant. We found items in the motel storage room used in the manufacture of methamphetamine. Items including gas cans, coffee filters, many packs of Sudafed."

"That room is full of all kinds of things. Regular cleaning stuff for the rooms and other stuff I haven't even looked at in years. And the boys, they used the room as extra storage for things from their shop."

"You are the legal owner of the motel. You can be legally held responsible by a court of law for what we found in the storage room."

"What the hell? Are you trying to turn a grieving mother into a criminal?" Ma Kane smiled bitterly. "Just how low would you go to get back at me?"

"This isn't personal."

"How can it not be personal?" hissed Kane.

Cassidy felt her emotions threatening to run away from her like wild horses. It took all her willpower to stay rooted to her chair.

"There are other things you won't have been told yet. Developments."

"Such as?"

"We found the body of Officer Kyle Ross in the trunk of one of the cars at Roy and Ted's garage."

"What?"

"He'd been shot. And in the trunk with him was the false license plate from the van that drove the school coach into Lake Vesper."

These few facts had an immediate and profound impact on Ma Kane. All the tension in her tough, spindly body and fierce face dissipated. The fire of resentment and suspicion that was her inner engine vanished.

"They...? They...? My boys were the ones who caused the accident...?" Ma Kane asked the question with a vulnerable innocence that Cassidy would not have hitherto thought her capable of.

"It looks that way. Though I guess a judge could argue the other way still, so it's not 100 percent."

"It is for me." Ma Kane had suddenly transformed, as if she had been struck hard by the greatest realization of her life. Cassidy didn't move, didn't speak. She knew through instinct now was the time to stand back. To not get in the way of what seemed to be coming.

"A mother knows," Ma Kane said and caught Cassidy's eye, who looked down at her notes. "The night of the accident, they were out. They came back to the motel in the early morning. They hadn't slept or washed. Said they'd pulled a late one at the shop and decided to sleep in the office. And I wanted to believe them so much that I didn't question it. The way they acted afterwards. The awkward looks between them. Calls on their phones they snuck away and took out of my earshot. Something changed with them that night, and I should have noticed. A mother should have noticed. But you gotta unnerstan'," she pleaded, "we was always up to all kinds of stuff. A dollar don't mean shit these days, you know how it is. But it was low-level business. Like the moonshine we was brewing and delivering—it was just kiddie stuff and nothing to get the feds piddling their pants over." Ma Kane stretched out a hand and laid her fingers on Cassidy's hand. "But I swear to you as the Lord is my witness, I knew nothing about the meth, about what my boys were doing. I shoulda done, but I didn't."

There was a silence, and Cassidy looked down at her notes once again.

"This won't be the last time you'll be interviewed.," said Cassidy. "The FBI are on their way and will want to look at aspects of this case that fall within their jurisdiction."

This time, there were no protestations from Kane. The old woman rose slowly.

"I'm glad it was you that gave me this news. I think it was meant to be you. It was holy justice. Maybe this is my punishment for what I did to you. I lost two boys because I didn't look after one little girl."

Cassidy felt searing emotions tear through her body. She grasped the side of the worn wooden table and, not looking at Ma Kane, spoke slowly and matter-of-factly.

"You left my terminally ill dad for another man when I was three. You wanted nothing to do with me or him. You made that decision for us both thirty years ago. As far as I'm concerned, what you did was irrevocable and everlasting."

Cassidy picked up her notes and left the room in silence.

THIRTY-THREE

"What can I do for you, Father?"

It was 9:00 a.m., and the hardware store had just opened. The guy behind the counter wore a grease-stained checked shirt. The sleeves were rolled up to the elbow, exposing thick, hairless forearms. Reading glasses were perched on the end of his nose. He scratched his shiny, domed head and looked Ramirez up and down.

"It's Nick, isn't it? Nick Stokes?" said Ramirez.

"Yeah, that's right. Do I know you?"

"No, no. But I was talking with Gary Burnett, who I believe you do know?"

"Oh, sure, I know Gary."

"Right. Good. So, Gary mentioned he'd spoken to you about the old people's home in Lyndonville, where your father is. About how some of the people there were experiencing surprising turnarounds with their health..."

"Surprising turnarounds?" Stokes gave a chuckle.

"What? What's funny?"

"Nothing, just an amusing turn of phrase, that's all. 'Surprising turnarounds.'" Stokes chuckled again.

"What's amusing about it?"

Stokes leaned on the counter and beckoned Ramirez in closer. "It's more than surprising turnarounds. The things I heard are anyhow. I was up to see my old man last week, and it was the talk of the place. All the old folk there are chattering about some of them having medical conditions they've lived with for years"—he snapped his fingers for effect—"nearly vanishing, just like that. I'm surprised no one else is talking about it."

"Did you see any evidence of this?"

Stokes shifted his weight and sighed. "Well, no. I didn't see anything directly. But they're all talking about it as if it were a fact."

"Why do you think more people aren't talking about it? People in Lyndonville and here in Hinkley?"

"Well..." Stokes's eyes wandered around as he mulled over the question. "Maybe the reason is this. A lot of the old folk a lot of who have dementia and such. So, what they say is taken with a pinch of salt."

"I guess that could be true enough. What's the name of the home?"

"The Meadows. It's called the Meadows nursing home."

MINUTES LATER, Ramirez was back in his car and heading out to the interstate. He got on the highway and drove south, taking the exit ramp for Lyndonville. The satnav took him through Main Street, into the southern suburbs of the town, then out into the countryside. He drove for a couple of miles until he saw a sign ahead of a turnoff for the Meadows Home. The turnoff was a short road that led to the Meadows' gated entrance. The gates were open, so Ramirez drove on through.

The Meadows Home was a two-story stretch of apartments surrounded by lawn and pines. There was a parking lot out front. A sign for reception and more parking pointed to a road by the side of the building that led around to the back. Ramirez took the side road and parked in a row of cars facing away from the building toward the pines.

He got out of his car and followed more reception signs that led him to a ramp and automatic glass doors. The doors clunked open, and Ramirez looked around. The large lobby was empty, apart from a nurse helping an elderly man into a wheelchair, but neither seemed to pay him any attention. The reception desk at the far end of the lobby was empty. Ramirez crossed the lobby and walked past the unmanned reception desk. Behind the reception desk was a short corridor that led into a long, bright room with floor-to-ceiling windows on each side. Residents were sitting in armchairs scattered around the room, facing a large TV on the far wall. *The People's Court* was playing to virtual silence. There was no staff around, so Ramirez walked back to the reception, where the nurse had managed to settle the old man into the wheelchair.

"Hi," said Ramirez. "I'm looking for the manager?"

The nurse stared at Ramirez. He looked tired and blank. His overalls were stained, loose, and hanging off him. "There ain't no manager around here today, Father."

"Oh, I see."

"She's in town meeting with the council."

"Are there any senior staff here?"

"Nope. Just the nurses like me and other carer staff."

"They all at the meeting too?"

"Yeah. It's an emergency meeting."

"Emergency? What kind of emergency?"

"The emergency here."

"What's happened here?"

The nurse sighed heavily. The man in the wheelchair stayed silent and looked even blanker than his carer, his eyes staring outward but his mind somewhere else. Both looked almost traumatized, Ramirez thought.

The nurse eyed Ramirez up and down. "You here to visit a patient?"

"No. I was contacted by a relative of one of the residents here who was worried about his father," said Ramirez, blending truth with lies.

"Which resident?"

"Mr. Burnett. I spoke to his son, Nick."

"Ed Burnett is out on a day trip to see a theater show in Burlington. And that's where I'd like to be too."

"Why? What's going on here? Why is there an emergency meeting?"

"Trust me, no one knows what's going on here. And no one wants to know."

"Try me."

The nurse put a hand on his hip and shook his head. "It's crazy here. We got residents who have been sick for years, some close to dying, saying they're suddenly getting better, the visiting doctor scratching his head and not having an explanation." The nurse looked at Ramirez for a reaction but got nothing. "You look like you're not surprised."

"No. I'm not. That's kind of why I'm here, actually. I've come from Hinkley, and we've seen the same thing happening."

"Hinkley?"

"Yeah."

The nurse shook his head. "Gotta be something in the water."

"You mentioned a visiting doctor. Is he around?"

"No. He isn't here today. Dr. Hudson comes here most Tuesdays though."

"Dr. Hudson? Dr. Rick Hudson?"

"Yeah. That's him."

THIRTY-FOUR

They had flown coach overnight from Seattle-Tacoma to Burlington International via a layover at Dulles. Eight hours, all told. In between bouts of sleep, the two guys in suits sat together and talked from time to time about football, cars, and distant European wars they had friends and relatives fighting in. Loban sat an aisle over from them and read the well-thumbed in-flight magazines from cover to cover. When he'd finished the magazine, he watched business news channels on his cell over the pay-to-use Wi-Fi.

After touchdown and security checks, they hired a BMW rental at Burlington for the drive to Hinkley. On the way, they picked up two new-in-box semiautomatics, three Springfield Hellcats, and enough ammunition for a week's hunting. The order had been made ahead of time through an online firearms website. No ID, no checks. It was just a happy coincidence that Vermont was a gun lover's free-market paradise. Tooled up, they took the I-89 and the I-91 across state and were sailing into Hinkley by breakfast time.

Loban was sitting in the back seat, staring out morosely at

the storefronts they passed by and then at the acres of flat, green land that followed.

"Where the hell are we?" muttered Loban from the back seat. "Everywhere in this godforsaken place looks the same. How do you even know where we're going? Or are you making it up, Gus?"

"I know where we're going," replied Gus confidently, the satnav on the dash tracking a path ahead.

"Do you have any water, Slava?" Slava dug down between his thick thighs into the footwell, brought up a bottle of water, and passed it over his shoulder. Loban twisted off the lid and took a glug.

Eventually, after passing nothing but fields and forest, a one-story white-brick building lying at right angles to the highway came into view. A sign for the Hideaway Motel advertising "Free Wi-Fi, HBO, laundry facilities and pets welcome" stood by a turnoff into a parking lot.

Gus pulled into the motel lot, and he and Slava squeezed their massive frames out of the front seats. They unpacked the luggage from the trunk. Loban crawled out and leaned against the side of the car. He took another glug of water, poured some in his hand, and patted it on his hairless scalp.

"What a terrible place this is."

He rolled off the side of the car and faced Gus and Slava. The two men dwarfed Loban in every way, like two gorillas looking down at a chimpanzee.

"Slava," said Loban. "Go check in."

Slava did as he was told and returned with a key attached to a large wooden key fob. "Rooms 103, 104, 105." He picked up a case. "This way."

Gus picked up the other case, and all three headed to their motel rooms.

THIRTY-FIVE

The calls had come first thing in the morning. Calls that worried Dr. Hudson. First, Archie Baker had called. Could Dr. Hudson come right over? Archie had said. Something was very wrong, Archie had explained. Very wrong indeed.

Dr. Hudson drove through the town and headed north to Archie Baker's place. He turned off the highway, navigated the rutted dirt track and broken appliances that littered the front yard, and parked in front of the porch. The front door was open, and Troy came slouching out, looking thin and dejected. He licked Hudson's hand and whimpered.

"Hey, boy," said Hudson. "What gives?"

Troy whimpered some more and nuzzled Hudson's leg.

"Okay, let's go see your master." Hudson entered the shack, and Troy dawdled in behind him. The room was dark, lit only by light that came through the gaps between the closed drapes and from one small window in the kitchenette above the sink.

"Archie...?"

"Over here."

Hudson's eyes followed the voice. His eyes were becoming accustomed to the gloom, and he saw the old man. He was wearing big Roy Orbison–style sunglasses and was slumped in a rocking chair in the corner of the room. By his side was a dusty table filled with dirty glasses, pill cases, and yellowing magazines. Troy had curled up at his master's feet.

"What's wrong, Archie? You don't sound so good."

"That's because things ain't good. In fact, they're downright awful."

"Why's that?"

Archie sighed. "Because I'm a damn fool, that's why. A damn fool that went up and down the length and breadth of Hinkley shouting about a damn miracle, and it was nothing of the kind. It was all phooey. Some temporary thing that went as quick as it came."

"Can I open the drapes and let some light in?"

"Yeah. I must have forgot they were shut. Go ahead."

Hudson pulled open the drapes, and a dull kind of gray March light illuminated the innards of Archie's shack. The usual state of chaos and neglect that greeted Hudson when he visited Archie's place had gone up a few levels. The smell had too. He looked at the round, slumped shape in the rocking chair. Squares of light marked out by the window muntins checkered Archie's face and body.

"My eyesight's gone," said Archie. "At least before the so-called miracle, I had a little sight. Five percent. It wasn't much, but to me, it was a big deal. Now... Now I don't see anything. Only a kind of darkness that's darker than I never knew existed." Archie raised a hand and removed his sunglasses.

Hudson, as hardened as he was from twenty years of experience, had to stifle a gasp.

Archie's eyes appeared to have caved in. It was like they had been sucked into his head, and the flesh surrounding them had puckered and collapsed.

"How bad does it look, Doc?"

"Are you in pain?"

"Yeah, I'm in pain."

"I'll give you some painkillers."

"And then?"

"And then I'm gonna call you an ambulance, Archie."

"It's that bad?"

"We need to get you to the hospital, where they can give you the care and treatment you need."

"What about Troy?"

Troy whimpered and looked up at his master.

"We can find a temporary home for him. Kind people who'll take in a dog like Troy. Leave it to me."

"Promise?"

"Promise."

AFTER THE AMBULANCE had collected Archie, Hudson locked the house up. Then, he led Troy up into the passenger seat of his car. Hudson got in the driver's seat and looked at the mutt, who looked back at him with big, brown, heartbroken eyes. He patted the dog's head.

"I know, boy, I know. It's tough. But I know someone who'll be glad to have you, and I'll get you some treats on the way."

Hudson checked his cell and saw he had a missed call. He dialed his voice messages and heard Jim Healy's voice.

"Doc, it's Jim Healy. You gotta come quick. Jean isn't well. She isn't well at all."

HUDSON PHONED AHEAD to a couple he knew who had three spaniels, a crossbreed, and an Irish wolfhound. They also had plenty of outside space and knew Archie Baker. They were enthusiastic about taking Troy in while Archie was in the hospital, so Hudson dropped the dog off on his way over to Jean Cassidy's.

He approached the V in the road, took the right lane, and turned into Jean Cassidy's yard. Jim Healy came out to meet him, looking like hell.

"How is she, Jim?"

"She's in a really bad way. It's happened so fast my head is spinning."

They entered the house, and Jim stopped at the foot of the stairs. He began to speak quickly and in a half whisper.

"Last night, she went to bed in the best spirits I've seen her in years. She looked great. She was twittering on about how good she felt. Her arm movement was getting better. It was all good news. Then, about five this morning, she called out in pain. She couldn't get back to sleep because of a pain in her chest and back. She's got a fever, and now she says she can't breathe easily... I'm scared, Doc."

"Let me have a look at her, Jim."

Jim Healy led Hudson up the stairs, along the hall, and into Jean's bedroom. Like the living room, the wooden furniture was dust-free and polished to a high shine. Fresh flowers in vases had been placed on top of the chest of drawers, and every surface had silver- and gold-framed photos of friends and family. Jean was tucked into a thin quilt and dwarfed by the large oak bed and plumped-up pillows. Her face was gaunt and washed-out, her hair matted and damp. Her tiny body was completely obscured by a light cotton nightdress that once, when it had been bought, would have fitted her.

Hudson set about examining her. But it didn't take long to come to the conclusion anyone, medical degree or not, would come to. She was desperately ill and not due to any one clean reason.

"What's wrong with her, Doc?"

Hudson said quietly but urgently, "Call an ambulance, Jim. Call it now."

With trembling arms, Jim took out his cell and dialed.

"What shall I say?" asked Jim.

"Tell them it's suspected multi-organ failure."

Jim pulled his cell out of his pocket and began to dial. Hudson listened to him hold back from weeping as he gave out the address over the phone. All the while, Hudson held Jean's cold, limp wrist and felt the last pulses of her artery pitter and patter away.

THIRTY-SIX

Devlin stood on the Wendigs' doorstep and waved to Elizabeth, who was sitting in the bay window, peering through a gap in the drapes. He rang the bell, and Kathleen Wendig opened the door.

"Father," said Kathleen. "Thank you for coming."

"Not at all."

Devlin stepped into the neat, well-kept hall. There were no shoes left hastily in a mess on the floor. No coats over the stair rails. No traces of outside dirt on the hall carpet. The walls were painted in calm, homely colors that led you gently through the immaculately kept house.

"Elizabeth asked to see you..." Kathleen pressed a hand against Devlin's arm, looked into his eyes with intensity, and said, "Thank you. I know your faith brought her back. Brought my daughter back. I am so blessed. Thank you." Then the intensity faded, and she stepped back. "Elizabeth wants to see you, but I'm afraid she won't tell me why."

A voice called through from the living room.

"She's impatient to see you," said Kathleen. "I would have let her see you last night, but she was so tired. She still gets tired easily. That's why I insisted you come over in the morning. She wasn't happy about it. Would you like anything to drink?"

"I'm fine, thank you."

Devlin followed Kathleen through to the living room. Elizabeth was sitting in her wheelchair in exactly the same place she'd been when Devlin had last visited with Ramirez, by the bay window with the drapes almost drawn, leaving a small space through which she could observe the street.

"Hi, Father," said Elizabeth.

"Hello, Elizabeth."

Devlin took an armchair, and Kathleen took a seat on the couch so that they both faced Elizabeth and the bay window.

"How are you feeling?" asked Devlin.

"Better. I can walk short distances, and the doctors at the hospital say I'm improving all the time."

"They're very positive," said Kathleen.

"I'm really glad to hear it," said Devlin. "We could all do with good news right now."

"Elizabeth," said her mother. "Do you want to tell Father Devlin why you needed to see him?"

Elizabeth's eyes flitted nervously from one adult to the other. She chewed on her bottom lip and frowned. "I... There's something I should have said before. Something I know... Maybe we could treat it like a confession...?"

Kathleen looked over at Devlin, who nodded and said, "I don't see why not."

Devlin's reply seemed to reassure Elizabeth, and she let out a sigh. "The last time you were here, you asked me what I remembered about the night I recovered. I told you that all I remembered was sleeping on the coach and then seeing you. And that was the truth. But as the days went past and I got better, I started to get flashbacks to the night of the crash. Images in my head that came out of nowhere."

"That's part of the trauma you've been through," said Devlin. "Your body's still trying to process what happened to you."

"Yes, it's like my mind has been holding things back from that night, protecting me until I can withstand them. And now it's drip-feeding me glimpses... A few days ago, I started to remember things that happened after I was thrown clear of the coach. I remembered seeing the white van, and for a second, while I was lying on the road in the snow, the van seemed to slow down. In the driver's window, I saw an arm with a tattoo. A blue tattoo. And I saw the side of Roy Kane's face. But it was difficult to tell if what I was remembering was real or dreamed... I didn't know if I should say anything in case it was my mind making things up... And then on the night Dad had Chief Garland and Kyle Ross over, Roy turned up too. He came into this room by himself and spoke to me. Maybe he saw me too that night, on the road, saw me seeing him. I don't know. But I asked if it was him in the van. He said yes, and he said that if I told another soul, he'd make sure I was sorry. He said..." Elizabeth's eyes watered over, and she sobbed. "He said he'd kill you, Mom...and Dad."

Kathleen rushed over to her daughter and took her in her arms. "Why didn't you say? Why didn't you tell me?"

"I was afraid. And then I thought I had to tell someone I trusted who could protect me. So, I called you, Father."

"You've been very brave, Elizabeth," said Devlin. "Incredibly brave. And you don't need to worry about a thing. Nobody is going to hurt you or your parents."

"Should we tell the police?" asked Kathleen.

"Yes. They're pretty sure already the Kane brothers had something to do with the van. Roy and Ted were killed this morning in an explosion."

Elizabeth and Kathleen became very still and looked at Devlin intently, trying to process this new information.

"What?" said Kathleen. "An explosion?"

"They had a meth lab out in woods east of Hinkley. It looks like they were in the lab making meth when the whole thing went up. They were both killed instantly. When the police searched the brothers' property, they found evidence that linked them to the van." Devlin held back on what had happened to Kyle Ross, figuring that announcement would be for the police to decide. "So, you should tell the police all about what you saw and what Roy Kane said to you, and you don't have anything to fear anymore."

Kathleen walked Devlin to the door.

"I'd call the police as soon as I leave," said Devlin. "Make sure to talk to Officer Lori Cassidy."

"I will," said Kathleen. "I guess this pretty much ties up everything that happened on that night? The Kanes were carrying illegal drugs and were trying to get away from the police. Then they covered it all up."

"Seems that way."

Devlin stepped out into the dull afternoon. A wind swept along the quiet street. He looked around to the Wendigs' bay window, but Elizabeth wasn't there. He lit a Cohiba and walked to his car. He leaned against the side of his car, smoked awhile, and thought for a while. He thought about everything that had happened that day and how the mystery of the van and the children's deaths had been neatly tied up. But the more he thought about it, the more he got the feeling it wasn't a neat resolution so much as everything being tidied away. Loose ends hadn't been tied up so much as cut off.

Devlin got in the car and wound his way back from the outlying residential roads through Main Street and out east to the police station. He pulled up outside and entered the lobby.

Devlin asked desk sergeant Esserman if Officer Cassidy was around. The desk sergeant made a call, murmured a few words, and put the receiver down.

"She's coming."

Less than a minute later, Cassidy appeared.

"You get a call from the Wendigs?" asked Devlin.

"Yeah, I did. Apparently, you were over there practically taking a statement. They don't believe in talking to the police these days?"

"I did tell them to call you. She talk to you about seeing Roy Kane in the van?"

"Yeah." Cassidy's cell rang. She looked at the screen, and her fair face screwed up. "Hi, Grandpa. Everything okay?"

Cassidy listened to her grandpa Jim speaking, and her face grew paler, and her eyes widened. "Okay, I'm coming over." She ended the call.

"Everything okay?" asked Devlin.

Cassidy's eyes had watered up, and the color had vanished from her face. "No... No, it's not okay," she said with a catch in her voice. "My nan. She's... She's dead."

THIRTY-SEVEN

Gus and Slava squeezed themselves into the front seats of the BMW, and Loban slid into the middle of the back seat. Gus and Slava hadn't bothered to change out of their suits after the long journey. Loban, though, had shaved, showered, and changed into a fresh shirt and pants.

"You smell like apes," said Loban disapprovingly from the back of the car. "Like farm animals."

"You want to get something to eat?" asked Slava.

"Yes. Take me to the best restaurant this crumby place has to offer."

Gus started the car, and they swung out of the lot. He took the road back west toward the town.

Loban cracked the window open and felt the breeze on his face.

"I want some surf and turf," said Loban. "We get plenty of carbs for strength. Because we will need it. And after we eat, then we go out to the lake. It's out at the lake we have to go, isn't it?"

"Yeah," said Slava, turning to face Loban. His boss had his arms out along the top of the back seat and his short legs spread open. His head was tilted back, and his eyes were closed. "The address we got is round the north end of the lake."

Loban rolled his head from side to side as they passed houses and stores that began to appear more and more frequently the closer they got to the town center.

"These poor, ignorant bastards," Loban said to no one in particular. "They have no idea at all what flows through the veins of this town. What strange narcotic runs like a river through their houses."

They came to a fork in the road. To the left lay the road back east, the area south of Lake Vesper, and the interstate. Gus took the right fork that took them toward the town center and became Main Street. Halfway along the main drag, Gus spotted a diner and swung into the parking lot beside it. The three men got out of the car, looking around them like tourists in a place they didn't understand.

Loban sized up the diner. It was a long, oval, one-story building. Cream with red details, it was pretty and neat. Straight, tidy hedges fenced it off from the sidewalk, and flowers in window boxes brightened up the facade.

Loban's eyes narrowed. "I hope it has a proper menu. With meat." The two other men grunted in agreement. "Not veeegan."

Inside the diner, the tables were empty, apart from two tables in the corner, which were surrounded by a group of college-age kids. Loban headed to a window booth and, without looking at a menu, beckoned over a waitress.

"I would like black coffee, and what steak do you have?"

"We have the Philly cheesesteak. It's very popular, and even if I—"

"Any other steak?"

"Er... No. Just the Philly."

Loban dropped his menu on the table. "Then it will be the

Philly." He nodded at Gus and Slave, who were squeezed into the booth seat opposite him.

"The same," said Gus.

"I'll have the western omelet," said Slava.

The waitress took the orders and went to attend to the kids who were making a din in the far corner.

"A western omelet?" Loban sneered. "What is a western omelet?"

"An omelet with ham," replied Slava. "And peppers."

"You're two hundred and seventy pounds, Slava, and you're eating like a schoolgirl?" Loban tutted and shook his head. Then he snapped his fingers and called the waitress back. "Please tell the kitchen that we don't want the omelet and want a Philly cheesesteak instead. So, three Philly cheesesteaks in total." The waitress gave a weary sigh and took the order as requested.

"An army marches on its stomach," said Loban. "A western omelet," he said once more and tutted, savoring the word "western." Then, he looked over at the college kids who were still making noise and acting up.

"Someone let the kindergarten out early," said Loban.

"You want me to go over and teach them manners?" asked Gus.

"No. No. Let the children continue with their folly."

The waitress came over with a glass carafe of coffee and filled their mugs.

"What's the next move, boss?" asked Slava.

"Next move is we need supplies, and then we go to the lake," said Loban.

The two larger men nodded, and all three fell silent and scrolled their cells while they waited for the food. The waitress served the three Philly steaks. The men placed their cells on the table and devoured their meals in short order.

All the while, the kids laughed and shouted. From the

moment the men had entered the diner, their appearance had attracted the attention and derision of the kids. Every so often, the kids would look over, make a snide comment, and erupt with laughter.

Loban finished his last mouthful. Gus and Slava had finished before him and drained their mugs.

"All good?" asked Loban. The two men nodded.

"Go have a look around, get what you need. I'll meet you outside..." Loban looked at his watch. "In half an hour."

The two men rose and left. Loban asked for his mug to be refilled and took his time drinking while looking over at the kids in the corner, who were still eyeing him up, smirking, and breaking out into laughter.

OUTSIDE, Gus and Slava walked up and down Main Street, peering into store windows, generally browsing. At the top of the street, Gus spotted something and got Slava's attention.

"What is it?" asked Slava.

"A sports store," replied Gus. "Let's go have a look."

The two men entered the store. A bell rang above the door, and a man, tanned and slim, in a polo shirt and chino pants, came out from behind the counter to greet them.

"Hi," he said as cheerfully as possible, hiding his uneasiness in the presence of the two huge, burly, and suited men.

The two customers grunted a hello back.

"You in town for pleasure? Business? Bit of both? Or to see relations?"

"Yes," replied Slava.

"We'll take a look around," said Gus.

"You suit yourself and take your royal time," said the store owner.

The two men spent a few minutes browsing the merchandise until they finally settled upon an item they wanted to buy.

LOBAN'S EYES, heavy-lidded, glassy, and cold, took in the young group sitting on the tables in the corner of the diner. This might, he thought to himself, be an opportunity for some fun. A few minutes passed, and eventually, the group began to get up and put away their cell phones and other accessories. They filed passed Loban, a few of them muttering "fucking Russki" and other similar insults. The last to pass was the tallest. He wore a ski jacket, jeans, and baseball boots. Instead of passing by, he slid onto the seat opposite Loban and grinned.

"Hi," said the kid.

"Hi," said Loban. The rest of the group had gathered outside the window right by the booth Loban and the kid were sitting in. Loban looked over the kid. Then, he turned to the group outside. Early twenties, thought Loban. Rich kids. Not who he expected to be hanging around an out-of-the-way place in Vermont.

"Where you from?" asked the kid.

"Where you from?"

"I'm from the USA." The kid leaned forward. "What country you from?"

"I live in Seattle."

"You're Russian, aren't you?"

Loban didn't reply.

"We heard your accent. So, I thought I better come over and tell you to be careful."

"And why should I be careful?"

"Because people will hear your accent, see that you're weird-looking, and maybe call the police. Or the FBI. Or decide to take matters into their own hands. So, maybe you'd be wise to have some protection."

Loban's thick, black eyebrows lifted. "Protection?"

"You give me fifty dollars, and I'll make sure a foreigner like you doesn't run into any difficulties. Guy like you needs friends in a place like this."

Loban nodded and smiled. Then, with surprising speed and agility, Loban slid out of his seat, swung around the end of the table, and planted himself next to the kid. Before the kid knew about it, Loban had a hairy arm over his shoulders. His heavy-lidded eyes and gap-toothed grin were right up in the kid's face.

"What the hell do you think you're—" protested the kid. He braced to push the older man off the seat and onto his ass but was prevented by Loban's arm squeezing around his neck with unexpected strength and brutality.

"I love friends," said Loban. Then, in one fast movement, he pushed his hand up into the kid's armpit. The kid's upper body spasmed, and he let out a low, hard moan.

"What's your name?" asked Loban, his mouth right up against the kid's ear.

"You... You stabbed me...?" The kid said it half as a question, half as a pathetic complaint.

"What's your name?"

"Ryan. My name is Ryan."

"Well, Ryan, I have inserted a small punch dagger into your brachial artery. But good news, you don't need to worry at all if you do exactly as I say. In a moment, I will get up and leave. When I do, you must remain seated and keep your arm clamped to your side so that the dagger will not fall out. When the waitress comes to take my money, you must calmly tell her to call you an ambulance. All the while, you must remain still and not let that dagger move right up until the point you are in the hands of a trained paramedic. If you don't follow my instructions, you will certainly bleed out and die before any medical assistance arrives. I think you have by now realized that I am a very dangerous individual. If you report this to the police or tell anyone I did this, I will come and kill you and any close relatives you have. You see, Ryan, I am what's known in the psychiatric journals as a psychopath. I have no fear or conscience."

Loban rose, threw some bills on the table, and left.

Outside, the other kids, unable to decide for themselves what had happened between Loban and their friend, cast puzzled glances at Loban, who got into the BMW rental and backed out quickly onto the road. The BMW roared up Main Street and pulled over next to Gus and Slava, who were coming back from their shopping spree.

"Get in," said Loban. "Let's go to the lake."

THIRTY-EIGHT

Cassidy and Devlin entered Nanna Cassidy's bedroom. Cassidy immediately went to sit by her nanna, whose tiny body lay coddled by the bed covers. Her face was nearly as white as the bed linen, but her expression was extraordinarily peaceful.

"I was calling an ambulance when she went," said Jim. He was sitting at the foot of the bed, slumped and defeated.

"So sudden..." said Cassidy, sitting on the other side of the bed just by her nanna. "Why was it so sudden?"

"I don't know," said Jim, shaking his head. "She'd been getting better. So much better. She thought it was a miracle."

Cassidy looked over at Devlin, who was standing respectfully back from the bed.

"We're not Catholics, but...would you say a prayer for my nanna? Give her a blessing... Or something...?"

"Of course," replied Devlin. "If that's something you want too, Jim?"

"Yeah... Yeah, I'd like that, Father."

Devlin sat on the opposite side of the bed from Cassidy and prayed over Jean's body. He held her hand for a moment and then genuflected.

"Thank you," said Cassidy.

"I'll wait downstairs," replied Devlin and left the room.

Cassidy turned to Jim. "Grandpa, we need to get an autopsy."

Jim raised his head a little and sighed. "Dr. Hudson said he'd arrange it. He's arranging the transport."

"Where is Dr. Hudson?"

"He had to go. He got a call that Archie Baker had died."

"Archie Baker?"

"Yeah, apparently, he had to be taken to the hospital in an ambulance and died before he got there." Jim slumped back down and pushed his face into his hands. "I feel like I'm in a nightmare, Lori." He began to sob, and Lori skirted around the bed and squeezed up next to him. She placed a hand on his back.

"I know it must be awful for you," she whispered. "I can't imagine how it feels to lose someone you've been with for over fifty years. But you got me, Grandpa. I'll do anything for you, like you and Nanna have for me, and I'll always be here."

WHEN CASSIDY FINALLY CAME DOWNSTAIRS, she found Devlin standing outside, smoking a cigar.

"You know how galactically bad those things are for you?" said Cassidy, wiping away tears with her cuff.

"I mostly don't think about it."

"Thank you for the blessing. Grandpa says Archie Baker died this morning. He was taken ill suddenly, and an ambulance came for him, but he'd died by the time he'd got to the hospital."

Devlin took a deep inhale of his cigar and sprayed the smoke out long and slow. "That's two of three."

"Two of three what?"

"Since I came to this town, three people have shown extraordinary signs of recovery. Your nanna, Archie Baker, and Elizabeth Wendig. Two have died suddenly."

"You think they're connected?"

"I'm not sure."

"Should we be worried about Elizabeth?"

"I only just saw her, and she seemed fine. Better than fine."

"I can't see how that's all connected. I think you're putting two and two together and getting...I don't even know what you're getting." As she spoke, the grief that had overtaken Cassidy had begun to transform into determination and anger. "You know what I want to do? I want to find that goddamned van. The van I chased through a snowstorm and disappeared the night those children died. This case won't be closed until that happens, as far as I'm concerned. You wanna come on a trip with me?"

"Where to?"

"I didn't have a chance to tell you, and we were keeping it quiet too—Franklin Kelly turned up. Franklin was one of the kids on the coach who we thought had died. Had his funeral planned and everything, along with the other children. Turns out he never got on the bus, and he was hiding out up past Frost Hollow, just like Archie Baker kept telling us. And as I was sitting with nanna, I got to thinking, maybe Franklin was the last person to see Kyle Ross alive. Kyle was processing Ross and looking after him the last time I saw him."

"Sounds like a lead. You sure you want me to come along?"

"Like you keep saying, you're an ex-investigator, right?"

"Yep."

"Ex-Air Force?"

"Yep."

"You found the Kane's meth lab."

"I wouldn't brag about it."

"You went head-to-head with a guy who tried to break your head open like it was a watermelon."

"I'm trying to forget that part."

"Well, the best officer on Hinkley PD's payroll was just killed. In my eyes, that creates a vacancy. If we were in an old-time frontier town, this would be the moment I pinned a bronze star to your chest and made you pledge an oath or whatever they did back then."

"I'm honored."

"That's sweet. Let's get in the car, Deputy Sheriff."

THIRTY-NINE

Hudson pulled into a space in the Hideaway Motel parking lot. He got out of his car and leaned against the driver's door. He was shaken to the core. He'd lost Jean Cassidy and Archie Baker. Two patients in the space of an afternoon. And truth be told, that wasn't even the beginning of his troubles. The sunlight and the world seemed to swim around him. For a moment, he felt faint and thought he might pass out. But the panic passed, and for a few minutes, he took slow breaths until he could face his next patient. At least this one was still alive.

The parking lot was near deserted, with only four parked cars in total, including Hudson's. There couldn't be many paying guests here. What with the bars, restaurants, apartments, and ongoing construction on the north of the lake, this area of Hinkley was beginning to feel more and more like a forgotten outpost. Now the Kane boys were gone, he wondered what would become of the unloved, fading building, its increasingly run-down rooms, and its charmless rattlesnake of an owner.

Hudson walked across the lot to the far end of the motel and entered the lobby.

The lobby was brown and dull yellow. The walls were

brown, and the carpet's maple leaf pattern had faded over the many years since it had been laid. The reception counter was painted to look like wooden timbers. An old landline phone and plastic spinners full of postcards sat on the countertop. Random oil paintings of eagles and seascapes hung on the wall.

Hudson rounded the counter and went through a door into the back office. No one was about, so he called out.

From beyond the office came a weak, croaking reply. "Come through..."

Hudson followed the voice through an open door and into a living room, which had the same muted colors and carpet as the lobby. Through an archway to his right was a narrow kitchen; ahead of him, a closed door. He heard the croaking voice again coming from behind the closed door. Hudson pushed the door open and stepped into a dark bedroom. A lamp on the nightstand lit up the thin, haggard face of Ma Kane. She was wrapped up in a comforter and blankets. False teeth, blister packs of pills, and vape cartridges lay on the nightstand under the lamp.

"Thank God you're here, Rick," said Ma Kane. "I feel just awful."

Hudson pulled up a chair and looked Ma Kane over. "I'm not surprised, Kay. No one should go through what you've been through."

"I lost my boys, Rick. I lost my baby boys." She curled up on her side with her fists in her stomach and wept.

"Oh God, Kay, I'm so goddamn sorry." Hudson lifted his case onto his lap and opened it up. "Here," he said. "I've got something to help get you through."

Ma Kane's sobs lessened, and she wiped her nose with a balled-up tissue. "Thanks, Rick. Anything. Anything to take away this pain."

Hudson took three small plastic bottles and placed them in

the tiny space available on the nightstand. Then he took a pen from the inside pocket of his jacket, wrote on his notepad, tore off the page, and gave it to Ma Kane. Ma Kane screwed up her eyes and read it over.

"I'm giving you antidepressants and anti-anxiety meds and something to help you sleep," said Hudson. "Those are the instructions for what to take and when." Hudson picked up two of the three bottles. "I'll give you the first doses, two of each. This is the antidepressants..." He rattled one of the bottles. Then, he rattled the other one and said, "And this one is for anxiety. Then you keep taking the same amount twice a day. Okay?"

"Whatever you say, Doc."

He nodded to the bottle still on the nightstand. "Those are sleeping pills. Take two before bedtime. I'll go get a glass of water." Hudson left the bedroom and headed across the living room to the galley kitchen, where he found a tumbler in a cupboard and filled it with water. He returned to the bedroom and gave Ma Kane the tumbler and pills. She gulped them back and shivered.

"Thank you, Rick."

"That's okay. You rest up, and I'll be back tomorrow. And it goes without saying, I won't be billing you for this."

Ma Kane put her hand on Hudson's. It was rough and hard. She gripped his hand with a strength he wouldn't have suspected her capable of.

"You know what gets me in the gut?" she said. "The real bitch of it all? My name. What everyone calls me... 'Ma Kane.' Well, o'course, I ain't no 'ma' now, am I?"

"You don't stop being a mother when your children die, Kay. You still brought those boys into the world, fed them, loved them, brought them up."

She looked at him like she wasn't sure of his answer. Then, she gave a tired smile. "But I just can't help thinking about it."

Hudson searched for something to say but found nothing, so a silence followed.

Then Ma Kane said, "How long you been in Hinkley?"

Hudson thought. "Eighteen months, I guess. Yeah, it'd be a bit over eighteen months."

Ma Kane smiled again, a kind of forgiving and understanding smile. "You won't know about Lori, then."

"Lori? Lori Cassidy?"

"Yeah, Lori Cassidy. She's mine."

"Yours...? You mean, your daughter?"

"Hard to believe, isn't it? I had her so young. And it was too much for me. I left her and her father. A mother abandoning a child. It's the worst thing, isn't it? People think it's the worst thing you can do. A mother leaving her baby behind. But I was so young, a child myself. Out of my depth. Frightened. So, I upped and left. But it was okay, I thought. The father, Jacob, he looked after her better than I ever did. Then he died from cancer only a few years later. People blamed me for that too. Said I caused his cancer. But the grandparents brought her up, Jean and Jim." Hudson realized Ma Kane hadn't heard about Jean's passing but decided this wasn't the moment to change that.

"Then I met Bill," Ma Kane continued. "Bill Kane. He owned the motel, and we had Roy and Ted. Then cancer took Bill too, and now, after all this time, I can't help but think my boys have been taken away from me because of what I did. Because I left my baby. Little Lori." Ma Kane started to weep again, rocking back and forth. "I'm being punished, Rick, and it's right that I should be..."

Hudson squeezed her hard, rough hand and said gently, "What happened isn't a punishment for what happened, Kay.

You're tying two things together that happened for completely different reasons. And when some time has passed, you'll maybe be able to see that."

Ma Kane held the balled tissue up to her thin, shiny lips and looked at Hudson like he was an angel.

"Thank you for your kindness," she said. She leaned forward and put her bony arms around him, pulling him toward her, and again, Hudson was surprised at her strength. For what seemed like an eternity, she held him and rubbed her hands up and down his back. Then, finally, she pulled away.

"I think those pills are starting to work," she said. "Or maybe it's you. Bless you, Rick. You're a good man."

Out in the daylight, Rick Hudson breathed a sigh of relief. He got into his car, but before he could start it up, his cell buzzed. A number he didn't recognize flashed up.

"Hello."

"Dr. Hudson. It's Father Ramirez. Could I talk to you? In person. It's quite urgent, I think..."

FORTY

Hinkley was a town of two halves. West of the town, where there was a good connection to the interstate, lay a crescent of large, more expensive real estate that ran from a mile or so up to where Frost Hollow began. This crescent was only a short drive and not such a long walk from the upper reaches of Lake Vesper. The lake itself was shaped like the face in Munch's *Scream*, wide and much shallower at the top and narrower and far deeper at the southern end. Over on the east was another crescent of housing. This crescent was higher density, made from cheaper supplies, and bordered onto forest and many acres of farming land.

Cassidy, with Devlin in the passenger seat, had skirted the south of the town and then turned off into the less affluent, eastern crescent. She traveled on for a couple of miles through the most populous part of the suburb and kept going as the houses grew further apart and the sounds of dogs barking grew more common. In this part of town, the weeds grew taller, and many of the houses stood empty and deserted. She drew up outside a house that was in a bad state and uncared for. The metal roof had rusted in great brown stripes. The dull green painted timber had darkened with years of hard weather. The wooden porch roof was rotting and hung down at an uneven angle. The drapes were stained and uneven. Next door was a bigger but just as dilapidated building. It was a store, and its sign read "The Smokin' Stop."

Cassidy and Devlin got out and took their surroundings in.

"You wanna stock up on cigars?" said Cassidy, looking at the store.

"I stocked up in Montreal. This Franklin Kelly's place?"

"Yeah, let's go knock."

Cassidy put a foot on one of the two planks supported by bricks that served as doorsteps and rapped sharp and quick. There was no response at first, and then came the thud of heavy feet, and the door creaked open. Standing in the doorway was a middle-aged man, around five ten and broad, wearing an unbuttoned grease-stained boiler suit and a food-stained undershirt. He was bald with curling tufts of thick side hair.

"Hi, Rufus," said Cassidy.

"Officer Cassidy. What can I do for you?"

"We'd like to talk to Franklin."

"What's it about?"

"Officer Kyle Ross."

Rufus scratched the side of his head and ran his fingers through his wayward hair. He looked upset.

"Yeah, I'm sorry about that...what happened to Officer Ross. He was a good man, and I owe him a lot for bringing Franklin back, and I'm sorry for you and the other cops. And for his family."

Cassidy nodded. "Thing is, Rufus, we think Franklin might have been one of the last people to see Kyle, maybe even the last person."

Rufus nodded, but he wasn't really listening. He was looking at Devlin.

"This is Father Devlin," said Cassidy. "He's been helping me with our investigations."

Rufus seemed confused. Then, he nodded. "You're the guy who brought Elizabeth Wendig back to life?"

"I was there when she came around from the accident," said Devlin.

"You were giving her last rites. That's what I heard."

"Anyhow," interrupted Cassidy. "Father Devlin worked as a detective previous to him being in the church. And Lord knows we need those kinds of skills in abundance right now. And you can see how important it is we speak to Franklin if he was the last person to speak to Kyle."

"Sure. Well, you better come in. He's out back in the yard."

They followed Rufus across an open-plan living room and kitchen toward the back door.

"I gave the kid hell about going AWOL," said Rufus angrily. "I mean, I set about beating the merry hell out of him for all the worry he caused."

"Hold on, Rufus. Just hold on," said Cassidy.

Rufus stopped by the back door, and Cassidy gave him a hard stare. "I hope you haven't been assaulting your son. 'Cause if that's what you're telling me..."

Rufus looked sheepish and rubbed at a fleshy earlobe. "Oh, hell, no. I just pushed him up against the wall and gave him a piece of my mind, is all."

"It better be. If it isn't, it's a police matter, and social services too, you hear me?"

"Sure, yeah. I do. I didn't lay a hand on him, I swear. Just gave him a few well-chosen words. About responsibility and such."

Rufus opened the door, and all three walked out into the yard. The yard was half paving stone, half balding lawn, and dominated by a sycamore tree in the corner, its bare branches zigzagging away like lightning.

Beneath the sycamore tree was Franklin Kelly. He was coiled up on an old rusty swing seat, wearing wireless earbuds and staring with hollow eyes at a tablet propped up against his knees. He looked up from his tablet to see the three figures looking down at him. First, he frowned. Then, he rubbed his face and took out his buds. He swung his feet onto the ground and blinked.

"Hi, Franklin," said Cassidy.

"Hi."

"How are you?"

Franklin shrugged. "Okay, I s'pose. Why are you here?"

"Did you hear about what happened to Officer Kyle Ross, Franklin?"

Franklin nodded somberly. "Yeah... Yeah, I did."

"Well, we wondered if we could talk to you about Kyle?"

"Why? Why talk to me?"

"We think you might have been one of the last people to see him."

"Me...?" Franklin seemed to give this some thought, then said, "Huh, I guess so."

"So, we wanted to ask you about the last time you saw him. What he—"

Cassidy was interrupted by the sound of intermittent pips and Rufus Kelly cursing. Rufus pulled his cell out of his boiler-suit pocket and stared blankly at the screen. "Goddamn. I gotta take this. It's work," he muttered and walked back into the house with his cell plastered to his ear, sounding like he was getting bad news.

Cassidy and Devlin pulled up two of the lawn chairs that were next to a garden table covered in burns, crushed beer cans, and cigarette ends. They planted the chairs in front of Franklin.

"I know you've been through a hell of a lot," said Cassidy. "More than anybody should go through, but we'd like you to talk through what happened the last time you saw Officer Ross."

"Okay." Franklin's brown eyes flicked over to Devlin.

"Father Devlin here's helping me find out what happened to Kyle," said Cassidy. "So, in your own time, just cast your mind back to what happened. To just after I left you and Kyle alone together in the office. Can you do that for me?"

"Uh, sure..." Franklin stared down into his lap for a moment and thought hard. "Ummm... Officer Ross was sitting at his desk typing, and I just sat waiting for him to finish." He looked up at Cassidy and Devlin and shrugged.

"That's it?" said Cassidy.

"Yeah. I just waited there till I could go."

"And Kyle was with you all the time?" asked Devlin.

"Yeah... No..." Franklin pursed his lips. "He took off before that. Yeah, 'cause of the van."

"The what...?" said Cassidy, hardly believing her ears.

"I told him I'd seen a van out near where I'd been hiding. In the hunting blind."

"Tell us more about the van," said Cassidy, trying to keep her voice level.

"It was a white van. Officer Ross wanted to know exactly where it was."

"And you showed him?"

"He got me to draw a map. And then he got up and left. And that was the last time I saw him."

Cassidy and Devlin looked at each other, then back at the boy.

"If I got you a piece of paper, could you draw the map for me?"

"Sure. I could give it a go. I mean, I did it before..."

CASSIDY AND DEVLIN stepped out onto the strip of sidewalk in front of the Kellys' house.

"Kyle must have gone to find the van by himself," said Cassidy.

"Yeah. And it looks like he found it."

"We need to find it too." Cassidy slid into the cruiser, and Devlin got in the other side.

She flattened the map Franklin had drawn onto the steering wheel and studied it. "It couldn't have been easy to find from what Franklin knew. I mean, this map..." She ran a finger over the roughly sketched drawing. "It's pretty rough and basic. It looks to be an area over from the hunting blind beyond Necker's Brook, but before you get to the fire trail. But that still covers a large area. It'd take days to find in a car. But Kyle had to have found it, otherwise he wouldn't have ended up dead, would he?" She looked over at Devlin, who didn't seem to be paying attention. He was staring out the windshield like he was a thousand miles away.

"Did you hear what I said?"

"Every word." Devlin turned slowly to Cassidy. "You said he must have gone out there by himself."

"Yeah. I did."

"You said it would have taken days to find it by himself."

"Yeah."

"But that he must have found it, otherwise he wouldn't have ended up dead."

"Are you just trying to prove you were listening?"

"Now," continued Devlin, off on his own track, "maybe he got lucky. He found it quick, he hit the jackpot. Could have happened. Or maybe he didn't find it, and instead, he ran into the Kanes, who made sure he never found it. Or..."

"Or what?"

"Following your logic, there's only one other alternative. He had help finding it."

"Help how?"

"What about the guy with the plane?"

"Marshall? You think Kyle might have asked for help?"

"It's what I'd do. I could be wrong, but I wouldn't want to drive out into acres of forest with a map drawn by a fourteen-year-old to guide me. It'd be a fool's errand. But if you knew someone who had a plane standing by, I'm guessing the only person in Hinkley that had one ready. That's who I'd talk to."

"But why wouldn't he have said something about it? Unless he was in on it too? With the Kanes?"

"I think we should go ask ourselves."

FORTY-ONE

Another day and business was picking up already. The irony was so biting Marshall almost smiled. He'd looked over his order book that morning, and the next few months were already filling up with retired anglers and comfortably off sightseers who fancied themselves as naturalists and photographers.

Marshall had just docked the plane for a two-hour sightseeing tour, done the usual chitchat as he walked the passengers back to the car, and took a handsome tip to boot. He'd been working his ass off to get this business off the ground, so to speak, and finally, it was turning a corner. Just at the point the rest of his affairs were threatening to go belly up. If only he was in a frame of mind to enjoy the success. Instead, he'd spent the day looking over his shoulder, wondering when he'd be paid a call.

A last-minute postponement by clients who had missed a flight out of Chicago meant Marshall unexpectedly had the afternoon free. He parked his floatplane in the hangar, closed up, took a good long look east and west along the lake road, then got into his pickup. On the way back, he checked his rearview mirror constantly. When he got home, he sat in the pickup for a long time, surveying the house for any sign of disturbance. Finally, he convinced himself that no one was waiting for him. He was about to pull the keys out of the ignition and slide out of the cab when a black BMW sedan appeared around the corner of the road and came to a screeching halt inches from his bumper.

The back door of the BMW swung open, and a huge guy in a gray suit emerged. Then the driver and front passenger doors opened, and an even larger guy in a gray suit got out on one side, and a much smaller bald guy with a pronounced gap in his front tooth got out of the other.

Despite the enormous physical size of the two men in suits, it was immediately apparent to Marshall the smaller man was in charge. Something about the smaller man's smile and ease of his manner told him that the two big men were just his attack dogs. The small man was the real danger. He wore a collarless shirt, braces, and canvas trainers. He had a mustache like a paintbrush and a strong five-o'clock shadow, which Marshall suspected was permanent. Thick, black, matted chest hair reached all the way to just below his throat. And his smile was a knowing smile, like he and Marshall both knew the same thing. But the smile made Marshall edgy because it was the smile of a lunatic, a psychopath.

"Mr. Marshall," said Loban. "Get out of the truck, please."

Marshall did as he was told. Loban stood in front of him. His hands were in his pockets, his feet were planted apart, and his chest was thrust out.

"What a lot of trouble you have caused," Loban said.

Marshall didn't have time to give the speech he'd rehearsed, to tell the story and make the arguments that might protect him. A kind of pain he'd never experienced before exploded in the middle of his leg, and for a moment, as he collapsed on the ground, he thought he'd been shot. Then, in his side vision, he saw the sun gleam off the silver clubhead of a golf iron. He was pretty sure his leg or his knee was broken or possibly smashed beyond medical repair. He was hauled up and into the back seat of the BMW behind his truck. And then he lost consciousness.

FORTY-TWO

Cassidy and Devlin had drawn a blank at the harbor. Marshall was nowhere to be seen. The owner of the dive shop on the front told Cassidy he'd seen Marshall tow his plane away an hour ago or more. Cassidy and Devlin found themselves standing out on the lakefront, planning their next move.

"Let's go out to his place," said Cassidy. "It's only a five-minute drive away."

They got back in the cruiser, and Cassidy took off, speeding west. They drove past the restaurants and lakefront properties out into the quiet, leafy outskirts, where buildings were few and far between.

"Marshall's place is up ahead," said Cassidy. "The next house on the right."

Cassidy pulled over and came to a halt, bumper to bumper with an old pickup. She and Devlin got out, and Cassidy headed up the steps to the door. She gave the bell a ring and knocked. No one answered, so Cassidy did the ring and knock again, but no one came to the door, and no one stirred in the house.

"This his car?" asked Devlin, who was standing by the truck, looking it over.

"Yeah."

Devlin tried the door handle, and the door opened.

"If he left his truck unlocked, he can't have gone far," said Cassidy.

Devlin leaned into the cab and pulled out a key and fob. "And if he left his keys in the ignition, he really can't have gone far."

Devlin looked over the set of keys he'd pulled out of the ignition. "Looks like the full set. Truck, house, planes even." He sat down on the passenger seat of the pickup, placed the keys in his lap, and lit up a Cohiba.

Cassidy folded her arms and looked up and down the road and back at the house. "So, maybe he walked off somewhere and just forgot. But I don't think so. Marshall is a squared-away kind of guy. Neat, tidy, professional. Ex-Air Force engineer who runs his own business, flies planes. He isn't some absent-minded professor type. This is out of his behavioral pattern... Unless there's a totally innocent explanation, and you've brought us out here for a featherlight reason... Devlin?" She looked at Devlin, who didn't answer and seemed miles away, pulled into his own thoughts. He was getting well into his smoke and his own thoughts. A form of concentration seemed to envelop him totally. For a long minute or so, he didn't say a word. Then suddenly, he let out a spurt of smoke and looked up at Cassidy.

"What if everything that's happened—the bus crash, the children dying, the Kane brothers blowing themselves up—what if all of that isn't about the meth?"

"What do you mean?"

Devlin took another toke of his cigar and studied the end of it. "You ever heard of dark matter?"

Cassidy puffed her cheeks and shrugged. "You mean the stuff that no one can find and makes up most of the universe?"

"Yeah, I do. Dark matter came about because scientists looked at the galaxies and worked out how much they should weigh. But the figure they came up with was too small. When they added up all the mass in a galaxy, it wasn't enough to create the gravity to keep it together. By their reckoning, galaxies should just fly apart. So they made up dark matter to fill in the blank in the equation. Kind of cheating, really, when you think about it."

"What the hell has this got to do with anything that's happened in Hinkley?"

"If you add up all of what seems to have happened here in this small town, it's huge. The Kane brothers drive a van of meth supplies into Hinkley, get into a chase with the cops, force a coach full of kids into Lake Vesper, and then go into the mother of all cover-ups. They hide the van and kill a cop. And after all that, they get blown up in an accident. All of that happens because they had a nickel-and-dime meth lab going?"

"Yeah, that's exactly it."

"There are meth labs the length of the country. Two-bit operations run by people who couldn't find their own ass with a map and compass. The Kanes may have been many things, but they weren't big-league criminals who would kill a cop in cold blood and put him in a trunk. For one thing, I don't think they had the brains. They were small-time, don't you think?"

"Yeah, they were. But then what is this all about?"

"It's about something else. Something darker with far more gravity. Like I said, dark matter." Devlin took a long, deep pull on his cigar and then looked at Cassidy through the smoke, blue eyes sparkling from under his dark brow. "And whatever it is, I think it was in the back of the Kanes' van. And it can't have been meth."

Cassidy nodded. “Nice theory.” She looked at Marshall’s truck and back at the house. “And Marshall? You still think he might have helped Kyle go looking for the white van?”

“Yeah. Yeah, I do.”

“Give me the keys.”

Devlin handed the keys over to Cassidy. She went around the back of the truck, unlocked the tailgate, and unclipped the tonneau. She rolled it back to reveal a mostly empty bed. There were a few tie-downs scattered around and a towrope, but that was about it.

“Not a whole lot going on here.”

She pulled out her Maglite and ran it around the bed, then climbed up onto the bed. She went onto her hands and knees and looked even harder with the Maglite. After a couple of minutes of an inch-by-inch search, something caught her attention on the edge of the bed. She took her gloves from the pouch on the back of her belt, put them on, and started to tug and wiggle at something in the join between the cargo floor and the side of the truck. She pulled free whatever it was she’d been yanking and held it up for Devlin to see. In her hand was a black strap about six inches long, with gold buttons.

“What’s that?” asked Devlin.

“It’s a belt tie. It’s from a cop’s duty belt.”

“You sure? It could be there for the same reason the tie-downs are. To secure whatever Marshall was carrying around.”

“I’m sure. Look...” She slid out of the tailgate and swung her hip around to show him the same black strap on her belt.

“It’s used to keep the under-belt and the duty belt together. ’Course, no one tells you when you’re training you need ’em. You only find out after you’ve been walking around hauling your belt up every two minutes and some other cop lets you in on the secret.” She pulled off the strap from her belt and held it up alongside the one she’d found in the bed. They were identical. "Only a cop would wear it. Only a cop like Kyle. Marshall is looking more and more interesting by the minute. I'll bag it up, then let's take a look around his place. I'm gonna put my neck out and say this little thing here is probable cause."

Cassidy opened the trunk of the cruiser, sealed the belt tie in an evidence bag, and closed the trunk. Then, she and Devlin opened Marshall's front door and went inside.

The hall was small and constructed out of dark wood. Heavy jackets and coats were hung on hooks, and mud-caked boots, left where they had been kicked off, cluttered up the floor. They moved through into the open-plan ground floor. The furniture was basic, like the place had been rented short term. Boxes that hadn't been unpacked were stacked by the couch and the kitchen table.

"Okay," said Cassidy. "Let's take a look around."

FORTY-THREE

The intense pain he had blacked out from brought him back around. All the way up the side of his leg and hip, pain ached and throbbed. At first, he was terrified because he didn't know where he was or why he was there. Then, when he remembered the answers to those questions, he was even more terrified. He was sitting on a double bed, his back against a wooden headboard with vertical slats. His arms were outstretched, and his wrists had been cable-tied to the slats. A strip of duct tape had been plastered across his mouth.

His vision unblurred a little, and he could see that he was in a motel room. The drapes had been drawn, and a lamp on the nightstand was giving limited light. Someone was sitting on the side of the bed, someone else was by the front door, and another person was by the window.

His vision unblurred some more. Loban was on the bed, and the two big guys were stationed at the door and the window. The guy at the door was slightly bigger, with a thatch of slicked-back hair that looked like a bad transplant. The guy at the window had thin, sandy hair that had been shaved down to stubble.

"Hello, Mr. Marshall," said Loban. "We are representatives of a number of major investors who have a stake in the business I understand you were employed to assist."

Marshall didn't answer. His mouth was as dry as rope. Loban seemed to sense this and nodded at the man with the sandy hair by the window.

"Go get Mr. Marshall some water. To loosen his tongue."

The man with the sandy hair went to the bathroom, and Marshall heard the faucet gush. Then, he returned and placed a chipped glass against Marshall's lips. Marshall opened his mouth, and the man tipped the glass. Marshall glugged down what he could. Some of the water went down his front, but enough went down his throat. When the glass was empty, Marshall's mouth was no longer dry, but his thirst wasn't quite quenched.

"I understand," said Loban, "that you felt things had gone wrong with the operation here and that you unilaterally decided to begin a cleanup operation in this shit-hole town. That you took it upon yourself to do this without informing anyone else."

"I... I thought it was the best thing to do," said Marshall. "I still think it was the best thing to do. The only thing to do... But sure, I'll tell you anything you need to know... I mean, if it'll mean I don't get hurt again..."

"If you don't tell me, you will definitely get hurt again. So, tell me. Tell me everything."

"I will. I'll tell you everything... I promise..."

"Yes, you will. And you must start from the very beginning. From where it all began to go wrong..."

FORTY-FOUR

"Sorry to take up your time." Ramirez was standing on Dr. Hudson's doorstep.

"Not at all," replied Hudson. "Actually, I've just got back myself from the motel you're staying in. I was visiting Ma Kane."

"Is she ill?"

"Ah," said Hudson, realizing he was about to give Ramirez Hinkley's latest breaking news. "You haven't heard, then?"

"Heard what?"

"The Kane brothers were killed today in an explosion. Apparently, they were producing and selling methamphetamine, and their lab blew up with them in it. Not only that, but Officer Kyle Ross's body was found in the Kanes' workshop. It's all over the local news. The theory doing the rounds is it was the Kanes who were driving the white van that caused the school bus to crash."

Ramirez stood blankly on the stoop, taking in this tidal wave of information.

"At least," continued Hudson, "we have an answer about who is to blame for the Lake Vesper deaths."

"I… I suppose so," stammered Ramirez, still taking Hudson's news in.

"Are you here about all that miracle business? I suppose you're still looking into that. Seems a little...trite next to today's events. But I suppose the church's work must go on."

Ramirez was impressed that Hudson had managed not to roll his eyes as he said "miracle business." The doctor closed the front door behind them, and the two men stood in the hall. Hudson in chinos, cardigan, and slippers and Ramirez in his clerical clothes.

"It sort of is, I suppose..." began Ramirez. "About the miracle business. A few more questions. That's all. To satisfy the archbishop."

"Come on through." Hudson led Ramirez through to the front room, which was half lounge and half office. Ramirez sat in an armchair by a table stacked with books and magazines. Through bay windows with open wooden shutters, Ramirez could see out over the lake. People were walking along the shore road, and boats were out in numbers on the water.

"Would you like something to drink?" asked Hudson. "I've just made a pot of coffee."

"Sure. Thank you."

"How do you take it?"

"Black, no sugar. Thank you."

Hudson disappeared into the kitchen and returned with two mugs and a plate of cookies, which he placed on a glass coffee table free of clutter. He handed Ramirez a steaming mug.

"Thanks, Dr. Hudson."

"Rick, please," said Hudson as he took a seat opposite Ramirez. Both were sitting side on to the bay window, the afternoon light across their faces. "What is it you wanted to talk to me about?"

Ramirez took a sip of his drink. He cleared his throat and thought for a moment. "Good coffee, by the way..."

"Thanks. I get it from a place online I like. I pay a bit more for it, but I can't abide bad coffee."

Ramirez nodded and smiled. "So, I've been reasonably busy these last few days. I've been around to all the homes of people who have claimed some sort of...unusual medical event. For the most part, I would say there is little to back up the claims made."

"I see. Turns out you're a healthy skeptic, then, Father?"

"Yes. Yes, it turns out that I am. To some extent. But I do think there are three cases that still puzzle me."

"Which cases are those?"

"Elizabeth Wendig, Archie Baker, and Jean Cassidy. They seem to exhibit changes that are exceptional and unexpected. And in two of those cases, Archie Baker and Jean Cassidy, their health has taken a turn for the worse."

Hudson's eyes flickered, his mouth twitched, and his hand tightened around his mug.

"Is everything alright, Doctor?"

"It's... It's been a trying day. You obviously haven't heard."

"Heard what?"

"Jean Cassidy and Archie Baker both died today."

"That's terrible news. What caused their deaths?"

"I'm not sure. In both cases, it was multiple organ failure. In the end."

"I see..." Ramirez thought for a moment. "They were all your patients, weren't they?"

"Jean and Archie were."

"And Elizabeth..."

"No. Not Elizabeth. Strictly speaking. Or at least she wasn't until she survived the tragedy. After the crash, I took Elizabeth on pro bono to help out, for obvious reasons. Before that, I had never been Elizabeth's doctor. Had never treated her."

"Right."

Hudson's answer seemed to throw Ramirez, who took a moment to get his thoughts straight and then continued. "I took a trip up to the Meadows, the nursing home in Lyndonville."

Hudson's body was now coiled with tension, and he seemed almost angry. Ramirez could sense the tension rising but continued.

"I spoke to an orderly there," said Ramirez. "He told me a very familiar story, that some of the people in the home had been presenting extraordinary turnarounds in health. But I believe you'll be familiar with these cases, won't you, Dr. Hudson?"

"If you're driving at the fact that I'm a visiting doctor there, then yes, I do go up to the home perhaps once a week to see specific patients."

"And you didn't think to mention what was happening at the home before?"

"I was only aware of it very recently."

"I see. I guess what I'm really beginning to believe is that I don't believe these cases have a spiritual explanation. I believe they have a medical origin, and you, Dr. Hudson, might be best placed to explain it."

FORTY-FIVE

Marshall was talked out, and his mouth was dry. He'd spilled everything he could spill. Loban was still sitting on the bed. The gorillas were still standing by the door and the window.

"That's it," said Marshall. "That's everything. I know I should have made the call, rung the alarm. But I had a plan, and I executed that plan and tied up all the loose ends."

Loban stared at Marshall, unimpressed and unmoved by Marshall's long speech. A chill went through Marshall's body as he saw clearly that he was another loose end now. One of two that remained.

"The doctor," said Loban. "He lives on the lakefront. Right?"

"That's right."

Loban nodded at Slava, who moved from the door and pulled out a knife. Marshall began to panic and wriggle as Slava approached. Loban laughed. Then, Slava gripped Marshall's chin and cut through the cable ties, freeing Marshall's hands.

"We will visit the doctor," said Loban. "Apparently, he stopped returning calls too. So, we need to have a proper catch-up."

Slava pulled Marshall upright and jabbed the blade into his side. "Behave, or I will skin you alive." He pulled a lamed Marshall off the bed, then held him up and practically dragged him over to the door and out to the BMW.

"Get in the trunk," said Slava.

"Wha... What?..." Marshall stammered.

Gus tapped the key fob, and the trunk opened.

"Get in," said Slava. "Or I shoot you in the head right here."

Marshall climbed into the trunk, and Gus tapped the fob. The trunk closed.

"Let's go deal with the other loose ends," said Loban.

FORTY-SIX

"I'm as in the dark about what's happening as you, I'm afraid, Father."

Ramirez looked at Dr. Hudson intently, trying to identify any telltale signs of deception. But the doctor's face gave nothing away. "You knew about the cases at the Meadows Care Home, but you didn't think to mention them?"

"I... I sent the samples I took off to the labs at Rutland, and I'm waiting for the results. They should tell us more than I could from purely speculating. If you don't mind me saying, I think you are suffering from a layperson's misunderstanding about what my professional role is."

"What misunderstanding is that?"

"I'm a doctor. An MD. I'm not an expert in any one field; I'm a generalist. If there is an explanation for what has happened that connects the very different cases in Hinkley and at the Meadows, then I am not trained nor have the experience, expertise, or instruments to identify it. I know that's an unsatisfying answer, but it's the truth. The mundane truth."

"But I can't get my head around the fact that you never thought to mention it. To anyone."

Hudson didn't reply right away. Then, he put his coffee down and stood. "I've explained as well as I can my role in this. The samples will be back from Rutland, and..." Hudson stopped talking. His attention was focused on the bay window. Ramirez turned to see a BMW pulling up outside. Hudson's face was suddenly pale, his breathing quick. He swallowed and looked at Ramirez.

"I'd leave now if I were you."

"What's going on?"

"The men getting out of the car are extremely dangerous. You need to go now."

Outside, three men were getting out of the BMW. They stepped onto the sidewalk and looked directly at Hudson standing behind the bay window. Two of the men were somewhere north of six four or five and broad as barns, and the third man was much smaller but looked no less formidable for it. Ramirez didn't ask any more questions. He rose, placed his mug down, and, without exchanging a word with Hudson, made for the front door.

He opened the door just as the three men were walking up the path from the sidewalk. Ramirez made to go past them but instead was blocked by a vicious punch to the gut and lifted by the arms backward into the house.

Ramirez was deposited with a thud onto the couch. Hudson had sat back in the armchair, resigning himself to what was to come.

"Let the priest go," said Hudson. "He's got nothing to do with our business."

Loban looked down at Ramirez, who was clutching his stomach and trying to get his breath back. "He does now. Gus, take his cell." Gus rooted through Ramirez's pockets and pulled out his cell and wallet. He threw the cell on the floor and stamped his heel down on it a couple of times till it cracked. Then, he pocketed the wallet.

"The syndicate called you," said Loban to Hudson. "You didn't call back."

"I didn't know if I should. If it was safe."

Loban looked around. "Nice place." He picked up the glass coffee table, tipping the plate and mugs onto the floor, and hurled it against the wall, casting shards of glass across the room. "What a pity." Then, he took the unoccupied armchair. Gus and Slava stood behind him, blocking the way to the door.

"It's over," said Loban.

"I know," said Hudson.

"It's a mess."

"It's a mess," Hudson agreed. "But it's not my fault."

"It's not about fault. It's about money."

"It is about fault. They started sending me stuff that was dangerous. Lethal. How was I to know?"

"It's not about fault. My job is to tie up the ends here. Reputation management. Secure investments. Steady the ship. Blah, blah, whatever you want. We clean up. We're just the cleaners. You did your job; now we do ours. End of story. We're going to take a trip, Doctor."

"Where?"

"Not far." Loban rose.

Hudson stood too. "Wait," he said. "What about the priest?"

"He's coming with us."

Hudson shook his head and avoided catching Ramirez's eye, then followed Loban out. Gus and Slava picked up Ramirez and followed behind.

FORTY-SEVEN

Cassidy and Devlin had come across nothing of interest at Marshall's place, so they had driven back to the lakefront and opened his hangar with the keys he'd left in his pickup. The hangar was a basic post-frame build with enough room for the two floatplanes parked there, wooden shelves and benches, and a long workstation.

"They'll cost some real money," said Devlin, admiring the floatplanes. "They're both in great condition. The Cub has to be fifty years old and cared for like a baby."

Cassidy and Devlin swept around opposite sides of the planes. They met between the propellers near the far wall, where they found a white cooler box sitting by itself on a long bench. It was plugged in, whirring and humming, keeping its contents cold.

"Fishing bait?" said Cassidy.

"Cold beers for the customers?"

"Let's find out."

She put on a fresh pair of gloves and opened the box. The contents of the cooler were nothing like beers or fishing bait. Instead, there were rows of labeled test tubes in racks. Not all the test tubes were the same. Some had different-colored tops and were different shapes. But most of the tubes contained dark red liquid.

"Blood?" said Cassidy. "Are these blood samples?"

Devlin bent down and took a long look at the different containers. "Yeah, they're blood samples. But the different colors mean they've been prepared for different types of analysis. Standards vary, but generally, the light green tops are prepared for routine chemistry tests. The dark-green tops are prepared for more specialized chemistry tests."

"How do you know this?"

Devlin shrugged. "Because I was para-rescue. I had enough training and more than enough experience to know what these tubes are for."

Cassidy picked out one of the tubes out and studied the label. "It's got a name on it, 'Archibald Baker,' and a date, 'March 18th'.' She replaced the tube, picked out another test tube with a different-colored top, read the label, and put it back. Then, she picked out another and did the same. She did this over and over until she came to a test tube label that stopped her in her tracks.

"What is it?" asked Devlin.

"It's a sample for Nanna. The label says 'Jean Cassidy.'" She held it up for Devlin to see. "What the hell is Marshall doing with my nanna's blood?" She put the tube back in the rack and looked at the box. "There are a lot of the same names here. Apart from Nanna and Archie, there are a few I recognize and a lot I don't. But they're all around the same dates, March 18th and 19th."

"That's over a week old and too old to be of any use. Stored at the temperature in the box, the samples would be scientifically useful for a few days tops."

"What the hell does Marshall want with blood samples?"

"It's the dark matter."

"What?"

"The stuff at the heart of all of the things that have been going on in Hinkley since the tragedy at the lake. Like I said, meth doesn't explain all of that. This is to do with what was in the van on the night of the tragedy."

Cassidy pointed at the cool box. "But this looks like it's meant to be shipped out. Not in."

"Yeah. It does. But something related to this was shipped in. What was in that van that night had to be more important than just meth. It was something going into Hinkley that had to be kept quiet at any cost. Even at the cost of the lives of the people on that bus." Devlin was suddenly struck by a thought. "What was the weather like the night of the accident?"

"Awful. Worse than it's been in a long time, in years. Blizzard weather. There was thundersnow."

"Were flights grounded?"

"Yeah. Burlington International had to put all flights on hold for a few days. I had a cousin stranded down in Florida who had to wait till the whole thing had died down before they could get on a plane."

"So what if Marshall is flying something into Hinkley?" Devlin pointed at the test tubes in the cooler box. "What if he's then flying these samples out? But on the night he's supposed to fly his cargo in, all planes are grounded. In desperation, he gets the Kane brothers to drive the cargo in. Maybe the brothers have their own cargo to ship in the van, maybe meth supplies. But they can't get caught. And more than that, when the accident happens and the coach goes into the lake, the Kane brothers know they can't confess 'cause of the meth lab. But Marshall, Marshall knows right that moment, he has to do whatever he can to cover it all up. Including killing Kyle."

"But Marshall can't be preparing these samples. He was an engineer in the Air Force."

"No. But Hudson could. And at least some of those names, including your grandmother and Archie, are his patients. We need to talk to Marshall and Hudson."

FORTY-EIGHT

"What's that banging?" asked Hudson, who was squeezed between Slava and Ramirez in the back seat of the BMW.

Loban, who was in the front passenger seat, holding a pistol, turned and gave Hudson a weary look. He waved the barrel of his gun toward the trunk. "Your business partner."

"Marshall's in the trunk?"

"Yes."

"What's he doing in the trunk?"

Loban didn't answer.

"He's not my business partner in any case," said Hudson. "I had virtually nothing to do with him. He was just the water boy someone at the syndicate found. He's the one who got those assholes the Kanes involved and messed everything up."

Again, Loban didn't answer. Instead, his dark, heavy-lidded eyes slid from Hudson to Ramirez. The priest was pale, his eyes were red, and he was holding his stomach.

"What's wrong with him?" asked Loban.

Hudson looked at Ramirez. "I don't know. Maybe the slug your guy gave him in the gut has something to do with it." Hudson shrugged. "Whatever, he's not my responsibility."

"What's wrong with you?" Loban asked Ramirez.

"I don't feel well. I don't feel well at all," replied Ramirez.

"Don't even think about puking on me," said Slava. "Or you'll feel even worse."

"Both of you be quiet," said Loban. "Or I'll stop the car, shoot you like dogs, and leave you in a ditch." Loban turned around and shook his head. "Worse than children."

Gus drove around the north of Lake Vesper, south on Route 5, and cut east around town, taking smaller, out-of-the-way roads until they got far enough east that it got quiet. Then, they turned back onto the main road back toward the Hideaway Motel. The banging in the trunk continued the whole way, and it made Ramirez feel even worse. Every thump, every bump in the road pushed his sickly body just that bit closer to the edge. He prayed and prayed for his stomach cramps and his throbbing head to ease off, but he feared they were only going to get worse. Just after they had got back onto the main road, Ramirez's body gave up on him, and he projected a jet of vomit over the backs of the front seats, the rear footwells, and Hudson's and Slava's pants and shoes. Part fire hose, part rainfall, it left no one in the car entirely unscathed. Though of the three occupants of the back seat, Ramirez seemed to be the one least blighted by his own vomit.

The car came to an abrupt stop. For a moment, nobody spoke. The engine ticked over, and the banging from the trunk went on. Then, Slava began punching Ramirez in the abdomen.

"*Slava*!" screamed Loban.

Slava froze, his hands around the priest's neck.

"Get the priest and Hudson out of the car," yelled Loban. "Now!"

Even in Ramirez's appalling condition, he understood that there was no one else on Earth whom Slava would so slavishly obey. Ramirez was probably still alive because Loban told Slava to stop hitting him.

All the while, the banging from the trunk had continued, and now the car was idling, Marshall's pleas to be let out could be heard from inside the trunk.

The back door flung open, and Slava pulled first Ramirez out and then Hudson and threw them both to the ground.

"You asshole," Slava shouted at Ramirez. "I'm covered in puke."

Loban got out and surveyed the situation. He gripped his forehead and tried to think, but the banging and Marshall's cries in the trunk were getting louder. Loban balled his fists up and hissed, "Someone stop that goddamn banging!" But the banging and cries got louder and more plaintive, and Loban's fuse finally blew. Realizing he'd left his gun in the car, Loban grabbed Slava's Hellcat from his hand, strode around to the back of the car, pointed the Hellcat at the trunk, and fired bullet after bullet into the bodywork until his temper was spent.

Finally, it was silent. There were no more sounds from the trunk.

"Peace at last! Thank God!" exclaimed Loban. He closed his eyes, took a deep sigh, and a moment to collect himself. Then, when he'd calmed down, he opened his eyes and handed the gun back to Slava. He was about to speak when his temper suddenly flared up again, and he bellowed, "Slava, you dolt!"

"What?" asked Slava incredulously. Then, he looked around and immediately saw the problem. Only the priest was on the ground. Hudson was gone. Slava turned to see a figure in the distance running for their life, already a good two hundred yards away.

Slava held up his gun and was about to make after Hudson when Loban intervened.

"Leave him! Leave him! We know how to find him now, and

most importantly, he doesn't know we know how to find him. Let's get rid of the body first, then go back to the hangar tonight and get rid of the evidence. After that, we catch up with the doctor."

Slava picked up Ramirez.

"No," said Slava. "You both stink. We're only a mile from the motel. You take the priest for a walk."

"Are... Are you going to kill me?" stuttered Ramirez.

"Get up," said Slava.

"Please... Please... Don't..."

"Get up, or I will definitely kill you."

Loban got back in the car, and Gus steered back onto the road. As they drove off, Loban watched Slava push the priest onto the field and march him away from the road and passing cars.

"What a mess," said Loban. "What a dumb mess. I simply cannot wait to get out of this hole of a town."

FORTY-NINE

Cassidy and Devlin pulled up in front of Hudson's lakefront house. A black Lexus with a tow bar and a roof rack was parked on the drive. Just ahead of them on the road was Ramirez's Toyota Corolla.

"That's Father Ramirez's rental," said Devlin.

"Why would Ramirez be here?"

"Maybe he's here about the report for the archbishop."

They got out of Cassidy's cruiser and went up the steps to the porch. Cassidy rang a few times, knocked some more, and rang a few times more. No answer.

Devlin was looking over the Lexus. "There's a tow bar on Hudson's car, but I can't see a trailer." He walked up to the bay window and looked in. "Well, this isn't right. Not right at all. Looks like the living room has seen some action."

Cassidy joined Devlin, peered in through the window, and saw the shattered coffee table and the fragments of glass covering the floor. Devlin took out his cell and called Ramirez's number. It rang a few times and went to voicemail. He rang again.

"Hey," said Cassidy, peering in through the window. "Look..."

Devlin looked through the window, and on the floor was a cell phone with a cracked screen, flashing and fluttering on the carpet and the shattered glass. The flashing stopped, and the cell stopped moving. Devlin rang again, and the cell flashed and vibrated again.

"It's Ramirez's cell," said Cassidy. "I don't like this. I don't like this one bit."

"First, we find Marshall's car but not Marshall, then Ramirez's car and no Ramirez. And no Hudson either, and his place has been turned over."

"If Ramirez isn't here, where's the next place he's likely to be?"

"Back at the motel."

FIFTY

Hudson was reasonably fit for a man in his late forties. He took his own advice and exercised regularly, drank moderately, and avoided high-fat food. But it was many decades since he had run cross-country. Back in high school, in fact. And back then, he hadn't been running for his life. His heart beat like it was screaming "stop," and his joints were aching from the unpredictable nature of the Vermont geography.

After running for what seemed like an hour but he was certain was much less, he had slowed to a trot and then to a walk. Drenched in sweat, stinking of vomit, and standing under cover of a dense copse of trees, he did a 360 sweep of his surroundings. There wasn't a soul to be seen. He had enough reception to get an approximate location on Google Maps. He studied the cell phone map and took his bearings.

Then, he thought through his options. He could walk toward the interstate and call a cab. That would get him away from Hinkley. He had his credit cards on his cell, so money wasn't a problem. But what if he needed to get out of the country? He needed that option open to him. The danger was that great. So he needed his passport. But he couldn't go back to his house. Not right now. But if he waited twenty-four hours or got someone else to pick it up for him, then with his passport, he could go wherever he liked. Loban would be expecting him to be getting as far away from Hinkley as possible. He wouldn't for a moment think Hudson had stayed put because he wouldn't know what Hudson knew. That Hudson had a safe place to go. He just needed to get to the safe place and wait it out. If he circled down further south of Hinkley, he could keep to the woods. Then, he could track around the western side of the lake and make for safety.

He set off following the map on his cell, wandering deeper into the countryside and away from human contact.

FIFTY-ONE

"How much further?" asked Ramirez.

"You don't want to know," replied Slava.

"I do. I do want to know. I'm being walked to the place where I'll die. I'm not afraid to die. I have my faith. I am at peace with my fate."

Slava sighed. He wasn't used to killing priests. These last few years, his trade had been mainly desperate businessmen at the end of their rope. Despite their begging and pleading, they were easy jobs. It had gotten so Slava pretty much knew all the beats of a man's last minutes. The priest, though, was different. Slava hadn't ever killed someone who was so down with being killed. So at peace with the act. And he didn't like it one bit. But still, a job was a job. And the sooner the priest was dead, the sooner he could get out of his vomit-covered clothes and shower. He smelled so bad he was thankful for the occasional breezes that took his stink away.

Slava scratched his head, looked across the flat fields, and pointed. "See that line of trees and the ditch in front?"

Ramirez looked in the direction Slava was pointing and saw

a pathetic line of barely leaved trees and drifts of dust coming up from a dry ditch below. "Yes."

"That's where we're going."

"Okay... Let's go."

Slava grunted. It almost felt like the kid was leading the way, and that was definitely unusual in these circumstances. In fact, Slava observed, once he knew where he was heading, the priest seemed to pick up his pace. It was like he was in a hurry to meet his God, and that made Slava jealous because he sure as hell didn't feel the same way about his own death, whenever that might come.

They reached the ditch in front of the line of trees quickly. Slava was considering shooting the priest in the back of the head a few yards short of the ditch when Ramirez suddenly stopped and turned around. He looked Slava square in the eyes with a frankness Slava found unsettling. The wind picked up, the branches creaked back and forth, and dust picked up around their feet.

"Before I die," said Ramirez calmly, "I'd like to have a moment to pray."

Oh, here we go, thought Slava. *In the end, businessman or priest, they're all the same. Bargaining for a little more time.*

"One Hail Mary. That's all you get. And make it snappy. It's short. I know all the words."

"You do? Will you pray with me?"

"Are you a complete moron? Get on with it."

"Let me genuflect at the end too."

"I'll let you genuflect."

Ramirez dropped to his knees, clasped his hands, and muttered to himself. Slava sighed and yawned. Using his free hand, he pulled a cigarette carton out from his inside jacket pocket, nipped out a cigarette with his mouth, and lit it up.

Smoke flared out of his nostrils as he waited for the priest to finish.

"Hurry it up."

The priest muttered some more words. Slava took the safety off his gun and waited for the priest's hands to come up for genuflection. Slava heard the words "now and at the hour of our death..." muttered, and the priest's hands came up.

This is it, thought Slava. *Game over.*

Slava pressed on the trigger, but instead of firing off a round, he was blinded by an explosion of grit and dust that filled his eyes nose and mouth. He reeled back, choking, fighting to clear the gravel and powder from his face. When he had finally wiped, snorted, and coughed away the filth, he could see through his watering eyes that the priest had gone. He looked around in a wild panic and saw that Ramirez was already halfway across the field they'd just walked through.

"Son of a bitch. You little..."

Raging with anger, he aimed and fired off a shot that whizzed well wide of his target. Then, he set off into a surprisingly fast sprint for a man of his size and bulk and soon was making up ground on the priest.

Ramirez had reached the bounds of the field where a line of trees ran. Beyond the trees was a narrow stream. He raced through the trees, jumped the stream in one bound, looked over his shoulder, and caught sight of Slava's hulking form gaining on him fast. Ramirez ran on, digging deeper to find more speed, and then came to a shuddering stop. His foot had struck a rock, and he went face-down into the grass. Grasping at the earth, he pushed himself back up onto his feet and set off again at a slower pace and carrying a limp.

Only some thirty yards behind, Slava saw his chance. He raised his gun and locked Ramirez's back in his sights. He stopped, drew a steady breath through his nostrils, and pulled the trigger, but instead of a boom and recoil, the gun clicked feebly.

Slava groaned, and his groan turned into a howl of anger. Loban must have nearly emptied the whole magazine when he shot Marshall in the trunk. He broke into a ferocious sprint. He'd wasted valuable time, but the priest was limping and struggling to keep running. They were both running up an incline now, and Slava was gaining a yard on the limping priest every ten seconds. The chase was almost up. The priest's hours were numbered.

FIFTY-TWO

The cavalry came out of nowhere.

Over the ridge of the incline appeared what at first sight looked like a herd of animals. Ramirez wiped the sweat from his eyes and realized that it was a group of people wearing shorts and trainers.

A running club.

Ramirez shouted and waved his hands. He stumbled and staggered up the slope in a diagonal that put him on a path to intercept the runner at the head of the group.

"Hey..." Ramirez pulled up alongside the lead runner. The runners all looked middle-aged and were jogging at a pace Ramirez found easy to fall in with, even with his limp. They must, he thought, be going for distance over speed.

"You okay, Father?" said the lead runner, a man who looked to be in his fifties or possibly older. Silver-haired and slim, he was in good shape.

Ramirez thought about his response. He considered explaining his whole situation, that he'd been kidnapped and chased, that he'd been almost killed. Then he thought better of it. The story would bring the runners to a stop, and that was the last thing he wanted. He looked around, and Slava was nowhere to be seen. He'd disappeared into the landscape. In the midst of this herd of runners, Ramirez was safe and could travel back to civilization and the police.

"Could I run with you?" asked Ramirez.

The lead runner looked him up and down. "You're in shoes and a suit, Father. You're hardly dressed for it."

"I know, but I'm a big trail runner. I'd just love to join you for the run. If that's okay? I'd just tag along and be no trouble."

"Well, it's a free country, I guess. We're headed up to the clubhouse. It's another mile and a half." The lead runner looked down at Ramirez's uneven stride. "You carrying an injury there?"

"Oh, just something my physio advised me to run off. This pace is just fine for me. In fact, it's just what I need. Honest."

SLAVA HAD WITHDRAWN into the tree line. Out of sight, he'd watched the priest join the runners and the line jog away. He sprinted to the top of the hill, and from the ridge, he spotted a farmhouse about half a mile away. In front of the farmhouse was an old truck, and poking out from underneath the van was a pair of legs.

He looked back toward the runners, now dots on the ridge beyond.

"You little bastard. You think you've got away, but you've only made it so much worse."

Slava looked back toward the farmhouse and made a plan.

FIFTY-THREE

Cassidy and Devlin parked in the Hideaway's lot and headed to Ramirez's room. They knocked but got no answer. Devlin peered in through a gap in the drapes.

"No sign of him," said Devlin. "Let's go speak to Ma Kane. See if she's seen him around.

Devlin started to walk to the lobby end of the motel, but Cassidy didn't follow.

Devlin stopped and turned back to a stationary Cassidy. "Something the matter?" he asked.

"It's fine. It's just that I have some history with Ma Kane."

"What history?"

"She..." Cassidy raised her eyes to heaven. "She gave birth to me."

"She's your mother?"

"Biologically. But she gave up any real claim to that title a long time ago. I told you that my mother left when I was three, and my dad died when I was four. Well, the mother in question was Ma Kane."

"Why did she leave?"

"Because she's a bitch. One of the worst people on the face

of the planet. She left because my pop was dying of cancer, and she didn't want to care for him or me. She went and jumped into bed with Bill Kane, who owned the motel and had more money than my pop, who was too ill to work and had to spend all his money on medical bills. If it hadn't been for my grandparents, I would've ended up in a home. They gave me all the love a child needs. They saved me. Ma Kane has always chosen to save herself. Bill was in his fifties when Ma Kane shacked up with him, and he died within ten years of their marriage and left it all to her. By then, she'd had Roy and Ted."

"Did they know you were their half sister?"

"Yeah. But we never talked about it. When Pop died, I was only a little girl, but I'd already made a decision she wasn't my mother and Roy and Ted weren't my brothers. I just made that decision as if it were a fact, and it became a fact. I thought that would mean it would all go away. And for a long while, it did. Now I'm a little older though... Turns out you can't make reality bend to even your most-wished-for wishes." Cassidy put her hands on her belt and let out a big breath. "So, now you know the baggage I got, let's go see the old witch."

The reception was empty, so Cassidy dinged the bell.

"I've been here five days, and I've hardly seen any other customers. Who stays here?" asked Devlin.

"People who come here for business. But that's not many. There's a hiking trail, so there's some tourist trade. But this place barely ticks over these days. Especially now they're building on the north of the lake."

The sound of a door opening and closing came from a room behind the reception, followed by steps across a hard floor. The door behind the reception counter opened, and Ma Kane's stick-like figure appeared. Cassidy's presence seemed to take her by surprise, but she recovered and stood defiantly, dressed in a nightgown, with her palms down on the hardwood countertop.

"Father," said Ma Kane, and then she looked across at Cassidy with her flinty brown eyes. "Lori. What can I do for you both?"

"We're looking for Father Ramirez," said Cassidy. "Have you seen him here today?"

Kane shook her head. "Nope. I've been around all day, in and out of my bed—in it, mostly, where I've been mourning my two boys—and I haven't laid eyes on him."

"What about Dr. Hudson?" asked Devlin.

"I ain't seen him either."

"Who else have you got staying here?" asked Devlin.

"What business is that of yours, Father?"

"It's police business," said Cassidy. "We got twelve dead people dead, including your boys. You of all people should want to know who's coming in and out of our town."

Ma Kane narrowed her eyes, and her sunbaked skin wrinkled. She swept away a stray gray hair away from her eyes and sniffed. "Far as I know, we got the answers to all of that, as heartbreaking to a mother as those answers may be. My two boys, God rest their gentle souls, were caught up in something terrible. Driven by the devil and that evil drug, meth."

"What if those answers turn out to be wrong?" said Devlin.

Ma Kane shifted her weight toward Devlin and eyed him up. "Since when did a priest have anything to do with law and order in this town or any town?"

"It's a small town," said Lori. "I need all the help I can get, specially since one officer and dear friend of mine was gunned down."

Ma Kane turned back to Lori. She shook her head, and her eyes suddenly teared up like a faucet being turned on. "And I'm as goddamned sorry as anyone could be for the appalling acts my boys have visited on this town. But we both know what this is really about."

"It's about why those children died in a cold, black lake. It's about why Kyle was killed and Roy and Ted died."

"No, darlin'. This is about me and you. About all the locked-up anger and sadness we have 'cause of what I did to you and your pop. Leaving a baby and a husband. But you gotta understand, I wasn't well. My mind and heart were as black as could be, and I was afraid I'd take my own life, and..." Ma Kane sobbed and covered her face. Then, she breathed in and restrained herself. "Even yours..."

"Oh, for God's sake." Cassidy turned her head away, unable to look at Ma Kane.

"It's the truth. I swear on the bible and all that's holy. I was in a dangerous place. And Bill saved me, and you know what? In a way, he saved you too. And after that, I couldn't come see you 'cause, and I know it was wrong, whenever I thought of you, let alone saw you, my heart was too full of pain. But...but I know, whatever happened...whatever happens, I am your mommy."

It took all of Cassidy's resolve to look at the woman in front of her. "That's not how it works," said Cassidy quietly, holding down a volcano of emotion. "You don't get to choose how you describe the role you play in people's lives. You play that role, or you don't. A mother is a mother because her child calls her that. I don't even know what I'd call you. I'm here on police business, so I'm gonna ask you again, who have you got staying here? And if you don't tell me, I'll get a warrant while you're standing there, shut down the whole motel, and turn every inch of it upside down."

Ma Kane wiped her eyes, sniffed, and straightened up. "Well, I'll say one thing for you. You're hard as granite and mean with it too."

"It's a real simple question, and you're beginning to look like someone who has something to hide."

"I ain't got anything to hide."

"Then tell me, who's staying here? Show me your register."

"It's my private records. It's got nothing to do with your investigation."

"I get to decide whether it has or not. If you don't hand the register over, I'll shut you down and have a team down here searching around, and you won't have any peace or guests for as long as it takes to bankrupt you."

"You little bitch. It's no wonder I left you."

"The register."

Ma Kane reached under the counter, pulled out a tray of registration cards, and slapped it on the counter. "We do things old-time here. Ink and card."

Cassidy pulled the tray over to her side of the counter and ran through the cards in the compartment at the front marked "Guests." There were about a dozen registration cards. There were cards for Devlin and Ramirez, three families, a couple of businessmen from Boston, and then three cards marked with the names "Mr. A. Smith," "Mr. B. Johnson," and "Mr. J. Williams." These last three cards caught Cassidy's attention. All three had booked in on the same date and time and were in adjoining rooms. Cassidy picked them out and laid them in front of Ma Kane.

"Who are these guys?"

"Some businessmen from out of state. Seattle. Like it says on the card."

"What are they here for?"

"I have no idea. I just take their money, and they take a room. They all had a driver's license, so I didn't blink or ask questions."

"How'd they pay?"

"Cash."

"How long are they staying?"

"Didn't give an end date. I don't see what the problem is here."

"The problem is the names: Mr. Smith, Johnson, and Williams. The three most common names in the country."

Ma Kane shrugged. "Like you say, they're common."

Cassidy looked at the cards and got her cell phone out. She dialed one of the numbers, listened to a recorded voice at the other end, and said, "Number's dead." Then, she rang another number from another of the three cards. "That one's dead too." The last number got a dial tone, and someone picked up and said, "Hello." It was one word, but Cassidy could still hear a thick, Eastern European accent.

"Hi, this is the Hideaway Motel," said Cassidy. "Is this Mr. Johnson?"

The line immediately went dead.

Cassidy stared hard at Ma Kane. "Where did you say these guests were from?"

"Out of state. Seattle."

"The guy I spoke to sure as hell didn't sound like he came from Seattle. He sounded Russian."

"Maybe he moved to Seattle."

"From Russia? Mr. Smith, Johnson, and Williams? I think we'll go pay them a visit."

"They're not in. You just missed them."

"Then open up their rooms."

"I got a duty to my customers. A thing called privacy. You might have heard of it."

"I've heard of obstructing police business, and I have a judge on speed dial who can give me a warrant faster than you could spin in your grave."

"Call him, then. I ain't letting police barge into my guests' rooms like there's no constitutional rights anymore."

Cassidy chewed her bottom lip. Then she said, "We'll be back. With that warrant."

Ma Kane smiled and said sweetly. "Goodbye, Lori."

Devlin and Cassidy stepped out into the weak March sun.

"What the hell is she hiding?" said Cassidy, ready to scream with frustration. "And where the hell are Marshall, Rick Hudson, and Father Ramirez?"

"We don't need the warrant," said Devlin.

"Yeah, we do. I can get one, but it won't be quick."

"No, we don't if you saw what room numbers they had?"

"I did. 103, 104, and 105."

"Those rooms are on the other side of the motel from where I am. Let's at least take a look through the windows."

Devlin and Cassidy walked past the rooms Devlin and Ramirez were staying in and around the bottom of the I-shaped building where the utility room was. As they rounded the corner, a black BMW sedan with tinted windows reversed at speed out of a parking space.

"Get back," said Devlin. He and Cassidy stepped back and out of view as the car roared out of the parking lot and turned right, gunning down the road back to town.

"Did you see that?" said Cassidy. "There were bullet holes in the trunk."

"Yeah. I'll bet real money they're Smith, Johnson, and Williams."

"Ma Kane was lying to us. You think she tipped them off that we were coming?"

"If I'd believe it of anyone, I'd believe it of her. Pity we don't know where they're going."

"I can put that right. I got the license plate." Cassidy pulled out her radio from her belt and called into the dispatcher. "This is Charlie 2-3 requesting a BOLO for a black BMW sedan heading west on Tall Pines Lane from the Hideaway Motel toward Hinkley. Vehicle suspected in relation to a 10-32." She read out the license plate, got a confirmation from the dispatch officer, and slid her radio back into its holder.

The three motel rooms were not far from the utility room. The first room's drapes were parted, giving a view of the room. It looked completely unoccupied: the bed was made, and there was no luggage or clothes visible or other signs of use. The other two rooms' drapes were shut and impossible to see into.

Devlin stopped at the door to the last room and pointed to the door handle. "See that?"

There was a smudged red fingerprint on the top of the silver handle.

"I say we call that and the bullet holes in the trunk probable cause and leave a judge to clear up the mess," said Cassidy. "Want to do that magic opening doors trick again?"

Devlin stepped back and sent his 250-pound mass into the door, which flew open on contact.

Devlin and Cassidy stepped into the room. Snapped cable ties hung on the bed frame, scrunched-up balls of duct tape lay on the floor, and there was blood on the sheets.

"Dear God... I'm calling this in." Cassidy radioed the precinct, and then she and Devlin looked around the room and bathroom.

"Everything's gone," said Devlin. "They've packed up and left. Whatever they were in Hinkley for, it's done or nearly done."

"I need to talk to Ma Kane. Right now."

Cassidy stormed back around the building. The lobby was empty, so she wandered through the rooms behind the reception, but they were all empty. Ma Kane was nowhere to be seen. Cassidy went back to the motel room where Devlin was waiting.

"She's gone," said Cassidy. "No sign of her. You don't think the blood could be Marshall's or Hudson's or, God forbid, from Father Ramirez?"

"I think it's gonna be from at least one of the three men we haven't been able to find."

They headed outside to wait for backup to arrive. Devlin started a cigar and wandered out into the middle of the lot. By now, Cassidy knew Devlin well enough to know he was going into his "deep thought" mode. Her radio hissed, and dispatch came through. She held the radio to her ear and listened to the dispatch officer, and then she raced over to Devlin.

"A patrol car has reported a sighting of the BMW over on the eastern side of Lake Vesper. It must have been breaking the speed of sound to have gotten that far over that fast."

"Are they following the BMW?"

"No. They lost it on Cooper's path. It's a narrow, winding road that snakes around the lake. Real bitch of a drive."

"Where does the path lead?"

"It doesn't really lead anywhere. It connects up about a dozen different fishing and mooring spots on the most remote part of the shore. Nobody uses it to get anywhere. People just use it for fishing and sailing."

"Wait," said Devlin. He blew out a cloud of smoke. "Hudson had a tow bar on his car. Does he have a boat on the lake?"

"No idea."

"Could that be why they're headed out to the lake?"

Cassidy's eyes lit up. "Hold on, you need a certificate of registration for any motorized boat. Let me check it out. We have access to DMV records." Cassidy got on the radio again and made the request for a check. It took a couple of minutes for the check to go through. "Hudson does have a boat registered to him. Let's drive out to Cooper's path and see if we can find the BMW."

They got into the cruiser. As Cassidy drove out of the lot, they met a Vermont state police cruiser on the way in. She leaned out of her window and updated the troopers. Then, Cassidy and Devlin drove off, leaving the troopers to wait for the crime scene techs and to find Ma Kane.

FIFTY-FOUR

Ramirez and his fellow runners had reached the clubhouse, a long wooden cabin with changing rooms and a small hall. The runners warmed down for a couple of minutes and then disappeared into the changing rooms. As the group filed in, Ramirez took the chance to get the attention of the lead runner and pull him aside.

"I wasn't quite telling the truth about joining you for a run," said Ramirez breathlessly. "But the truth is kind of unbelievable."

"Okay..." said the runner, his brows already knotted in confusion. "So, what's the truth?"

"I was actually being chased by a man who had kidnapped me and tried to kill me."

The runner stood open-mouthed and gabbled out a "W... What...?"

"I know, it sounds crazy. But it's true. I just need to get to the police, as soon as I can. He's out there..." Ramirez swung an arm out to indicate the countryside. "The man who tried to kill me. And I won't be safe until I get to the police and report what happened. I don't have a cell phone, so if you could just phone the police?"

For a moment, the runner didn't say anything. The only sounds were the talk and laughter of the other runners coming out from the changing rooms. When the lead runner did speak, it was decisive and short.

"Stay there. I'll do better than call the police—I'll take you to them myself. Let me grab my change of clothes." In less than a minute, he was back with a gym bag over his shoulders and still in his running gear. "Come with me."

He led Ramirez around to the parking lot at the rear of the cabin.

"My car's over there. I'll drive you to the police station."

"Thank you. Sorry, I don't know your name."

"Randy. Randy Blake. I know Chief Garland too, so we'll make sure we talk to him personally."

"I'm so grateful for your kind help. The name's Ramirez. Father Ricardo Ramirez."

They got into Blake's sedan and swung out of the lot and onto the road toward town.

"What on earth is going on, Father?" asked Blake, who was picking up some serious speed.

"I honestly don't know. It's... I can't even begin to explain. But there are some dangerous men in Hinkley, and the police need to know about it."

Blake nodded, concentrating on the road ahead. They were approaching a junction, and Blake put his foot down, speeding through a red light.

"I heard a couple of priests were looking into people reporting miracles in Hinkley," said Blake. "You anything to do with that?"

"Yeah, that's me...and Father Devlin."

Blake turned to Ramirez. "I've lived around her all my life, and I've never known anything so strange as—"

Blake didn't get to finish his sentence. The collision that stopped him was colossal. An old truck with a rusty fender shot out from the grassy roadside at tremendous speed, slamming into the driver's side and sending the car into a sideways roll. For a long time, Ramirez lost all sense of direction. There was only rolling and the wrench of metal as the car spun viciously. Eventually, it settled right side up about ten yards from the road, one wheel spinning and the bodywork groaning. The old truck approached slowly, groaning to a stop a few feet from the wreck of the sedan, and for a moment, its clanking engine idled.

SLAVA KILLED the engine and got out. He looked through the driver's window first. The old man's head was a mess. He was dead, Slava concluded with complete certainty. He walked around to the passenger side, where the priest was unconscious but breathing.

Slava pulled at the door handle, and the door fell open. He unclipped Ramirez's seat belt, pulled him out, and threw him into the truck's passenger seat. Then, he reversed back onto the road and drove the clanking truck away.

FIFTY-FIVE

Night had fallen by the time Hudson had got to his destination. It had been a twelve-mile hike orbiting the town and the lake. The spot he had come to was a quiet cove about halfway up the eastern shore of Lake Vesper.

A basic wooden hut stood about two hundred yards from the water's edge. Directly in front of the hut on the bank of the lake was an equally basic, weathered jetty. Moored to the jetty was a blue-water sailboat. Hudson stood for a moment and marveled at the quiet, the occasional breeze, and the lapping water. He breathed in and looked up at the gloriously clear night sky.

Then, a darker mood took hold. He shook his head. Why the hell had he ever gotten involved in this crazy venture? He must have been out of his mind. He thought back to the moment he was approached. He had been at a low ebb. He was a doctor with a practice in West Virginia who had fallen from grace after an allegation of improper behavior from female clients. He'd pleaded his case to anyone who would hear him out. It was, after all, low-level stuff: overfamiliarity, a flirt too far, a risqué joke, and, yes, sometimes a lingering touch on the back of the hand. But that was it. Nothing criminal, he would say to anyone who would hear him out. It didn't matter though—the rumor mill did for him, his business, and his marriage. His reputation and his work vanished. So, when a representative from a wealthy private research fund approached him, he was already a soft target. The company would hire him, no questions asked, set him up in business, and deploy him to a town where he could start afresh. The money was three times what he could hope to make as a doctor under usual circumstances. And he knew the likelihood of him getting a doctor's job under usual circumstances was astronomically low. It wasn't just an offer he couldn't refuse; it was a damn near miracle. And like all miracles, it turned out to be too good to be true.

He looked around the cove and out onto the lake. Not a soul about. From where he stood, he could make out the line of lights that came from the buildings on the northern shore. On the lake, he could see the navigation lights of half a dozen boats out on the water.

He walked back to the hut, punched four digits into the key-safe buttons by the door, and took out the hut and the boat keys. Inside the hut, there was some rudimentary furniture and fishing gear. He found a battery-powered lamp and took it with him.

Hudson walked along the jetty, boarded the boat, and descended into the cabin. He placed the lamp on the table and filled a cup with water from the galley sink, which he downed in one go and then refilled. There were fresh clothes folded away under the settee berth and tins of food in the galley, but he was too tired to cook or change out of his clothes. He lay down on the settee, and within seconds, the gentle rocking of the boat had sent him into a deep sleep. In his sleep, he dreamed of Elizabeth Wendig's miraculous recovery, of being chased by dark figures through narrow hallways, and of his ex-wife, who had left him for a friend who was also a doctor.

FIFTY-SIX

Cooper's path was hardly even a path. It started as a poorly maintained road branching off from the highway south of Lake Vesper. Within a mile, it petered out into a dirt track carved out by use rather than construction. Cassidy's cruiser wasn't built for off-roading and made hard work of the drive, but she was a good driver, sure-handed and confident. She drove with care and efficiency, avoiding the ditches and traps a lesser drive would have hit. There was no sign of the BMW, so they slowly worked their way north, searching for a sighting of the car.

The path ran the eastern length of the lake and never veered more than a few hundred yards from the bank. Every so often, they'd come to a point in the path where a smaller, worn path in the dirt would turn off toward the lake. At each of these points, they'd get out and scout the route to the bank. Mostly the smaller dirt tracks led to fishing spots and empty jetties.

"What was that stuff you were saying about dark matter?" said Cassidy as she steered back and forth, navigating the winding path in the ebbing daylight. "You said all of this isn't about meth."

"Yeah, I did.

"Then what is it about?"

Devlin thought for a moment as the car rocked and bucked over the uneven earth. "It's about the cover-up. Kyle Ross, the Kane brothers, Hudson...Father Ramirez going missing. So much energy expended and risk taken to cover something up means that it's not meth. People coming into town with false identities and forged documents to back that up—that's high-level, professional. Those kinds of people are not interested in homemade meth."

"What are they interested in, then? 'Cause I have no clue."

"How long has Hudson been in Hinkley?"

Cassidy took a moment to think about the answer. "Couple of years."

"Where was he before that?"

"I think he said Boston."

"You ever check that out?"

"Why would I?"

"No reason, I guess."

Cassidy glanced over at Devlin, then back at the road. "What is it you're driving at?"

"These guys with the false IDs and maybe Eastern European accents came here and seem to have taken Marshall and Hudson and possibly even Ramirez. So it stands to reason Marshall and Hudson are involved in whatever's going on. Ramirez I have no answer for at the moment, but it's likely he has just caught up in the whole thing by accident. Marshall can fly cargo in and out, so that's likely to be his role. On the night the coach drove into the lake, all flights statewide were grounded due to bad weather. So maybe Marshall paid the Kanes to drive it in. After all, the Kane brothers were likely already running meth and supplies to make meth in and out of Hinkley. But what was it that Marshall had to get into Hinkley if not meth? It had to be related to the blood samples we found in his hangar. And in all likelihood, it related to Dr. Hudson."

"I know all this. You going anywhere with it?"

"I got a theory."

"Okay, then, let's have it..."

"What if Hudson is being paid to trial medicines on his patients?"

"What kind of medicines?"

"Untested medicines. Medicines they aren't allowed to test on people anywhere else. Medicines so experimental and powerful that they are capable of causing Archie Baker, Elizabeth Wendig, and your nanna to temporarily seem like they're miraculously recovering and then decline incredibly quickly."

"What kind of medicine would do that?"

"I don't know for sure, but maybe experimental treatments that aren't passed by the FDA. There are strict regulations on trials of new drugs and treatments. And you need to get permissions to undertake the trials, which can take time and have to have regulatory and federal oversight. But if you had doctors in remote spots all over the country who were quietly testing medicines on old, weak, and vulnerable patients and then sending samples back to labs...well, that data would be extremely valuable. Medical data is huge business. And medical data you can't get legally...that could be worth enormous sums of money."

Cassidy hit the brakes, and the cruiser lurched to a stop. "Here's another path to the bank. Let's go check it out."

FIFTY-SEVEN

For a moment, he wasn't sure where he was. It was pitch-black, and he couldn't see a thing. It took a few long seconds to remember what had happened that day. Slowly, the realization came to him that he was on his boat, and the lamp must have gone out. Hudson propped himself up and rubbed his face. Then, he froze. Somewhere in the boat cabin, something creaked, and he suddenly knew in his bones that he was not alone.

"Who's...?"

A light exploded in his face. It hurt his eyes and blinded him. He recoiled, and a hard object glanced across his forehead. Then the lights flickered on, and bit by bit, Hudson shook off the shock and pain until he could see who his visitors were. The cabin was suddenly very crowded. The settee Hudson was lying on was U-shaped. Next to it was a table, a chair, and then a narrow space up and down the cabin between the table and the kitchen equipment. Sitting on the settee by Hudson's feet was Loban. Leaning against the sink and countertop were his two henchmen. Hudson heard a groan coming from below him. He looked down to see Father Ramirez lying on the floor. He was in a bad way, bloody face and swollen features.

"Why did you run away, Doctor?" asked Loban.

Hudson moved into a sitting position and rubbed his tender forehead. "Because I thought you were going to kill me. How did you find me? No one else knows I have this boat."

"The old woman at the motel."

"Ma Kane?"

"I believe that's her name. When you went to visit her, when she was ill, she planted a tracer in your jacket and one in your medical case."

Hudson remembered the hug she'd given him. How long and unnatural it felt. What a dope, he thought. What a class A dope.

"Why would she help you? You...them." He pointed to Gus and Slava. "You were all part of it. Part of the whole thing that killed her sons."

"We didn't kill her sons. Marshall killed them with his stupid plan. When I told her it was Marshall who killed them, she was very agreeable to my plan to kill Marshall. And we paid her an awful lot of money to keep quiet. Of course, when you are an old woman without money or morals, it's an easy deal to make."

Ramirez groaned again, and all four men looked down at him.

"What the hell have you done to him?" asked a horrified Hudson.

"He pissed Slava off," replied Loban. "Pissed him off quite a lot, actually."

"I'll kill him too," said Slava. "Out here. And leave him all alone in an unmarked grave."

Ramirez groaned, and Slava kicked him like a dog.

"Get him off the floor," said Loban.

Slava picked up Ramirez and dumped him in the chair next to the settee and Hudson. Despite his physical condition, Ramirez managed to sit upright. He tried to lick some of the blood from his swollen lips. Then, to Hudson's surprise, he spoke. The words were difficult to get out and muffled by his swollen features, but still understandable.

"What... What were you giving them, Hudson? What... What was in your patients?"

Hudson was lost for words. He looked around at Loban, who was smiling.

"Well?" said Loban. "What are you waiting for? Tell the priest what you were injecting into those people."

"You're kidding me? Why would I tell...?"

"Tell him," Loban said. "Tell this greenhorn priest-child how bad the world can be. Maybe he'll see then why there is no God."

Hudson looked uncomfortable and thought about what he should say. Then he shrugged and turned to Ramirez. "Stem cell therapy. They were given stem cell therapy that's still in an extremely early experimental stage and hasn't yet had human trials. The investment fund we work for... They work for..." Hudson gestured at Loban, Slava, and Gus. "It specializes in funding cutting-edge research in areas that are most likely to bring high returns. Stem cell therapy has immense potential. It could cure multiple sclerosis, type 1 diabetes, Parkinson's disease, and macular degeneration. And that's just the start. There are many private groups around the world with a great deal of money who are desperate for medical trial data to further their own therapies, but the laws are incredibly restrictive, and getting permission is slow and mired in bureaucracy. So a ring of powerful investors found a quicker way—people like me. Doctors practicing in small towns with private clients, particularly older clients, clients in nursing homes, who are vulnerable. We are sent the harvested stem cells regularly. We administer the harvested cells to our patients under the guise of injections for pain or anti-inflammation or whatever reason we can come up with. Then, a few days later, we start taking samples and send them back to the lab to analyze, and that data is sold on for millions of dollars to private medical research groups and other interested parties. It's a license to print money."

"There are other doctors like you?" asked Ramirez.

"A whole network supplying samples and raw trial data nobody knows about."

"But... Why not pay people? Like in clinical trials?"

"Because," Hudson replied wearily, "the FDA oversees all clinical trial. They would hit the alarm soon as they knew we were rolling out drugs to patients that haven't even been through preclinical trials. This research isn't about being safe. It's about making mistakes fast."

"What happens to the patients you give the therapy to?"

"Surprisingly nothing, mostly. Sometimes a minor improvement. Sometimes a small decline. Sometimes a death that we cover up. As I say, it's mostly elderly patients. People whose death is expected, anyway."

"Like Jean Cassidy and Archie Baker and the people at the old folks' home?"

"Yeah. All of them." Hudson looked over at Loban. "I don't know what they put in the last batch, but it sure wasn't what they were sending before."

"They took a chance with some new developments," said Loban. "Something called polygenic gene disorder therapy. Sticking stuff they only just cooked up in a high-tech lab into a retired accountant in this dead-end town, or in Suckville, Ohio, or someplace else, and getting instant data results," said Loban.

"The last samples you sent back will be like gold dust to the lab people."

"It was incredibly unstable. It shouldn't be used again," said Hudson.

Loban shrugged. "They'll tinker with it, make it better, send it out to another country doctor to test on stupid old people, and maybe it will be better. Who are we to stand in the way of science?"

"They'll use it again?" asked Hudson.

"Of course! This trial has been a success. Okay, lots of people ended up dead, and this town is a mess. But from our side, it's been a triumph. Whatever they've made is powerful stuff. They'll want to see more data so they can adapt it. Finesse it."

"It's lethal. What if they kill more people with it?"

"Then we clear it up. That's our job. Not that moron Marshall's. We protect the investments." Loban smiled. "What you Americans don't know is how much money is made out of your bodies already. You know that blood from low-income families is the USA's tenth most valuable export? It beats semi-conductors, corn. If data is the new oil, medical data is the new diamond. We're in the golden age of biology, and this is the gold rush, baby. And it is a rush. In ten, maybe twenty years, people will be able to set up a genetics lab in their garage."

Hudson looked at Loban with contempt. "I gave treatments I didn't understand from people I've never met. I'm the smallest cog in this."

"We're all small cogs in this, you idiot," Loban snapped back. "That's the whole point. Each stage is separate from the next. Each cog turns when they're told to. That's the cardinal rule. That's where that dumbass Marshall went wrong, and that's why we're here now."

"Wait," said Ramirez, who, despite his condition, had paid

close attention to Hudson and Loban's conversation. "What about Elizabeth Wendig? She wasn't old. You said she wasn't your patient before the crash. Was she part of the trial?"

Hudson and Loban exchanged glances, and then Hudson said, "No. No, she wasn't."

"So how come she came back from the dead?"

"I don't know," said Loban matter-of-factly. "And I don't care." Loban nodded at Slava, who grabbed Ramirez by the collar and dragged him to his feet and out of the cabin.

FIFTY-EIGHT

It was mostly Slava's brute force that got Ramirez from the chair out to the deck. Once out on the deck, Slava let Ramirez try to find his balance, but almost immediately, the battered priest slumped to the floor. Ramirez's legs were weak, and his head was dizzy from the cruel beating Slava had given him.

"Get up," said Slava.

"Just shoot me here and get it over with."

"I give the orders. Get up, or I'll cut your fingers off one by one."

Ramirez sighed. Then, he slowly brought his knees underneath him and pushed himself onto all fours. From there, he got himself into a kneeling position and scrambled to his feet.

"Let's go, onto the jetty," said Slava. "And no last prayers this time."

Ramirez stumbled toward the side of the boat and managed to roll over the gunwale onto the jetty, where he lay exhausted. Slava followed and stood over Ramirez.

"Sit up."

Ramirez just about managed to follow Slava's order. Slava pulled his gun from his waistband, and then he paused, looked around, pulled out a metal tube from his jacket pocket, and attached it to the barrel. He pointed the gun at Ramirez's head.

Ramirez looked up at Slava with bloodshot eyes. "I forgive you," said Ramirez. "I love you."

These unexpected words jarred Slava for a split second. "Jesus," hissed Slava. "Why is killing priests so exhausting?" Slava thumbed off the safety and wrapped his finger around the trigger.

The priest stopped breathing, closed his eyes, and sat waiting for the silence to be split by a bullet to his temple. Slava pushed down on the trigger, then stopped. From somewhere out in the night came the low hum of an engine. Slava looked around, scanning the dark woods beyond the hut, trying to detect where the engine noise was coming from. Then, he heard a splash and turned back to see Ramirez disappearing like a seal into the black water.

"No! Not again!" In desperation, Slava let off six rounds into the water as the priest sunk from view. A huge bloom of red spread out like a slick on the surface of the water. Certain that he'd hit the priest, Slava waited on the jetty for a good five minutes. The priest didn't reappear, and Slava was satisfied that this time, the priest was gone for good. He spat into the water. "That's where forgiveness and love get you." Then, he stomped off into the woods to find the car that had wandered too close.

FIFTY-NINE

"How far along the lake are we?" asked Devlin.

"About halfway. We've passed seven fishing spots, and I'd guess there are about the same number again along the rest of this side of the lake. To be honest, it's not a part of the area I'm that familiar with. I'm not often needed out this way, and the satnav isn't reliable here either."

Cassidy jigged the steering wheel back and forth to follow the path as it zigzagged. After about another twenty yards, the path stopped zigzagging and curved gently toward the shore.

"Looks like there's another fishing point coming up," said Cassidy as she turned the wheel to the right.

"Stop."

"What?"

"Stop the car. I thought I saw something. A light, maybe."

Cassidy brought the cruiser to a halt.

"Turn it off," said Devlin. "Let's go by foot from here."

SIXTY

"What about me? What are you going to do with me?" The boat swayed and creaked on the calm lake water, and Hudson eyed the two men nervously, waiting to hear his fate. "If you're going to kill me, just do it. Shoot me in the head. Get it over with... Please..."

Loban and Gus exchanged a look, then both smiled.

"Go to the car, Gus."

Gus didn't need to ask why he was going to the car or what for; he left like he knew exactly what he had to do.

"Hudson," said Loban. "What I need from you is to tell me exactly where everything you have relating to our project is. Where all the equipment is held, where all the samples are held, and anything else we need to remove."

Hudson nodded. "Sure. Absolutely... Of course. I'll tell you everything. Where all of it is."

Loban took out his cell and placed it on the table. "I'm going to record what you say."

"Okay. Okay, that's fine. I'll tell you everything. If... If I tell you everything, will you let me live?"

Loban smiled. "Yes, I will."

There were footsteps along the jetty outside and then the sound of heavy feet on the deck. Loban tutted and smiled.

"Gus. He's such a clumsy oaf. Good job he didn't want to be a ballerina."

Gus descended the stairs into the cabin. He was holding a roll of electrical tape in one hand and a jerry can in the other.

"Is that gasoline?" asked Hudson, his voice quavering.

"Please don't ask questions," said Loban. "From now on, your job is to answer my questions."

Gus put down the can, pulled Hudson off the couch, and threw him onto the chair Ramirez had been sitting in. He started to pull strips of electrical tape from the roll, which he bit off with his teeth and used to secure Hudson to the chair. When he was done, he stepped back, and Loban inspected his work.

"Very good, Gus. Hudson, I need to know that you will tell me everything, so I'm going to introduce a little motivation into the situation." He nodded at Gus, who picked up the jerry can and tipped it over Hudson's head. Hudson gasped and choked on the liquid and fumes as gasoline cascaded over his body and drenched every inch of him.

After he'd finished coughing and gagging, Hudson yelled at his captors, "You'll set the whole boat alight, you crazy bastards."

"We'll get out okay," replied Loban. "Please don't worry about us."

Loban produced a brass cigarette lighter and laid it on the table by his cell. Then, he smiled a broad smile, his thick, black mustache spreading over his upper lip. "Now, if you don't want to burn alive, you'd better make sure I believe you are telling me everything. Do you understand?"

Hudson nodded somberly. "I understand."

SIXTY-ONE

The freezing black water had almost killed him. He had fought with every ounce of will he possessed to remain conscious as the weight of his body took him below the surface of the water. Then, he'd felt a sharp burst of pain as a bullet grazed his shoulder. Blood immediately began to trail above him. Blood in huge quantities. He watched his blood cloud around the blurred disc of the moon visible underwater and began to feel a wonderful warmth envelop his body. The trauma of the recent past evaporated away and was replaced by the most profound peace.

Then, he saw a light.

The light was at the end of a dark tunnel. Ramirez felt the pull of pure love, and he knew all he had to do was give up, and he would be pulled toward the light. It would be the easiest thing to do. So what was holding him back? He felt a presence behind him and understood that this presence was the force holding him back. Slowly, it dawned on him that the presence had the shape of a broad, tall man in clerical clothes. It became clear to him that the presence was Devlin.

The older priest was holding out a hand and beckoning him back. It occurred to Ramirez that there was no one else on Earth who could make him doubt whether he should give up his mortal body and accept eternal grace and peace. He could see now quite clearly Devlin holding out a hand. Ramirez felt the warm light begin to fade, the tunnel begin to shrink, and the feeling of pure love begin to withdraw. He understood that he had moments before that path would close and not open again for many decades.

Ramirez turned away from the dissolving light and stretched out to hold Devlin's hand. At first, it seemed that Devlin's hand was too far away to touch, and a sudden panic took hold of him that he might not reach Devlin and be suspended in the dark forever. In infinite emptiness. He stretched out as hard and as far as he could and brushed fingertips, which gave him the encouragement he needed to strain that half an inch further. He felt the solid mass of a hand around his and pulled himself toward it. The hand that had encompassed his and was dragging him back toward the blurred red disc of the moon was changing, becoming colder and harder. Devlin, Ramirez realized, had gone, and in his hand, instead of Devlin's hand, was a slimy piece of wood.

The water broke above Ramirez's head, and a breeze of air ran over his face and neck. His body spasmed. He took in a burning lungful of air and in return ejected a gut-full of sickeningly brackish water through his mouth and nose.

Frantically, he looked around to work out where the hell he was.

SIXTY-TWO

About thirty yards from the cruiser, Cassidy and Devlin found the black BMW parked close to a line of trees. The trunk with the bullet holes was open, and dried, pooled blood had collected and congealed on the carpet.

"That's a hell of a lot of blood for someone to lose and still be alive," said Cassidy.

Devlin tried the driver's door, which opened.

"Keep a lookout," said Devlin. "If they left the car unlocked, they might be nearby." Then, he dove in and rooted around, searching the footwells and the glove, door, and console compartments. He came out of the car holding a wallet. He placed it on the hood of the BMW, and Cassidy illuminated it with her flashlight. Devlin flipped out an ID card.

"Father Ramirez's ID," said Cassidy.

A line of trees screened the lake from view, and beyond the trees, the ground looked like it dipped in the direction of the lake.

"I'd guess we're a half a mile from the lake," said Cassidy. "Let's follow the path down to the front. Maybe Hudson's boat is moored down there. That's the only reason I can think that they're out here."

The path wound in a haphazard manner through the tree line and ran down the dip to the lake. Once they were through the trees, they could see the landscape in full. About a dozen navigation lights shining from boats night sailing were dotted across the lake. Over to the left was the north bank of Lake Vesper. The lights of the marina and of the bars, restaurants, and apartments lit up the two-mile stretch. Directly across the lake, the eastern shore was dark, with only the occasional car headlight visible. To Cassidy's and Devlin's immediate left was an old wooden hut, and down on the bank was a wooden jetty with a thirty-foot sailing boat tethered to it. Light from the cabin below seeped onto the deck.

Cautiously, Cassidy and Devlin made their way to the hut first.

"No lights on..." said Cassidy. "Stand back, and I'll take a look."

Glock in hand, Cassidy approached the hut, pushed open the door, and swept her flashlight around.

"No one here," she whispered back to Devlin. She slipped inside the door while Devlin looked down toward the boat for activity.

Inside the hut, Cassidy did a more thorough search. There were no electrics, no light switches, only a wooden table, two chairs, and fishing rods and nets. Up above her was a ledge constructed out of half timbers. It was built out to about six feet with about four or five feet of headroom. She stepped forward, and the floor creaked beneath her. She froze and swept her flash around again.

"Nothing doing here," she murmured. She snapped her gun back into her holster and turned to exit the hut, but before she got to the door, a crushing weight came down on her like a sack of bricks. Cassidy hit the floor with enough force to push all the wind out of her lungs. Whoever had ambushed her must have hidden, lying on the timber ledge, and rolled straight off it. There was a split second of dread before Cassidy felt hot, rank breaths on her neck.

"Make a sound and I'll put a bullet through your spine," said Slava.

Cassidy realized the accent was the same as the one she'd heard on the call from the motel. A man's voice, thick and Eastern European. She felt a hard object jab into her back.

"Get up slowly," said Slava. "With your hands where I can see them."

The crushing weight lifted, and Cassidy, still recovering from the sudden ambush, got to her feet. Her assailant was behind her, and the gun barrel was still digging into her back.

Slava began whispering instructions into Cassidy's ear. "Hands in the air."

Cassidy did as she was told. Slava reached around the right side of her duty belt and felt for her gun holster.

"Very slowly," Slava whispered, "I want you to take your gun out of your holster and drop it on the floor."

Again, Cassidy did as she was told. Her Glock hit the wooden floor with a thud.

"Who else is with you?" asked Slava.

"No one," said Cassidy, her heart racing and her breathing shallow and erratic. The barrel moved from her lower back to the back of her head. The toe of Slava's shoe touched her right heel.

"I'm going to ask you only one more time," said Slava. "If you lie, I'll kill you where you stand. If you tell the truth, I'll only shoot you in the leg."

Cassidy could feel panic threatening to overwhelm her. With brute force, she willed herself to calm down and to think with absolute clarity. She knew she had one option. She had to keep him talking and be prepared to execute that option clinically and flawlessly.

"One other person is with me," she replied.

"Where are they?"

"Outside. I think they're headed down to the lake. They're not a cop though. They're civilian." She could almost feel her attacker's thought process through the minute movements of the barrel against the back of her skull. For a moment, the pressure on her skull eased off fractionally. Then, she felt the metal push against her head again.

"Are they armed?"

"No. No, they're not. I swear. If you want, I can call them." She felt the pressure ease off.

"No. You don't need to call them." The barrel was pulled away from her head, and she knew she had the smallest sliver of an opportunity. Cassidy swung her right foot back hard and made contact with a hard shin. Simultaneously, with her right hand, she cross-drew her Taser, thumbed the safety, swung low, and twisted, discharging the Taser and praying for a hit. The sound of the probes clicking told her she had hit something, and the sight of a massive guy in a suit freezing and falling backward confirmed she had got her target. She pulled the trigger again and sent another brutal shock through her target's body. Then, she dropped the Taser and ran out the door. She got twenty yards before her foot twisted in a rut in the ground, sending her face-first into the dirt. Dazed, she lifted her head to see that despite pumping the guy with two loads of charge, he had managed to get to his feet and stumble to the doorway.

Slava's eyes lit up when he saw Cassidy on the ground. Cassidy attempted to get up, but a flash of agonizing pain from her ankle told her she was in real trouble. She was pinned to the ground by bad strain or maybe a break.

Slava immediately lurched away from the hut toward Cassidy. He'd only taken a couple of steps before he was slammed sideways by a charging figure coming from out of the dark.

DEVLIN STOOD OVER SLAVA, who was laid out on the ground, recovering from Devlin's ambush. Slava's gun was no longer in his hand.

"Where are Hudson and Ramirez?" barked Devlin.

Slava didn't answer. He got to his feet and smiled.

"Another priest. How lucky for me."

"Not on this occasion," replied Devlin.

Slava expanded to his full height and width. He balled his fists and jutted his chin forward.

"You are so out of your depth you can't even imagine," said Slava.

"Educate me."

Slava approached Devlin, his balled fists prepared. He was a couple of inches taller than Devlin and maybe twenty or even thirty pounds heavier. Devlin had to think quickly. He had to come up with a strategy that gave him, however marginal, an advantage. His opponent was larger, heavier, more powerful. Devlin instinctively drew on his boxing days when he had occasionally faced bigger boxers.

Slava came in at speed and attempted to ram Devlin. It worked pretty well. Devlin was surprised at the strength and force his opponent hit him with, and he barely managed to stay on his feet. Slava followed up with swings at Devlin, which Devlin managed to evade. Instead of trying to square up to Slava, he bent his knees, even crouched, inviting him on. Slava took the bait and laid into Devlin. Blows rained down, but

Devlin was able to come in under the bigger man, weather the impacts, and send a rocketing punch into the side of Slava's jaw that made him see stars.

In the back-and-forth of the brawl, they had moved away from the hut. Devlin's blow had given Slava pause, but he shook off Devlin's slug and went back on the attack. Again, Devlin crouched low, forcing Slava to come down to him. This time, the tactic was less effective. Though Devlin attempted to duck and dive, Slava sent his slabs of fist into Devlin's head and shoulders. The power of each blow drained Devlin's strength. He couldn't weather this kind of brutal assault for long, and he had to make the short time he had count. The first blow he managed to connect was right into the gut, and it landed like a peach. The follow-up was a clean uppercut, the kind that Foreman used to finish off Frazier in '73. It didn't lift Slava off his feet, but it sure as hell poleaxed him. Slava listed backward, and Devlin did what Foreman couldn't have done and kicked him as hard as he could in the nuts. The huge man dropped to his knees, and Devlin went about butchering him with his bare knuckles, punch after merciless punch, until there could be no doubt that Slava would not get up again that night.

Devlin stood over Slava's unconscious body, panting, but he didn't have time to recover. Movement in the periphery of his vision caused him to turn lakeward. Stomping over the brow of the slope was a suited figure very similar to the man on the ground but, if anything, larger.

Gus stopped to survey the scene before him: his comrade, Slava, laid out on the ground and covered in blood; the priest with bloodied face and knuckles; the cop lying on the ground. Trying to comprehend the situation, he cocked his head like a dog not understanding the instruction it had just been given. Then, he raised the gun he was carrying and pointed it at Devlin.

There was a muffled shot, and Gus was slammed backward but did not fall. A red patch grew on his chest, and he raised his gun again. Another muted shot split the silence, and Gus stumbled backward again. Then, three more shots popped in quick succession, propelling Gus's body onto the ground, where he lay still.

Devlin watched Gus fall and then turned to the source of the gunfire. Cassidy, still on the ground, had managed to retrieve Slava's gun, silencer still attached, and was holding it in her trembling hands.

"I had to..." she said.

"Damned right," Devlin replied.

SIXTY-THREE

Loban smiled, baring his gapped teeth. He played with his brass lighter, twirling it between his fingers.

"That's all... I swear..." Hudson, covered in gasoline, shivered and choked. "You have to believe me... Please, you have to... I've told you everything..."

"I believe you."

"Then... Then... Will you let me go?"

Loban said nothing. He slipped the cell phone and the lighter into his pocket.

"What...?" Hudson's eyes were wide with terror. "What are you doing...?"

Loban picked up the half-full jerry can and held it over Hudson's head.

"Please... No..." gasped Hudson.

Loban ignored Hudson's pleas. He poured a couple of lugs of gasoline over Hudson, then backed out of the boat, pouring a line of gasoline as he went. Up on deck, he flung the empty jerry can into the lake. Then, he stood on the jetty, holding the lighter in his hand. From below deck, Hudson could be heard screaming and wailing.

"Hey."

The voice came from behind Loban, from the banks of the shore. Loban turned to see who was calling him. To his surprise, he saw a priest coming down to the lake's edge. This priest was older, Loban observed, and looked a hell of a lot tougher.

"Your men are dead and out of action," said the older priest. "And we know what Hudson and Marshall were doing to Hudson's patients. We have the evidence from Marshall's hangar."

"Who are *you*?" asked Loban.

The older priest didn't answer. He stopped short of the jetty and glanced down at the jerry can floating in the water. "Smells like there's been a gasoline spill. I'd be careful with that lighter. The winds up and flames can go ways you don't predict."

"I know where the flames will go," said Loban.

Hudson's screams and shouts for help came from inside the boat.

"It's all over," said the priest. "There's nothing left to kill for."

Loban smiled his gap-toothed smile. "I don't think so."

He flipped the cap off the lighter and struck the flint wheel with his thumb. A flame danced in his hand. He raised it up and prepared to swing it into the boat, but something stopped him dead. Loban glanced down at his foot.

"What the hell?"

An arm had appeared from beneath the jetty, and a hand was wrapped hard around his ankle.

"Get off me!"

Loban shook and kicked his foot to get free from the fingers that were grasping and pulling at his ankle. The hand jerked his leg sideways, and he only just managed to stay on his feet. But the wet, slimy, reed-covered hand had no intention of stopping and dragged him inch by inch over to the side of the wet, slick jetty. Loban cursed as he saw the owner of the hand, Ramirez, appearing from beneath the jetty. With one furious wrench, Ramirez yanked Loban's foot from under him. Loban's legs swung up, and he tumbled off the jetty, hitting his head on the wooden edge on the way in.

For a few silent seconds, Loban was completely submerged and had no clue as to what was up or down. Suddenly, his throbbing head broke the surface of the water, and he frantically took in gulps of air. He began to thrash wildly, attempting to get back to the jetty, but Ramirez pushed him back, first with his arm, then with a foot.

"Get out of my way," Loban screamed between panicked breaths. "I can't... I can't swim...!" But Ramirez didn't move, and nobody else came to help. Loban knew the water was winning, lapping up over his mouth, then his eyes, and then his head. He had had his last sight of the world above. His wild lashes and kicks were futile. There was nothing he could do to stop his slow fall into the cold, indifferent deep. His lungs screamed to be filled with air, but only water came.

IT WAS all Ramirez could do to drag himself along the side of the jetty to the bank and get himself ashore. When he looked back, Loban had disappeared beneath the water. Two strong hands had gotten hold of Ramirez and lifted his sopping body entirely out of the water. Devlin carried Ramirez up the slope and laid him on the ground. "Stay there," said Devlin. "You're safe. I'm going back to get Loban. Drowning's too easy a way out for him."

Devlin raced back to dive into the lake. He was underwater for what seemed like an age, and when he resurfaced, he was empty-handed.

"Nothing," he shouted up to Ramirez. "I couldn't see him anywhere."

Devlin hauled himself onto the jetty, climbed onto the boat, and disappeared below deck. Moments later, he appeared with Hudson over his shoulder. He took him, still with hands bound with tape, to the spot where Ramirez lay. Cassidy limped over with great difficulty and joined them.

"How are you?" Cassidy asked Ramirez.

"I'm cold, I've been shot, and I hurt everywhere..." said Ramirez faintly. "That's how I am."

"And what about you, Rick?"

"I'll live," muttered Hudson.

"How are you?" Devlin asked Cassidy.

"A twisted ankle," replied Cassidy. "That's all. I've radioed for paramedics and backup. You stay here. I'll get a first aid kit from the cruiser." Cassidy turned to Hudson. "Dr. Hudson, you have the right to remain silent and refuse to answer questions. If you give up the right to remain silent, anything you say can and will be used against you in a court of law. I'd cuff you, but you're already pretty well tied up."

"I want a lawyer," Hudson replied, looking grim and unrepentant.

"That's your right. But, Rick, there's not enough money in the world to buy you a lawyer that's gonna do you any good. Get to your feet." Cassidy limped away, taking Hudson with her, hailing dispatch on her radio as she went.

Ramirez's eyes were slits, but they were just about open. He turned to Devlin, looking utterly bewildered. "Who are you?"

"You know who I am."

"No... No, I don't think I do." Ramirez looked toward the lake. "I was in the water, drowning, falling to the bottom. I saw the tunnel, the light, the whole show, and then... Then you appeared and guided me back."

"I assure you, I was here on land all the time."

"No," said Ramirez with total conviction. "You brought me back from the dark. Just like you did with Elizabeth Wendig. I remember how she described it—the gentlest, strongest hands I'd ever held. It was exactly the same. Exactly the same..."

"Maybe Elizabeth coming back had more to do with whatever Hudson was giving her."

Ramirez shook his head vehemently. "No. That's not right. You're wrong. He didn't treat Elizabeth with the experimental therapy. Up until the crash, she wasn't even his patient. Hudson told me. You did it. You bought both of us back. The rumors about you... They were right... And I think I knew it from the moment I met you. So tell me, please... Who are you?"

Devlin looked at Ramirez, then looked away. For a moment, he seemed lost in thought. Then, he turned back to Ramirez. "You want to know?"

"Yes."

"It's downright crazy."

"Just tell me, for crying out loud."

"Okay. I'll tell you, then."

Devlin sat on the ground with a sodden, bloodied Ramirez and began to tell him the whole story. He started by telling Ramirez about his pregnant wife, who was murdered by a heroin addict. About when he became a priest and, unable to forgive the killer of his wife, hunted him down and took his life. He told Ramirez about the nightmares every night afterward, in which he was visited by a demon called Azazel. How Azazel asked every night if Devlin would atone for his sin. And every night, Devlin replied that he would not. Eventually, Azazel accepted Devlin's answer as final and cursed him. The curse would be that wherever Devlin went, evil would rise up. And that's exactly what happened. Until one day, Devlin was given the opportunity to be released from his curse. For Azazel to leave him. And he chose to keep his demon and his curse because it had become the one thing that defined him. That gave him a mission on this Earth. And so, wherever he would go, evil would continue to find him out.

Ramirez listened intently throughout, and when Devlin was done, he thought about what Devlin had said for a good while before he finally spoke.

"Yeah," said Ramirez. "I thought it might be something like that."

Devlin laughed. Then Ramirez joined in, and they both laughed hard. The laughter faded, and Ramirez looked at Devlin and frowned. "You must be a very dangerous man to be around."

Devlin shrugged. "A moment ago, you were thanking me for saving your life."

"Is that everything? I know everything about you now?" asked Ramirez. "Or are there more surprises?"

Devlin shut his eyes as if trying to listen to something within him. Maybe, thought Ramirez, it was Azazel. Then, Devlin's eyes opened, and he stared out at the lake and began to speak in such a calm, detached, and almost otherworldly voice that it sent shivers through Ramirez's battered body.

"There is something else you should know."

"What?"

"That... That I have seen things happen that are beyond rational explanation. Extraordinary things beyond even the most devout faith. These things have happened in my presence. And ever since the moment I stepped foot in this town, I have had a very profound and real sense that truly extraordinary things would happen here too."

"Like Elizabeth?"

"Like Elizabeth... But everything that happened here is not

just because of me; it's because of Hinkley. Because its people's need was so deep and raw."

The sound of sirens grew closer, and there was another sound too. To begin with, Ramirez thought it was clapping—that, absurd as it was, somewhere out on the lake, a group of people had begun to applaud. The clapping grew loud and thunderous, and Ramirez turned to see the surface of the lake lifting into the sky. Then, he saw it wasn't the surface of the lake but thousands of birds, a great sound and motion as every waterbird instantaneously took to the air. They covered the sky and the moon, the lake grew darker, and there was a deathly quiet. The quiet only lasted seconds and was broken by shouts from people on their boats. All the engines of the boats on the lake seemed to have stopped; their lights had gone out, and they drifted and swayed lifelessly.

"What's happening...?"

The astonished voice came from behind Ramirez. Despite the pain, Ramirez managed to turn a little and saw Cassidy. She was holding a first aid kit and had stopped still. Her whole body had frozen, and her mouth was wide open.

"Dear Christ..." Cassidy gasped.

Cassidy was looking beyond Ramirez out into the lake. Ramirez swung around to see what had transfixed Cassidy.

A mist had formed, hovering over the silvery-blue surface of the lake, and further out, moonlight had laid a wide carpet of gold across the main body of the water. As he squinted through his swollen eyes, he caught sight of movement about ten yards from the shore. He blinked and focused again, and this time, Ramirez could see a figure staggering out of the water. His heart sank, and he felt a dread in the pit of his stomach.

"Oh, God..." muttered Ramirez. "Loban's back..."

"No," he heard Devlin saying. "It's not Loban."

The figure had stopped, and his features were becoming

clearer in the moonlight and the mist. He was a slightly overweight, middle-aged man wearing a tie with a clip. His shirtsleeves were rolled up.

Ramirez felt his arm being clasped. It was Devlin.

"Listen," said Devlin in an urgent whisper. "I'm going to tell you to do something, and you have to promise me you'll do it."

"Wh... What?"

"When you write up what happened here tonight, keep me out of it. Okay?"

"Keep you...?"

"Okay?"

"Yes. Okay."

"And somehow, you have to get Cassidy to do the same for her report. Okay?"

"Why...?"

"Okay?"

"Yeah. Okay."

Devlin stood and began walking out to the lake. Ramirez watched him approach the slanting bank and then carry on down it, walking across the thin strand of mud into the edge of the water. Devlin kept on going, wading out until the water began to lap around his waist, and Ramirez realized he was going to greet the figure that had appeared from the lake. The man seemed to talk to Devlin, and Devlin nodded and laid a hand on his forehead. Then, they embraced. From out of the mists on the lake, more figures appeared. Eight of them. The older man looked around and waved to them to follow him. He began to walk through the water and the mist toward the shore, and the other eight younger figures trudged on behind them, looking pale and utterly astonished.

"Hugh..." Ramirez heard Cassidy say weakly. "It's Hugh Varley, the science teacher... And... Oh, Jesus, sweet Jesus... It's the kids... All seven of them..." Tears were streaming out of

Cassidy's eyes. Her cheeks and chin were wet with tears. She was full-on weeping, helplessly like a child. "Oh, dear God, they're back... They've come back..."

Dozens of paramedics, cops, and firefighters had appeared on the banks of the lake. All of them had either stopped in their tracks or slowed to a halt to take in the extraordinary scene unfolding on the lake.

Cassidy, limping as fast as she could, hobbled down to the bank, into the water, and embraced the older man, who held her tight to him. Ramirez managed to stand, almost forgetting to breathe. Pain surged through his tired body, but he hardly noticed it. He hardly noticed it because finally, he was witnessing a miracle.

The other thing he didn't notice was that Devlin was gone.

EPILOGUE

Three Months Later

He didn't intend to end up at Holy Cross church. He was on his way back from the New York State Catholic Conference in Albany, where he'd been invited to give a talk. That happened a lot these days. After the events in Hinkley, he'd attained a celebrity that was quite unexpected and not unpleasant. Invitations came often, and a book was in progress for which one of the big publishing houses had given him a six-figure advance following a fierce bidding war. Of course, in all his talks and the book to come, there would be one significant omission.

The town of Avery, Massachusetts, was not far out of his way, and curiosity, as it had before, got the better of him, so he took the exit ramp. Quiet country roads led him into the valley of Avery and then up a steep incline to Holy Cross church. It was a route he knew well by now. Glorious summer was at its height, the sun was up and hot, and the sky was clear and blue.

Parking was easy; there was a mostly empty lot to the side of the church entrance and in front of a ramshackle hall.

Ramirez got out of his new Volkswagen ID., the rusty Nissan long gone, and stood for a moment in front of the church. In the half dozen visits Ramirez had made to Holy Cross, his impression of it hadn't changed much. It was a mid-twentieth-century stone build, plain and efficient rather than anything eye-catching and in need of love, care, and a lot of money.

The door to the dilapidated hall opened, and a large figure stepped out. He was a tall, rough-looking man with broad shoulders. He saw Ramirez and nodded.

"Hi," Ramirez called over. The man gave a hint of a smile back, and Ramirez walked over to him.

"Back again?" said the man.

"Yeah. I am, Hoyt. But I guess there's no news."

"No," replied Hoyt Tanner, the church sexton. "Not a word."

Ramirez had met Hoyt Tanner a couple of times on his visits to Avery. Like the church he was sexton for, he had seen better days. His face was pitted, his eyes were bloodshot, and he had a couple of teeth at the front missing. Even so, with his height and broad shoulders, he was a formidable-looking guy.

"The bishop is still as mad as hell," said Tanner. "He never wanted Father Devlin here in the first place. It was all arranged over his head."

Ramirez felt a pang of sadness. He felt empty, betrayed by Devlin's disappearance. And he still felt profoundly unsettled by the events in Hinkley. He doubted that feeling would ever leave him.

Ramirez and Tanner talked awhile. They talked about what people now variously called "The Hinkley Manifestation" or "The Great Return"—the raising from the dead of seven children and one man. Ramirez took pleasure in regaling Tanner once again with all the details of the great event, except, of course, the one significant omission. Like the rest of the world, Ramirez had never told Tanner about Devlin's part in what had happened in Hinkley.

After they had exhausted the subject of Hinkley, they discussed the new Holy Cross priest and Ramirez's new and eventful life, and then about how much they both missed Devlin.

Tanner had repairs he needed to attend to, so he said goodbye, and Ramirez wandered back around the front of the church and then into the cemetery. He stayed there for a while, roaming through the headstones and reflecting on the shortness of life. Then, realizing the day was running away from him, he decided he had better get back on the road. As he turned to make his way back to the path to the parking lot, he saw another figure standing in the cemetery. She was small with blonde hair and hadn't seen Ramirez.

"Hi," said Ramirez.

Lori Cassidy turned around, and her eyes lit up. "Father Ramirez?"

"Officer Cassidy."

"Call me Lori."

"Call me Ricardo."

"What are you doing here?"

"Same thing as you, I think?"

Cassidy pursed her lips and nodded. "Looking for the big man."

"Looking for the big man."

"How many times have you been down here?"

"Half a dozen."

"Yeah, it's about the same for me." Cassidy shook her head. "Where the hell is he? It's like he vanished off the face of the Earth."

"I wouldn't put it past him. Not Devlin. If anyone could vanish off the face of the Earth, he could."

Cassidy smiled. "Not like you though. I saw you on TV. Being interviewed. You're kind of an authority on the whole Hinkley Manifestation."

Ramirez blushed. "Yeah, seems that way. But people just keep asking me, inviting me to speak and write books..."

"Write books?"

"A book. I've written...well, am writing a book." Ramirez paused and was suddenly taken by a thought. "You know, he almost predicted it... The big man. He said I had a bright future, and I joked that he could see into the future." Ramirez chuckled. "But maybe I'm making too much of it."

"After Hinkley, who knows? You gonna tell the whole story?"

Ramirez leaned in a little. "No. Not the whole story. There's a certain person who won't be mentioned."

"The big man."

Ramirez nodded. "The big man...and the people at the heart of the story too—the kids, their parents, Varley, they've clammed up. Not talking to anyone. Not to me or the press. They've made a pact of silence."

"I heard that. I guess they want their privacy, and who can blame them?"

"Maybe. But the other side of that is it's allowed every kind of conspiracy theory to spread like wildfire. Theories about Hugh Varley being in a cult and taking the kids off somewhere to be brainwashed, theories that the town was in on faking the whole thing. I even heard a theory that they survived in an air pocket in the bottom of the lake."

"People will believe what they want to believe. It's the time we live in."

"Yeah, ain't that so. So, how are you? I heard you moved out of Hinkley."

"Yeah. I got an attachment with the FBI. A promotion, actually. I'm part of the federal investigation into Loban's operation. I'm living and working in DC. That's how I know Devlin can't be found. I've taken advantage of every database I have access to, and there's nothing. No sign of him on any federal or state database since he went missing." Cassidy looked back at the church and sighed. "God, I miss him."

"Me too... Me too..."

"Where you going now, Father?"

"Boston. I'd better make a move now, or else it'll be crazy late by the time I get back. You?"

"I'm down in Lowell doing some training at the FBI offices there. I'm gonna have to get driving too."

They lingered for a moment, not quite wanting to say goodbye.

Then, Cassidy said, "Say, how about we do this again? Make it a thing?"

"Sounds like a great idea. Every year, on this day, we'll meet back right here at exactly this time."

"We'll call it Devlin Day."

"After the big man."

Cassidy and Ramirez walked back to the parking lot and shook hands. Then, they got into their respective cars and headed off, each one asking themselves the same question over and over.

Where was Devlin?

The End.

Printed in Great Britain
by Amazon

44389965R00178